For my family and friends wherever you may be, and Queenstown, oh Queenstown, oh how I miss thee.

Lister Verdi Whitwam

WHAT TO DO WHEN THE WORLD ENDS

AUSTIN MACAULEY PUBLISHERS™

LONDON · CAMBRIDGE · NEW YORK · SHARJAH

ISBN 9781528982580 (Paperback)
ISBN 9781528982597 (ePub e-book)

www.austinmacauley.com

First Published (2020)
Austin Macauley Publishers Ltd
25 Canada Square
Canary Wharf
London
E14 5LQ

Author's note

Firstly, a massive thanks to our amazing, selfless NHS, and to the key workers and volunteers all around the globe. These are dark days in which we live. The world, it seems, is losing the plot, and given the current climate, I realise that tales of woe are the last thing that most people will want to hear. As such, I apologise for the potentially inappropriate timing of this release. The project began ten years ago, midst the apocalyptic theories that were abound at the time, but it is my hope that the light-hearted nature of the telling, might put a smile on at least a few solemn faces. Maybe add a little joy to what has been a joyless time.

A brighter day will come. Stay strong and pass the pipe of peace, metaphorically of course, or at least having sanitised it thoroughly beforehand. No more passing the dutchy to the left-hand side for the rebellious little scamps amongst you.

Play the game and be safe, but free your mind, question everything, be excellent to one another, and do the right thing (Particularly you, Mr Banker. I know you have a conscience hidden deep within you somewhere.)

One love.

Author's note

Firstly, a massive thanks to our amazing, selfless NHS, and to the key workers and volunteers all around the globe. These are dark days in which we live. The world, it seems, is losing the plot, and given the current climate, I realise that tales of woe are the last thing that most people will want to hear. As such, I apologise for the potentially inappropriate timing of this release. The project began ten years ago, midst the apocalyptic theories that were abound at the time, but it is my hope that the light-hearted nature of the telling, might put a smile on at least a few solemn faces. Maybe add a little joy to what has been a joyless time.

A brighter day will come. Stay strong and pass the pipe of peace, metaphorically of course, or at least having sanitised it thoroughly beforehand. No more passing the dutchy to the left-hand side for the rebellious little scamps amongst you.

Play the game and be safe, but free your mind, question everything, be excellent to one another, and do the right thing (Particularly you, Mr Banker. I know you have a conscience hidden deep within you somewhere.)

One love.

Chapter 1

Queenstown
New Zealand's southern lakes

'Bollocks...' grumbled Digsy with a resigned huff, his gaze fixed pleadingly on Mary's as she beckoned him over to the pub's exit.

'Run along Digsy!' someone called out mockingly, and Mary frowned as Digsy hesitated, swigging the last of his pint, he slammed it down onto the bar, smiled apologetically at the barman, and then trudged begrudgingly through the crowd towards her.

Oh woe is me thought he, shoving his way through the throng.

Dusk was falling, but beer still flowed and the night was yet young. It had been a fun night too, abound with much-needed merriment and laughter, and a chance to frolic for the first time since the earthquakes had ravaged the area three months earlier.

A chance to forget.

A chance to put those horrific days to the back of their minds.

So many had died. So much heartache. Half of Queenstown had been flattened, and beer just hadn't been a priority for most people. More important matters had been at hand.

The first pub had just reopened though, and was packed with revellers. Free out-of-date beer for everyone, all night. Woo-hoo! The recent horrors were all but forgotten for that briefest of moments, swept away on a tide of indulgence.

But yay, it couldn't last, and all too soon for Digsy, it was time for home.

Disobedience would not be tolerated.

Clicking the umbrella into place, Mary took him by the hand, dragging Digsy into the night, and the jubilations haunting his every step were soon but a faint whisper on the strengthening breeze.

A light rain was falling, a thin veil of mist hanging midst the cliffs, glowing almost in the scant moonlight, shrouding the suburb in a mysterious sheen.

Their house was at the end of the street on the right, not far from the cliffs that'd crushed those to the left. It stood solitary between the ruins of its neighbours now, a large crack traversing the near side where it propped up the pine that'd fallen into it.

Only a few lights shone in the houses still standing. Huge fractures lined the street before them now, puddles of filth festered under clouds of flies and mangled cars sat twisted midst a sea of shattered glass.

The scene was unrecognisable. It looked like a warzone, not the quaint alpine suburb it'd been just three months earlier. An assault course of grime and rubble stretched up the road before them, fallen trees and boulders, crushed cars and debris of every description littering its length.

It was a sight to sadden the hardest of hearts, but on Digsy strode, mindless of the surroundings, the streetlights sparking frenziedly as he staggered past them in a haze of beer-soaked indifference. The hard times were gone from Digsy's mind. Lost in the moment was he. Feeling the love and loving the love, the gentle patter on the umbrella like an army of drummers to Digsy's ears, the rain's caress as he strayed from under it like angels' kisses.

How sweet life suddenly seemed.

How poetic.

To groove forth was all that Digsy wanted. To ignore the devastation. To ignore the sorrow. To ignore it all and rave the night away with the moths zipping about under the lamps. And given the previous few months, it didn't seem like too much to ask for, but the ground lurched abruptly and he staggered forwards instead, a haunting groan filling the air like a thousand hungry stomachs rumbling in unison.

Pushing himself to a crouch, Digsy turned to check on Mary, the ground swaying gently now, the din harrowed and quickly growing louder, rising up through the earth in a symphony of bad tidings.

Does one duck, or cover? wondered he.

Or perhaps both?

It was an important distinction to make he knew. There very lives might well be in its hands, and this most tantalising of musings, dear reader, could indeed have gone on for a while longer too.

Rooted in reality, Digsy was not, and he intended to thoroughly make the most of it, but then all of a sudden, all hell broke loose.

Utter chaos suddenly in every direction. Utter terror.

Car alarms screamed to life all down the road as fresh cracks crept up it. Roofs caved in and walls toppled.

The ground was shaking like Stevens now. Elvis turned in his grave.

'Digsy...**Digsy!**'

Mary was beside Digsy again, but her scream sounded distant somehow, and otherworldly, and Digsy felt dazed suddenly, bewildered and sick. Everything was moving, everything shaking.

People ran screaming into the street, confused and terrified, bloodied and covered in dust, running around like headless chickens or stood transfixed at the carnage unfolding around them. A car swerved to avoid one of them, smashing into a wall to the right as another was skewered to the left. It was horrific. The world was falling apart before their eyes. Parents screamed for their children and children for their parents. Cars were swallowed and trees uprooted. Power lines lay sparking across the street and water fountained high from burst pipes, animating the shroud of mist that choked the scene as sparks cut through it like tiny comets through the night.

It was like something from the movies, something from a nightmare, and it sobered Digsy up instantly. Grabbing Mary's hand, he looked for an exit. There was no way out though. No way through the barrage of death engulfing everything now. Escape was futile, their efforts in vain no matter which way they turned, which way they fled.

'**We need to get away from the cliffs!**' cried Mary, barely audible above the chaos, her black locks now a dusty grey and a trickle of crimson running down her cheek.

But it was too late.

The cliff before them started to crumble and a tree fell behind them, blocking their way back. They were trapped. Hemmed in like hipsters in a half price hat shop. There was nowhere to run, nowhere to hide. The end appeared nigh. Frozen to the spot, they gripped each other tighter, rocks crashing down like huge hailstones all around them now, bouncing back up like exploding landmines and littering the air with shrapnel.

And it was at that point, that Digsy noticed one particular boulder that required attention. It had broken free from the cliff and ricocheted away from it, and was rushing down directly above them now. So displaying admirable aptitude for one so impaired, Digsy shoved Mary from its path and dived left like he'd never dived left before.

He felt the boulder slam down, driving deep into the ground where he'd stood, and heard the scream that'd forever haunt him as he scrambled desperately for safety, and then… then he was back in his bed again, shivering and dazed to begin with, but no longer in the street he knew, and no longer facing death. There were no boulders rushing down to crush him, and no Mary there to be crushed. He was drenched to the bone and confused, but safe he quickly realised as his senses conjoined from the mess they'd awoken to, and rescued from the nightmare that plagued him most every night still.

Or the memory to be precise.

The memory of that terrible night six years earlier.

Chapter 2

April 2050

Sweet Santa's shrivelled sacks…. it's so cold! thought Digsy, welcoming the day with a weary, fateful sigh. Or thoughts to that effect, and he stretched out his arms till his fingers touched the cold wall behind him and wrenched them back impulsively, shivering as a chill coursed down his spine.

And indeed it was cold, even for an autumn in the mountains, so he pulled the blanket up over his shoulders and rolled onto his side, pulling his feet back under.

Drip

The noise echoed around the walls, teasing and tormenting Digsy, like water torture for beginners.

Drip, drip

And then he felt his knee, throbbing suddenly, like his knee was expanding, straining to break free from the skin that imprisoned it.

The pain had been growing worse recently too, and more frequent, in unison it seemed, with the water which seeped in through the ceiling, the days wetter of late, and noticeably colder.

Why Digsy had chosen to live in a cave was a particularly pertinent question to him, given the pain and ill feelings his cave seemed to inspire. A foul mood washed through him, unimpeded and unapologetic, but he was quite used to his own cloudy disposition now after years of coexistence, and had indeed, developed somewhat of a soft spot for it. He'd learnt to embrace his moods, and to cherish them sometimes even. That same dream, that same nightmare, had plagued him most every night for the last six years, and it was almost comforting at times to him now.

It wasn't this morning though. It was just *so* cold. Digsy's entirety was tense and tender. His happy sacks had retreated from whence they came and his manhood was suddenly in question.

Opening his eyes, he regretted it instantly. Even his eyeballs were cold. Even the floaters he could see when he closed them again seemed frozen to the spot.

Digsy hated the cave he lived in suddenly. It was a truly miserable place – dark, damp and musty, and cold beyond belief now as the winter quickly encroached.

To the rear of the space, a dim glow radiated up the cave's walls from the dying fire there. Other than that, there was no light but for that which seeped in through the small holes in the ceiling, which conversely let the rain in too though, and water would seep down the walls on rainy days, pooling in the moat that circled the space before emptying through the entrance shaft at the front.

Everything was wet, everything cold, and the air was playing on Digsy's lungs more and more now. He'd presumed the fire would suffice in warming him when he'd first moved into the cave, and it did at night, when it was blazing away, all warm and fiery, but the mornings…

He could barely feel it now, crackling and gasping away, flames leaping sporadically up from its depths like hands reaching up from hell to drag Digsy back down.

For such had been his frame of mind of late. Forever dismal and morbid. Barely a slither of hope left to cling on to.

Oh how Digsy missed his amore, his Mary. Her gentle caress and her warm, loving smile, her memory invariably fresh in his mind the very instant he woke each day. No longer did he relish the prospect of the day ahead without her. No longer did he welcome each new morn with a sense of wonder and potential, but foreboding and dread.

Needless to say, living in a cave hadn't helped in that regard, but the cave was well hidden and quiet, which were prerequisites for Digsy. There was plenty of room for his brewing equipment too, with ventilation and a water supply, hence why he'd moved into the cave in the first place. Brewing was Digsy's livelihood.

Throwing back the blanket, he stepped into the day, quickly donning his hoody, and then slid into his boots, and once the more intricate of the morning's necessities were done with, he stoked the fire, adding fresh wood from the pile that was drying out beside it. The branches didn't take to begin with, so he blew on the embers and they crackled suddenly, roaring like a tiny passing train, flickering orange and black with a calm fury that was almost mesmerizing; and then the fire flared into life, the damp walls of the cave glistening suddenly under the new orange hue.

After a moment, Digsy's shivers eased, so he picked his hipflask from the table and took a swig, the nectar warming him further, and he sighed, stroking his beard to its tip as his thoughts went to the day ahead.

It was delivery day.

The last batch of the season, the most important day of the year for Digsy, and a disaster waiting to happen he couldn't help but think. His latest batch of moonshine was all bottled up, and waiting only now for him to deliver it to The Order's warehouse, where he'd trade it for the supplies he needed to see him through the winter. A shiver suddenly traced his spine at the thought of it. At the thought of dealing with The Order. It was a risky business he mused, scratching his stubbled head as the day's prospects suddenly dawned on him.

Suffice to say, they weren't great.

The Order you see, had ruled New Queenstown since attacking the town three years earlier, and still did so with an iron fist that Stalin would've been proud of. Just another bunch of power hungry, self-serving secretion stains, growing fat off the suffering of others. They used the moonshine Digsy made for fuel, which was scarce otherwise, and therefore highly prized. Digsy was their only supplier, but The Order had fenced New Queenstown off recently, cutting his trade routes, and were now his sole supplier of most everything else too.

It certainly was a tricky one, and somewhat of a catch 22 that Digsy had found himself in.

Without The Order's supplies though, he would struggle to survive the winter he knew. *Needs must,* he mused, fastening his body armour beneath his jacket, picking his air pistols up from the table, placing one in each pocket and then sliding a knife into his boot.

He needed The Order's supplies as much as they needed his moonshine, and since the town had been fenced off, he'd been left with no choice. There was no one else left for him to trade with, and The Order were now his biggest, nay, only client.

But it wasn't just The Order that Digsy was worried about. Oh no. It was a scary world out there now. A dangerous world, which Digsy preferred to avoid where possible. Miscreants and vagabonds roamed, robbing, raiding, rioting and ransacking, and an outing these days required planning, preparation and lots of it.

A leisurely stroll was simply no longer possible. Or even an aimless meander for that matter. Those days were sadly long gone, and Digsy remembered them with a strange fondness now. Times of real hope, before The Order arrived, when it'd seemed realistic to dream that something good could be salvaged from the ashes.

The survivors in Queenstown had pulled together not long after the earthquakes, and there'd been a new hope about the ether suddenly. A new beginning.

At that point, Digsy still lived in Queenstown, and a year or so after the "big one", he'd built a still from a few scraps of copper and an old boiler he'd found whilst out scavenging, and he'd started making moonshine, trading it for whatever he needed to get by. Business had actually boomed too, for a little while at least, the fuelling, sanitary, and other obvious benefits of his moonshine proving more than popular in these strange new times. He'd had the freedom to come and go and trade with whomever he pleased. There'd been no red tape, no taxes and no problems.

Life had almost been good again.

But of course it couldn't last. Of course it had to end, and those days seemed like a lifetime ago to Digsy now. Such joys were but a memory of a more hopeful time nowadays, mere ghosts of yet another world gone by.

The world had changed yet again. The streets of New Queenstown were dangerous now, and had been since The Order arrived.

Chapter 3

Her Ladyship was a harsh woman. She knew that, *and so fak'n what? It's a harsh fak'n world,* thought she, gazing out through the truck's window, out over the luscious bowl of rolling green and meandering blue that she so proudly called home.

It'd been a mite harsh on Her Ladyship lately as well though, and she was beginning to feel her age suddenly.

Being New Queenstown's governor had taken its toll on her she knew. The people were just so demanding. The responsibility, the pressure and the incessant whining had been grinding her down, but as a princess called unto duty, she'd stepped up, and was more than willing to forgive herself for her intemperate temperament at times.

Today though, she found herself particularly irked.

Ten minutes earlier, she'd been inspecting her new watchtower, which was still under construction, rising up through the ashes of the old ski centre near the summit of Coronet peak. It had been disappointing though. The facility was slowly but surely taking shape, but it was taking too long, and the workers' reactions as she'd screamed at them had taken her aback. Was it her fault they were behind schedule? Was it her fault they had the work ethic of crackheads?

No it fak'n wasn't, she decided as the dead one's face before she shot him sprang into her mind.

Keeping her thoughts to herself though, she studied the back of her driver's head instead. It was a big head she noted, olive skinned, bald and bulbous, with rolls of loose skin drooping from under it that she was tempted to pull. However much she wanted to though, she resisted the urge, as the head was attached to the oaf that was driving her down a rather treacherous road.

The road wound across the eastern face of Coronet Peak like a string of spaghetti stuck to a child's face. It was battered and riddled with pot holes, which didn't help Her Ladyship's nerves, and the wonderous view ambled by mostly ignored. She couldn't take her eyes off her driver's head now. The head had her transfixed. It was just so big. Raul was the head's current owner, and would remain so until she decided otherwise she'd delighted in reminding him on a few occasions.

Raul was a glum fellow, with a large chip on his shoulder, but he'd proven useful recently, following her orders without question no matter how heinous they be. Indeed, it appeared to Her Ladyship, that his ambition far outweighed any moral doubts he might harbour in doing what she often made him, and it was a weakness she enjoyed to exploit.

She'd first encountered Raul three years earlier when her Order first attacked Queenstown. He'd lived in the town at the time, and had fought valiantly by all accounts, but he'd soon surrendered, and been easy to turn, easy to mould into The Order's ways.

Her ways.

His choice of attire though, frankly bemused her.

A pirate suit? A fak'n pirate suit! He looks a tit! thought she, turning her attention back through the truck's window, her eyes glazing over as they gazed out at the peaks meandering past in the distance.

The ground dropped away steeply to the left, a meter beyond the truck, spilling into a vast trough of rugged green which sat like an oasis in the mountains. The Wakatipu basin was a glorious sight to behold, shredded by deep gorges and ravines through which brilliant turquoise waters raged. Abandoned suburbs and scattered mansions lay in ruin midst the nature that had reclaimed much of it, and a wall of wintery peaks rolled around and surrounded it all. The view soon succumbed to the tree line though, their way lined suddenly by a blur of windswept skeletons, the mountains looming ever higher beyond them, dominating the horizon under a patchwork of brooding clouds.

It all appeared barren and cold to Her Ladyship though. She saw not the beauty in the naked trees, ushering them ever onwards. Nor the magnificence of the basin laid out beyond them, but a blur of brown and a mass of sprawling limbs clawing at her path, which made her ponder her own ageing, and depressed her. She hated the winter more each year now she was finding, and at eighty-three, she was definitely starting to feel it more.

Still though, she wasn't one to bemoan her lot, and of that she was certain.

A smile crossed her face as her thoughts skipped to the power plant, that all going to plan, would soon be operational.

Oh, the possibilities!

It had been so long since Her Ladyship had had a hot shower, that the mere prospect of it sent a tingle shimmering through her. All she had to do, was find the plans for the original facility, repair it, and Bob's all of a sudden your mother's pet ferret—Electricity, and all the wondrous comforts that come along with it.

The prospect was a tantalising one, and one that couldn't be happening soon enough for Her Ladyship. Her machines were just sat there, ready and waiting to go, waiting to build, but the fuel had run out six months earlier. All they had to power them now, was the moonshine that they were forced to trade, and that supply was tenuous to say the least.

A power supply would change everything.

Adjusting her wig, which had slipped slightly to the left, she considered her options. Only one sprung to mind. The plans for the original facility, which drew water from a creek in the town's infancy, were somewhere in the area her informant had told her, but Her Ladyship suspected he knew their whereabouts more specifically than that, so she'd had his daughter kidnapped and was on her way to meet him.

With The Order energised she knew, with electricity, they would be unstoppable. The whole of the Wakatipu basin would be hers for the taking, and she allowed the thought to blossom for a moment, picturing herself sat on a heated throne forged from the gold in the mountains surrounding.

Her own little piece of paradise. Her Eden, and she'd defend it to the end.

'Raul!' she snapped, slapping her hand down onto her driver's shoulder, to which he flinched and Her Ladyship sniggered. 'Have ya found me those fak'n plans yet mate? Yooouu poncy fak'n fak!'

The truck slowed as they reached the mountain's foot, where they turned to the right, back through the ruins of Arthur's Point, and back towards New Queenstown.

'Plans, ma'am? Which, erm, w…which plans, ma'am?' stammered Raul, stalling, trying to find the right lie. Sadly for Raul though, lying had never been one of his fortes. He well knew she meant the plans for the hydro-plant that'd powered the town in its goldrush days, as she'd been ranting on about them for months now, but the plans had been proving elusive, and Raul wasn't quite sure how best to relay the news of his failings to her.

'You fak'n know which fak'n plans mate.' she returned bluntly.

The truck bounced through a pothole and Raul braced the steering wheel. The truck wobbled slightly and Her Ladyship coughed, winding down the window, and spat the filth she'd coughed up through it.

'It's outa your fak'n hands now anyway…'

She pulled a glove from her hand, and then the other, sliding them into her pocket.

'You fak'n failed Raul mate…' she went on after licking the spittle from the corner of her mouth. 'Fak'n useless…' Reaching out, she grabbed the headrests and pulled herself forwards, so that her mouth was by Raul's ear.

'My snitch says he knows where the fak'n plans are, and we're off to meet 'im.'

She flicked his ear lobe, grinning again as he flinched accordingly, before going on, 'We still need more moonshine though mate. And I think it goes without fak'n sayin', I'd prefer not to pay for it.'

Her voice dropped to a whisper, sinister yet warm, and oh so disconcerting.

'So you've only got one job now Raul mate, ya cockeyed fak'n lard-arse. Find that fak'n cave.'

Chapter 4

The sun was up, only the tenderest of glows piercing the gloom above Digsy now. A solitary moth fluttered between the narrow shafts of light that hung like light-sabres from the ceiling, battling against the smoke that bellowed up all around it to the air holes above. The fire was struggling again, so Digsy grabbed his backpack and swung it over his shoulder, gripping the rope that hung from the wall, and then lowered himself gingerly down the shaft at the front of his cave, dropping to the ground with a wince as his bad knee took the brunt of the landing.

A slight frost coated the grasses here, thicker in places, and forming tiny white sculptures which lined the foot of the cliff.

Stooping from under the cliff's ridge, Digsy stood, the air crisp and clean suddenly, and he could feel the cold caress his lungs as he drew in deep, revitalising breaths. It was a pleasant morning and he didn't want to rush, so he stretched his pains away, stepped to the edge of the plateau, and surveyed the descending scape before him.

At the bottom of the slope, which dropped away at his feet, just before it met the road, his truck was well hidden, and already loaded with moonshine. The plateau he stood on jutted from the mountain and stretched out ten metres either side of him, before re-joining the rocky slope and dropping steeply. An army of pines straddled the slopes around it, blocking the view of the mountains behind them, sunlight blazing through them in shafts of wispiness, spotlighting the pine needles that carpeted the ground like a duvet of bronze.

Behind him, the cliff rose almost vertically above the entrance to his cave, which was concealed beneath an overhang.

It was a beautiful little spot. Nice and quiet, and away from it all. It had been Digsy's home ever since The Order first attacked Queenstown, though he'd known about it for a long time before that. An old friend had shown it to him in the old world. Shortly after, he'd brought Mary to see it, and they'd shared a bottle of wine on the plateau before it.

Again he tried to shake the memories that invariably popped into his mind, but there she was again. Always there. Always lurking, always ready to brighten or darken Digsy's day.

Mary.

He'd lost her quite literally. No trace had he seen of her since the apocalypse.

She'd simply vanished.

Now, some may argue at this juncture, that to use the word *apocalypse,* is to overstate the situation to a degree. The naysayers may cry **Nay!** The world yet lives on, nay thrives as the hemp army might claim in righteous indignation, unencumbered as it is by humanity's excesses, and Digsy would certainly have been the first to voice his accord Dear reader.

He remembered watching it all unfold as he sat with Mary, glued to the holo-telly as he lovingly sipped his home-brew.

The Apocalypse. The end of days.

It hadn't seemed like anything out of the ordinary to begin with. More something that was happening elsewhere. New Zealand seemed to have escaped the worst of it. There'd been a few more earthquakes of course. A couple of volcanos smouldering in the north island and a spot of flooding and unusually high winds. A few hundred dead here, a thousand there, but that was all merely par for the course in those days. The world had grown jaded by then, and the people complacent.

Such was life.

Digsy had warned people though. Prepare yourselves and get stocked up he'd preached. Be ready, but people just laughed it off when he casually dropped the subject into an otherwise pleasant chit-chat, or looked at him like he was crazy.

'It's nothing to worry about,' they'd retort with a nervous chuckle before wandering quickly off.

The thought never ceased to amaze him, and it didn't again as he made his way down the trail to his truck, careful to leave no evidence of his passing. How lucky he'd been. Fortunes had been favouring our Digsy before the apocalypse you see, and he'd found himself by chance in one of the few places to remain habitable since it.

He'd moved to Queenstown in 2030, and was instantly enamoured with its natural majesty, untouched for the most part by the incessant destruction of progress. Indeed, one of the few semi-spoilt places the world could yet boast boasted most everyone that lived there, and splendid it certainly was— a picture-perfect paradise no less, nestled lakeside midst an array of snow-capped peaks, thundering turquoise rivers and vistas to blow even the most well-versed of minds.

It had been such a happy place. So full of joy and wonder at the world around them. But yay, it wasn't to last.

Digsy remembered roadblocks being posted there a few months before the "big one", and armed guards manning them, the airport being closed and curfews imposed when word of another pandemic started to spread. The first case had just been reported in the north island. Restaurants closed and busses stopped. People avoided each other in the streets. Looting and stockpiling, paranoia and fear.

And if that wasn't enough, the quakes began in earnest not long after that, in Queenstown and most everywhere else. The oil had been drained, the planets lubricant dried up, and her plates ground together like never before. Nowhere escaped it. Nowhere was safe, but it's nothing to worry about so they were told. Batten down your hatches and everything will be okay they were assured as an advert for the brand new I-bot came on and the world went, 'Ooooooh!'

That pitiful theory was laid to rest along with three billion souls in early 2044.

Old mother nature spat her dummy. She'd had enough of humanity's lecherous ways, and Hollywood had gotten it right too. A chain reaction of disasters, seemingly coordinated, rocked the world. It was absolute pandemonium. Volcanoes erupted as one across the globe, the air choked as ash clouds circled and day turned to night almost everywhere at once. It was the perfect storm. The seas smashed the coasts and the rains the land, the wind ripping everything in its path to shreds as reactors failed and vast swathes of land were rendered uninhabitable. The power was cut, the crops dried up and the teabags ran out. Untold suffering, untold heartache, untold devastation and untold loss.

Help didn't come for most though. Disease, starvation and depravity.

'Where are you when we need you?' cried the banners.

'Get back,' retorted the police surrounding them.

Needless to say, it quickly turned ugly, and most everything fell apart from that point from what Digsy remembered. It was just too far gone. Too much damage done for society to simply claw itself back from. Fresh water ran out and the survivors grew desperate, and violence captured the world as the fortunate few watched on like it was some epic tale they didn't realise they starred in. Revolution and mayhem, and nothing could stop it. Nothing could repair the damage that had already been done, but the bombs dropped anyway.

It seemed humanity didn't need any assistance in its own demise from there, but then came the nail in the coffin for most.

The big one.

The fourth of April 2044.

Such dark days, which sadly for Digsy, he still remembered well. The end of the world, or at least the end of the world as it was known at the time.

Oh the things he'd seen and the things he'd done. The things he'd had to do. Often, he'd shudder at the mere thought of the heinous acts he'd committed in the name of survival. Violent acts, depraved acts, and embarrassing acts too. He'd helped bury the dead, and thrown up on the first maggot ridden corpse he'd seen, and again he forced the memories from his mind, ducking under an overhanging branch and tripped on the adjoining root, making a mental note not to drink his moonshine for breakfast.

The ground began to level off, the undergrowth thicker suddenly, growing around, and hiding the ruins that sat rotting beneath it, and Digsy could see his truck now – an old Toyota Hilux, battered but reliable, and perfectly suited to the rugged local terrain - riding low under the moonshine he'd stacked on her the night before.

He'd named the truck Vera, after his grandma, and had the engine converted to run off his moonshine too, much like his grandma. She was grey, tatty, flaking and bruised, much like his grandma, but well-looked after, and not looking bad at all for forty, which was where the similarities ended.

The truck was hidden behind a stone wall with the surrounding foliage draped strategically over it. Stacked on the back, the moonshine was protected by reinforced plates which rose along the sides from behind the cab to the rear.

Placing his air pistols on the seat beside him, he started her up, and she roared reassuringly to life.

First he would complete the trade, and then he'd find a real gun.

The warehouse was a twenty-minute drive away, just beyond the marsh at the town's limit.

Chapter 5

Passing through the marsh without word, Her Ladyship was lost in contemplation of the shit that the day no doubt held in store for her. The morning haze was thick here, and sat just above the marsh, shrinking her world perceptibly around her. Once through the roadblock at New Queenstown's limit, they passed a steep adjoining road to the right, leading up towards the warehouse where Raul was soon to meet the moonshine delivery, and Her Ladyship instructed him to slow as a man emerged from behind a burnt-out car on the left and hailed them.

Of average height, he was lean and muscular, standing upright and proud, with neat blond hair and circular glasses that complemented his stereotype perfectly. He stood tense and clearly nervous, in beige military fatigues that were slightly too small for his frame. Tomas was the man's name. One of the town's vast immigrant population, which Her Ladyship considered a blight. He was ex-military too though, and would make a good edition to her ranks she knew.

The truck shuddered to a stop on the verge beside him.

Her Ladyship pushed the door open.

'**My God!**' she croaked, writhing back in disgust at the stench suddenly invading the truck. The newcomer smelled like a wombat's arse. He ducked through the door and slumped down beside her. Her Ladyship felt sick and indiscreetly wound down her window, making a show of sucking in the fresh air and then overdoing a coughing fit.

'So, fak'n soldier boy.'

She turned to him with a sigh, folding her arms across her breast, and looking him over with glaringly obvious distaste. 'What's the fak'n word mate? Have ya found me those fak'n plans yet?'

Looking to her from behind the rim of his glasses, Tomas dropped his eyes, avoiding her amused gaze. His knee was pumping up and down, like he was psyching himself up to do what his every instinct told him not to. He was understandably tense thought she, eyeing him warily now, but he seemed more so than usual. He seemed angrier, and hostile even, which Her Ladyship supposed was understandable, given that she'd kidnapped his daughter, but still though, his fists were clenched and he was shaking, beads of sweat forming on his forehead.

'My... my daughter,' he started after a moment, his tone timorous yet resolute, a defiant look in his eyes now though as he turned his head to face her.

'Your fak'n daughter...' Her Ladyship cut in. 'Will be fine, yoooou Nazi baaastard! As long as ya do what I say. Alright?'

'Zat is not fair. I am not...' began Tomas, but she stopped him with a finger to his lips.

Smiling a fake smile, she brushed pretend dirt from his shoulder, and he huffed, slumping into himself, and then dropped his head like a scolded child. Gazing at his knees, he was resigned it appeared, to his treacherous lot, and gave a barely discernible nod of his head.

'Well...?' Her Ladyship continued, her eyes probing him as her patience in her snitch quickly waned. Still Tomas hesitated though, clearly agonising over the decision he was being forced to make.

He knew his friend Sinead had the plans in question, but The Order had kidnapped his daughter. It was a simple enough choice obviously, but the thought of betraying his friend though, betraying his love, was an absolute nightmare that was real for Tomas suddenly.

He had no choice though.

'I tsink I know where ze plans are.'

But he also knew that Sinead would never let The Order have them, so a cunning plan of some description was called for.

Sinead would be wondering where Tomas was now he knew. The raid would be going down soon, and Tom was supposed to be on lookout duty, but he'd had to meet Her Ladyship.

If only Her Ladyship knew what they were about to do. The thought buoyed Tomas for a moment, but he could feel her gaze fixed on him, so he held his smile. Soon he'd see his daughter again. Her Ladyship had promised him that much, once he'd delivered the plans. Somehow he'd get the plans from Sinead, and without involving her in any way, after their raid on The Order's warehouse.

Chapter 6

The compound Sinead gazed at sat sparse, but for a few bits of rusted machinery lining the warehouse at its centre. It was a chilly morning, and an eerie gloss hung midst the trees, hanging a few feet above the ground, but rising quickly and twinkling in the sunlight that broke sporadically through the clouds.

It all looked so pretty, so peaceful, and yet ill omens danced on the ether. Sinead's Ominositor, had she had one, and had such a thing ever existed, would've undoubtedly exploded at the extra-sensory badness permeating the air. Her nerves were tingling. She felt terrible suddenly, and oh so weak, worn to the bone through The Order's oppression her Da had always preached whenever she'd bemoan their lot.

Hence why they were about to raid the warehouse.
Sinead wasn't ready though. None of them were. There were so many ways in which she could see the raid going wrong. Their crew were untrained, undernourished and arguably unhinged. It was a huge risk she knew, especially considering the guards she could see patrolling the compound, the weapons they carried and the muscles they wore.

One of them was big and fat for want of a more fitting term, more than muscly, and bore a striking resemblance to the warriors of old Sinead had seen pictures of in books—The Sumo if she remembered correctly. A strange craft it seemed to her, in which the combatants indulge in a spot of vigorous hugging whilst trying to remove each other's loincloths. He carried a rifle which he held like he were on parade, and stood around six-feet tall, with a black tracksuit clinging to his girth.

The route he'd walked since dawn remained unchanged – clockwise around the warehouse, and patrolling in the opposite direction, was his partner. He stood well over six feet, his broad shoulders rolling forwards under their own weight, with muscles upon muscles and pock marked skin draped over sharp, angry features. He wore a black T-shirt and shorts under a long beige overcoat, dirty and tattered, with a red band tied around his right arm, as did all The Order's militia. An eye patch covered his left eye, and a mass of thick dreadlocks sprouted from his massive, square head.

She could see his sword's hilt rising up behind his shoulder, the pointy end jutting out behind the opposite thigh, and a pair of sawn-off shotguns nestled in his belt.

Sinead's stomach rumbled and captured the mood. How could they get past the guards?

Shooting rabbits was one thing she'd mused as she pondered the conundrum. The furry little yokes had done nothing to her, but needs must as her Da had always reminded her whenever she'd question the morality of the murder she was to commit. They had to eat somehow, and at least the rabbits didn't shoot back.

The Order's guards would shoot back though she suspected.

It was a disaster waiting to happen she knew, but they needed the food.

The supplies they were to rob were inside the warehouse that loomed before Sinead. A couple of smaller sheds sat nearer the compound's perimeter fence, and beyond that, a patch of woodland gave way to the marsh at New Queenstown's limit. That was their escape once the job was done. Tomas had cut a hole in the fence the previous night, and they were all but ready to go now.

Apparently, Tomas knew the place well. At least that's what he'd told them. He'd been scouting it daily. It was poorly guarded he'd said, and full of supplies, supplies that their people were in desperate need of, and with a harsh winter looming, robbing it was the only way they could see to survive.

It wasn't poorly guarded now though.

Tomas was perched behind an outcrop in the cliff, twenty metres up behind Sinead. She could see his head poking up from behind a cluster of rocks, and smiled as he nodded back down at her, a twinkle of sunlight catching his glasses as he did.

In the old world, he'd been an officer in the German army. A sniper or some such. He was their protector now though. Their lookout, and he prided himself on his prowess with a rifle.

He could see most of the yard from his position, and keep a vigilant eye out.

An hour earlier, he'd vanished without word, which Sinead had thought strange, and somewhat disconcerting given the occasion, but he'd just returned and resumed his position. He'd seemed flustered at first. Distracted, and a little shifty, though he'd assured her that everything was fine.

He'd been to see his man on the inside apparently. An old friend of his, and all was well.

'Ve should go now. Stick to ze plan,' he'd insisted on return.

The plan itself was the problem though.

'Fill yer pockets an' run,' Sinead's Da had laughed when she'd enquired as to their strategy the day before. Something had seemed different about her Da suddenly though. He'd seemed twitchy and erratic, and the plan he'd unveiled seemed thrown together at best.

'Boob, Dobbin, d'ye hear me lads? Come on now boys would yis. Pay attention so...'

He'd seemed disconcertingly jovial too, continuing, 'You lads create a distraction. Tomas, you cover dem boy, and Sinead luv, you can get us in.'

His speech hadn't inspired much confidence, but Sinead had just put it down to nerves. Today was a different story entirely though. Today her Da seemed entirely unsure of himself and verging on manic.

The guards by the warehouse flicked their smokes to the ground, a gentle breeze tickling the air as a wave of golden leaves fluttered from the trees.

Everyone was in position.

No one was ready.

It would be going down soon.

Chapter 7

Pulling into the market square, which was surrounded by five storeys of cracked mirrored windows, balconies on every second one, on all sides but the dock, Her Ladyship stepped from the truck and slammed the truck's door behind her, strutting off towards the steamboat that was moored at the lakes' edge. That was Her Ladyship's HQ, *Uppity cow,* thought Raul with a sneer as he watched her hobble off towards it. She'd been in a terrible mood all week, and she was driving Raul nuts. Being her number two, he'd borne the brunt of it, and good riddance.

With a crunch, he forced the truck into gear and rolled on, ignoring the rabble and toil that lined the narrow streets he passed. A busy day lay ahead. Raul was due to meet the moonshine delivery, so he set off back the way he'd come, north out of town towards the warehouse, ignoring Her Ladyship's face as it heckled him from the back of his mind.

Oh how Raul loathed Her Ladyship. She was a beast of a woman, vile, ruthless and vindictive, and wasn't the kind of employer he'd envisaged when she'd forced him into service three years earlier.

She'd promoted Raul recently though. Now he was the head of her elite guard, and he wasn't enjoying his lot at all. Twenty blood thirsty, deranged lunatics comprised the guard, and Raul was in charge of them.

Pulling away from the buildings that cast the town centre in eternal shadow, he ignored the guard at the first roadblock, just beyond the town centre, and stopped a few meters before it. Mo was the guard's name if he remembered correctly. He was a stout fellow, and had served The Order well, but he was objectionable too, and insubordinate at times almost. He'd always seemed so happy with himself, like he could see what nobody else could, and Raul had never liked him, so after a little nod, he kept his eyes forward and drove on as Mo opened the gate and waved him through.

More important things were at hand than rogue employees this day. At last, precious moonshine was on its way. More moonshine meant more machines, which meant more progress and more power, and oh how Raul longed for a taste of Digsy's moonshine again. Indeed, he remembered it well from the old days, before The Order had enslaved him. Raul had helped Digsy with some of his early brews, and had indeed developed somewhat of a taste for it, but Her Ladyship soon stamped that wee pleasure from existence.

The thought of it unnerved Raul suddenly, and he looked to the 44 Magnum lying on the seat beside him. It had once been Digsy's. The long barrel glistened as the sun caught it, shining on the evil ideas popping into Raul's mind almost it seemed.

Ideas which he'd been straining increasingly to supress of late, which was becoming increasingly strenuous.

At one time, he and Digsy had been the best of friends, but things had grown tense between them of late. Digsy had been getting in the way. Raul had relayed Her Ladyship's offer to him of head brewer within The Order's ranks, but Digsy had refused it, and drip fed them his moonshine whenever it suited him instead. Now Raul was tasked with finding Digsy's cave and stealing his equipment, which had strained their relationship somewhat.

Without Digsy's moonshine though, The Order would have no fuel. All of their machines, all their plans and all of their dreams would be redundant. The truck shuddered as if to emphasise the point, and Raul tapped the fuel gage, as pointless as it was. The tank was almost empty he knew. The moonshine couldn't be coming at a better time.

Chapter 8

It would be too cold to brew for the next few months, and Digsy's moonshine was running low, so he kept the truck in neutral, rolling down the road as quietly as the morning. The road wound back and forth through the devastation, hairpin after hairpin, obstacle after obstacle, much of it reclaimed by nature now, and barely visible through it. The sun caught brief glimpses of metal and stonework through the brambles, corrugated roofs or telegraph poles poking up through the foliage like relics of another time.

Near the foot of the mountain, the road met another, where it emerged from beneath the canopy, and the foothills loomed all around suddenly, meeting beyond the road where the ground fell away into a deep gorge.

To the left, a bridge crossed the gorge, the road cutting north through the basin towards Arrowtown, so Digsy turned right towards New Queenstown, the road barely passable, cracked and still littered with debris, winding up and away from the gorge, and then back down again, up and down, left and right, vivid autumn shades shimmering on the breeze all along its length.

Five minutes later, the slopes retreated from the road, giving way to a valley that stretched towards the town and onto the lake beyond it.

It was a stunning view to behold normally, but the morning mist and smoke from the town's fires blocked the view entirely now. Just a blanket of grey sat atop the marsh, which stretched across the valley, riddled now with the remnants of the homes it'd swallowed six years earlier.

Beyond the marsh the road met an incline, before cutting down through New Queenstown towards the lake. At the crest of the incline was a roadblock, with a wire fence stretching from both sides of it, all the way to the foot of the mountains surrounding. The guards there hadn't always proved cordial in the past, but with this being a sanctioned visit, Digsy presumed all would be well.

He was to meet his friend from the old world, Raul, who worked for The Order now, and was indeed one of their top dogs Digsy had heard. Raul had brokered the initial deal, and Digsy's relations with The Order had been generally strained otherwise, so Raul had become his only contact with them.

The warehouse was at the top of the hill beyond the marsh, to the right after the roadblock.

Raul would see him.

Chapter 9

A cool breeze whipped up the leaves and rustled the foliage that Kieran was crouched in. The day was warming up, the sun just poking up from behind the peaks, its bite ferocious and oppressive almost though, and far more so than Kieran ever remembered it being. It was so confusing to Kieran suddenly, but he couldn't understand why. Everything was confusing to him, and that in itself scared him to the point of even more confusion. His aged muscles ached along with his bones, which had been the case for years now, but that too seemed amplified suddenly, and he feared to stand lest he not be able to.

What was happening to him?

A few meters before him, his daughter, Sinead, was crouched in the tall grass which kept her hidden from the compound, her gaze fixed on the guards who were patrolling it beyond the tree line. The guards would be growing tired now, so soon they would launch the raid. That much Kieran knew at least, that they were about to raid the warehouse, but he couldn't remember why suddenly. Pushing himself up, he smiled at his ability to do so, and then cringed at the sudden pain in his lower back, easing himself slowly upright.

'Are ye keepin' an eye on d'road now Da?'

Sinead craned her neck to face him, but she was frowning at Kieran now for some reason. Ah yes, the road. Kieran remembered Sinead asking him to watch the road suddenly. That's what he was supposed to be doing. Where was the road though? He couldn't see it. Had he left it somewhere? And what was he supposed to be watching it for? He didn't answer Sinead, as he knew she'd be mad at him, and tried to remember where the road was instead.

Sinead's Da was the only family she had left in the world. Her Ma, and most of her family, had either been killed in the quakes, or slain by The Order, but her Da had always been there. He'd been a good leader to the people he'd adopted too, and been instrumental in the forming of their camp after they'd fled Queenstown. He was an honourable, strong-minded and resourceful fellow, of compassion, humility, fortitude and dignity, thus why he was the chosen leader of their raiding party. Something seemed wrong with him now though. There was something different about him. He was worrying Sinead, and starting to unnerve her, pacing around and muttering to himself, tugging at his filthy white beard, on edge and avoiding eye contact.

He'd gotten much worse since the morning too though it seemed. Confused and incoherent at times almost now. Smiling a sad smile, she tried to catch his gaze as his eyes darted this way and that, settling on hers for a split second before jumping on again. He crouched after a moment, staring intently at her through the mass of tangled hair between them, a sadness in his eyes which displayed no hope, but had an urgency too as he struggled to find the words, slumping against a birch to his side lest he lose his balance.

'Ders a truck cumin luv.'

Kieran could just see the truck now, on the road, which he was very happy to see, emerging from the foothills and approaching the marsh from the north. Coughing violently, he brought his hands up to his mouth and lowered his eyes in shame, slumping back against the birch again lest he loose his balance. Sinead brushed the matted locks from his face and smiled, fighting to keep back the tears at her Da's demise. She knew he shouldn't be with them in this state. He should be resting, but he'd insisted he lead them, and he'd seemed okay before they set off.

'Okay, Da. You wait here now,'

A tear crowned her eye, 'I'll go and see.'

Kissing him on the forehead, she turned back to the warehouse.

'We'll hafta wait, Sinead luv,' her Da wheezed, placing a hand on her shoulder. 'Ders too many guards, luv, and a truck cumin so der is.'

Nodding, she placed her hand on his with a sigh, and then stood, signalling to Boob, who she could just make out tucked behind a shed on the far side of the warehouse, pressing down with both her palms to stay put.

Kissing her Da on the cheek, she slipped her Ma's gold chain back inside his ragged Parker, and then crept back through the hole in the fence to the shrub-line beyond it.
'Sinead luv. Ders a truck cumin, luv. Abort! Abort luv!'

Chapter 10

A lone sentry patrolled the walkway that split the marsh in two, wispy and wraith-like, and floating it seemed, on air through the mist. He was of no consequence though, and the truck passed through the marsh and met the incline at the far side, chugging up through the mist again, the scene bathed in tenderness suddenly as the haze thinned and sunlight poured through it.

The air felt warmer too, the peaks either side of Digsy channelling him up towards the roadblock that he could see at the crest of the hill before him now. The guards there remained unmoved as he pulled up before them. There were two of them, with two battered cars, their bumpers almost touching blocking the road behind them.

'Greetings…'

Stepping from the truck, the sun hung low behind Digsy, casting his shadow to the feet of the guard on the right, who looked to the shadow, and then back to Digsy with a frown. He wore brown dungarees and a tatty camouflage jacket, the sleeves too short and riding up his arms. The red band tied around his arm was faded and wrinkled, and he chewed a stick as he pushed himself from the car he leant against. Bringing a second hand to his rifle, wiry strands of auburn flopped over his unfortunate face, and he smiled, a smile intended to leave no doubt as to the sender's ill will. He was around five-foot-nine, with a gut that circled his mid-section from naval to groin, but was strangely slender otherwise. He looked like a seasoned taxi driver to Digsy. Digsy recognised him too. He was a former officer of the law of the road-bound persuasion in the old world. He'd arrived in town just before the quakes, transferred from his station in Alabama.

Red was the guard's name if Digsy remembered correctly.

'No trespasin. Yawl git,' came Red's reply.

'Splendid…' Digsy's.

A dog barked somewhere in the distance, and then yelped. All was quiet otherwise.

'I come bearin' gifts mate. I've got your grog, Raul's expectin' me.'

The air was growing much warmer now, and the haze clearing, the sun rising quickly and shimmering like a nugget of gold on a riverbed. It appeared that Red was studying Digsy now, with what appeared to be thought, and an uncomfortable silence ensued as Red pondered his repose.

'I know,' it came.

He didn't elaborate from there though, and the silence resumed, the guards grinning as Digsy frowned, folding his arms at his chest with a 'Hmmm'. Being the bringer of booze, Digsy had expected a more amiable welcome, and he was a mite put out. He went to speak after a moment, when the second guard sniggered suddenly, snorting as he did, and then stepped up beside Red. He was tall and slender, his skin golden and cracked by the sun, with greasy blonde hair, a face like a ferret, and a long, crooked nose. Reaching back, he took an arrow from the sheath there, notching it on the bow he held, and in some danger of being collected on a passing breeze.

'Good then, great…' Digsy went on.

'Would y'move so I can drop yer booze off then please?' he enquired.

'Maaay…be,' replied Red, his drawl prolonging the syllables almost beyond comprehension.

'Was thinkin' bout just tak'n it though.'

The skinny guard sniggered again. A couple of his front teeth were missing, so he whistled with a lisp, as he added:

'Can I shoot him, Red? Can I mate?'

This wasn't the start that Digsy had hoped for. He was unsure how to proceed, but he did so nevertheless, and with a witty retort too no less, which in hindsight, clearly wasn't chosen carefully enough given the dicey nature of the situation, and his suspicions were confirmed with a startling bang as a tiny hole appeared in the truck door beside him.

Stumbling backwards, he reached out and grabbed the truck's door to stop himself, startled and shaken slightly, but unharmed, and watched on as Red raised his rifle up to him again. He could see Red's finger twitching on the trigger, itching to pull it, the sneering eyes just waiting for an excuse. Waiting for Digsy to say the wrong thing again. It wasn't to be though. A car horn honked out, shattering the tension in an instant.

'Bro!' boomed a familiar voice that seemed to echo more than the horn had, yelling from every direction in turn like a Mexican wave as it rippled around the valley; and a most welcome interruption it was indeed.

'Digsy bro, ged up here!'

Raul had a roar that could flatten a tidal wave. He was fifty meters up the road to the right, and barely visible above the foliage but for the hat that he waved in the air above it.

Barking instructions at the guards, Raul stepped into the orange truck behind him and set off up the hill.

'Today yow lucky day boy.'

With a sneer, Red stepped into one of the cars blocking the road, the skinny guard the other, and once the roadblock had been cleared, Digsy rolled on. Turning off the main road, which sloped towards the town centre, he turned up to the right, both sides of the street littered with derelict workshops and warehouses here, and followed Raul's Land Rover up the hill towards the fenced compound he knew his meeting to be in.

It should be a simple enough matter from here. Digsy's moonshine for The Order's supplies.

But it was all on this deal.

Digsy's surviving the winter depended on this deal.

Chapter 11

The warehouse loomed twenty meters before Sinead, with only open ground before it, but for the derelict shed that stood crooked ten meters before her. Only moments before she'd heard a gunshot, and the guards patrolling the warehouse had moved off towards the compound's gates, and were out of sight now. The shot's echo still lingered, and Sinead could hear a vehicle approaching now, from beyond the compound it seemed, and getting closer.

Her instructions had been to wait until an hour before the changing of the guards, which wasn't far off, but she was intrigued and growing impatient, so she crept onwards, across the open ground towards the warehouse, and crouched behind the shed as an Orange Land Rover pulled in through the compound gates.

She heard its engine shudder to a halt, and then heard a door slam.

The two guards were speaking to the newcomer now, but their voices were muffled and too far away for Sinead to hear properly, so after a moment, she crept to the shed's corner and peered around it. The orange truck was parked at the warehouse corner, and three of The Order's guards were stood beside it, the newcomer shorter by far than the other two, and podgy. He was wearing a black pirate suit it appeared, clean but ragged, and stood before the taller guard, glaring up at him, his finger in the guard's face as he thrust it up at him.

Once again, that all too familiar sense of pervading doom washed through Sinead. The raid's prospects were looking worse by the second. Again she heard an engine growling in the distance, dropping gear and whining as it hit the incline leading up to the compound, and then moments later, another truck, grey and battered, pulled in through the gates and parked by the warehouse next to the first.

A fourth man stepped from it, nervous and hurried, a long leather jacket draping to his knees with the hood beneath it up, so she could see nought of his face but for the nose poking out from under it. It was broad, hooked and proud, and perched above his beard which hung ragged to his chest. Of average height and bulk, he was maybe in his early thirties, but he was covered up mostly, so it was hard to tell.

He stepped hesitantly towards the guards.

'Digsy bro…'

Raul was grinning from ear to ear, his teeth glistening in the morning sun as the samurai sword at his hip did likewise.

'Ow are yu?' he enquired, extending his hand out, which Digsy strode forth and accepted with genuine warmth for the friend he'd lost touch with.

Time, it appeared to Digsy, had not been kind to Raul. His face was more lined than he remembered, and weathered. His bald head sported a black, tri-tipped naval hat with a bedraggled red feather tucked into it. He wore a Georgian naval officer's jacket, black with blood-red trim, and knee-high boots with his trousers tucked into them. A far cry from his humble former self.

A moment passed as Raul appraised Digsy in kind, with a contradictory frown quickly replacing his smile. He ushered the two guards away and they stepped back a few paces, just out of hearing range, but close enough to step in should the need to castrate Digsy arise.

'Not too shabby cheers mi hearty…' Digsy replied with a wry smile, and before his brain could intervene, he went on,

'You're lookin'… err… extravagant. You off to a fancy-dress party?'

Raul's brow dropped and he squeezed Digsy's hand, his deep-set eyes penetrating Digsy's before he dropped his hand abruptly. The dreadlocked guard stepped closer again, putting his hands to the sawn-off shotguns tucked into his belt.

'Cheeky bro. In Bra-siil, we cut off your bolls for this.'

Raul made a cup with one hand and scissors above it from the other, closing his fingers in a chopping motion.

At one time, Raul would have laughed at such audacity Digsy couldn't help but muse. The two hadn't seen much of each other since the upheavals though, though he'd known Raul from the old world, and things had obviously changed. They'd both arrived in Queenstown twenty years prior, backpacks and instant noodles in tow, and shared many a drunken moment and hilariously debauched jape. But whilst Digsy had been in the hills when The Order attacked, Raul had been in Queenstown. He'd battled hard to begin with from what Digsy had heard, but The Order had quickly captured him.

Being a resourceful fellow though, and with mouths to feed, before Raul knew it, he was a fully pledged colonel in the "New Wakatipu Order".

The two of them sat on opposing sides of life now, and Digsy knew he'd have to tread carefully.

'Force of habit captain. Not in fronta the troops, I know,' he conceded, gesturing at the guards, one of whom grunted at a rustling sound that came from near the shed, raising his rifle, and shuffled off towards it to investigate.

Moments passed as Sinead cowered behind the shed, her heart pounding faster, sure she'd been spotted by the guard she could hear approaching her now. The cover of the shrub-line was only a short dash away, but the ground lay open before it. She was trapped. She'd gotten too close. The rotund guard was just beyond the shed now, and getting closer. She chanced another glimpse around it's corner, and ducked back as she saw him coming towards her, bouncing from side to side like a flicked Subbuteo player. Slowly she stood lest he see her knees poking out, and pressed herself tight up against the timbers, the footsteps softer now, on the grass and closer still.

There was no escape. The guard had stopped just around the shed's corner, warping the very time around him. She could see his gut sticking out like a half moon, his sheer size almost drawing her towards him, and hear his shallow breaths.

He held his rifle out before him, which he strafed in a flat arc which was swinging back towards Sinead now. He was so close. Were she to move, she would be seen. Were she to cough, she would be heard. But it wasn't her own life that Sinead was concerned for. She didn't care too much for that these days, and she knew Tomas would put a bullet in the guard's head as soon as he stepped around the corner; but then the game would be up. The Order's guards would find them, and the others would die.

Time stood still. She dared not breathe.

One more step from the guard, and all hell would break loose.

Chapter 12

Raul's gaze followed the fat guard, and he smiled, as if laughing off the same trail of thought that Digsy had embarked upon, and maybe the guard had only seen a leaf flutter, but it unnerved Digsy. The guard was stood by the corner of the shed, twenty metres from them, his rifle held out before him, strafing it left to right.

What had he seen?

Whatever he'd seen didn't appear to concern Raul however, who'd turned his attention to the large stack of moonshine on the back of Digsy's truck, adopting as indifferent an air as he could muster.

'So…' he started, pausing for effect as he eyed the tarpaulin covered hoard rising up behind the truck's cabin.

'How is tha booze?'

This was more the conversation that Digsy wanted to have. Strictly business. Smiling a wary smile, he released the straps holding down the tarp.

'The booze my friend…' he replied with an inadvertent smug note as the stack of vats slid into view. 'Is as good as always,'

Unabashed pride washed through Digsy, and he forgot for a moment that he resented giving his moonshine to The Order.

'It'll knock yer bollocks off…' he went on with unintended gusto. 'Twenty kegs of…'

Bang!

The crack of a gunshot filled the air and the fat guard by the shed crumpled, the blast echoing mockingly as a fountain of red gushed from his head.

For a split second, there was a confused pause, perplexed eyes searching each other for answers. Raul and the dreadlocked guard were glaring accusingly at Digsy suddenly though. The dreadlocked guard stepped towards him, reaching for his guns, but then a second shot grazed the ground between them and they all pounced for cover between the trucks.

Shot after shot followed, an air of confusion as bullets thumped and zipped around them, slamming into the plating protecting the moonshine, driving into the ground or thumping into the truck they hid behind, and not fired in haste it seemed, but at a steady rate, measured and considered.

What the hell was going on?

Digsy had never been in a gunfight before, and he was terrified. He wrenched his legs to his chest as a bullet pinged into the asphalt, slamming into a burnt-out car by the fence. He felt queasy suddenly, light headed and out of his depth.

'Is this yo doing, Digsy?' growled Raul, flinching with every shot, holding his hat in place with one hand as the other sought the gun in its holster.

Digsy protested his innocence, but the shooting drowned him out, so he shook his head and Raul snarled.

'In the cliffs boss bro…'

The dreadlocked guard was crouched beside Raul with his back to the orange truck, dreadlocks swaying as he turned, facing Digsy's truck with the warehouse to his right. He pulled the two sawn-offs from his belt, pointing one of them over his shoulder up at the cliffs beyond the truck they cowered behind.

'There's a sniper up there.'

So Raul nodded and the dreadlocked guard grinned. His eyes were sparkling, and turning slowly, he rose, looking through the truck's window, and dropped back down again as another shot followed and the window shattered above him.

Another volley erupted, but amidst the onslaught, the dreadlocked guard spotted one of the assailants by the far corner of the warehouse, so he stood quickly and levelled his sawn-offs, and Digsy heard a scream follow the blast as the guard ducked back down again with a smile on his face.

Thump!

The bullet drove harmlessly into the warehouse above the guard as he ducked back out of sight, and the empty casing sprung into the air, clinking down the cliff face before Tomas. Tom's pulse was racing. This wasn't supposed to be happening. It was supposed to have been a clandestine operation, but the fat guard had seen Sinead, so Tomas had to shoot him.

Now it was kicking off, and Boob was dead.

Fumbling with the bullet in his hand, Tomas slid it into the chamber, resting the stock in the crease of his shoulder and the barrel on the rock before him. His instincts weren't the finely tuned death machines they once were he was finding. He'd never fumbled over a reload, and never missed his target.

The dreadlocked guard had given Tom a huge target, and yet he'd missed!

Scheisse!

He pushed the rifle's action forward and felt the bullet drop into place, and then looked back down to the yard sprawled out below him, hoping beyond hope that Sinead had used the distraction to retreat whilst she still could. But there she was still, crouched behind the shed a few feet from the guard he'd shot.

Moments passed as the shots battered back and forth, each one ripping Sinead's nerves to shreds, and it was all her fault she knew. She'd gotten too close and the fat guard had seen her. As soon as she'd seen his foot stepping around the shed, she'd known it was a dead foot. It was poking around the shed's corner now, and twitching, a pool of red quickly engulfing the leg attached to it.

Now they were in a firefight they couldn't win though she knew. Their numbers were even, but her crew were out-gunned.

If only she hadn't ventured out so far…

The whole valley was awash with noise, the blasts rippling like machine guns, echoing wildly in a continuous volley of death that terrified Sinead. She dared not move, dared not retreat from the shed.

For a precious few seconds though, she found the time to catch her breath and focus. She could escape if she was careful she knew. Tom had the guards pinned behind the orange truck still, so she backed slowly away, keeping low as she crept back towards the fence.

Just as she reached it though, she saw something moving through the bushes. She couldn't make it out to begin with. It was hunched over, and moving towards the warehouse in a manner somehow familiar to her, oblivious to the danger it seemed, ragged and old and approaching the truck the guards hid behind.

She recognised him then though, and screamed out to him, but it was too late.

Her Da was metres from the orange truck, and doddering towards it.

'Sinead luv, are ye der?'

The voice was old and croaky, and sounded to Digsy like it came from just beyond the truck, frail and wavering, with another shot from the sniper accompanying it, and then another, and another, the far side of Raul's truck punched with hole after hole suddenly as bullets started tearing into it.

'Sinead luv?'

Again Digsy heard the voice, though he couldn't make it out over the racket, and he thought he heard footsteps next, and then a scream. Such a haunting sound thought he, which was followed by an elderly gentleman who'd vaulted over the truck's bonnet and launched himself into Raul, knocking him to the ground with a startled yelp.

The old man bore down at Raul like a rabid dog, snarling and drooling almost, and his foot caught Digsy on the brow, knocking him back into the truck behind him. All Raul could see was the knife-point quivering inches from his eyes. His assailant was frail but incessant in his onslaught, his strength impossible for his age, all of his limbs attacking at once as he thrashed relentlessly down.

He was like a scarecrow on cocaine, a hobo on hooch. His assault was short lived however, and it was a valiant effort, but Rodney levelled his sawn-offs and a deafening boom rattled the scene as the old man's head exploded, decorating the scene in a delightful deluge of death.

It took Digsy a moment to adjust from there. His world was awry suddenly, distorted and chaotic.

The blast from so close had knocked him for six, the scream that accompanied it but a whisper on the wind now as the next shot from the sniper drowned it out.

His world seemed to pulsate as he strained to ignore the corpse that was quickly draining beside him. The gap between the trucks seemed to shrink. The puddle of blood crept closer. It engulfed Digsy's feet and he felt sick. The ground between the trucks was gleaming, the corpse twitched and Digsy stepped back, stumbling as the sniper spotted him and tried to pick him off again.

They were still pinned.

'Don't worry, bro.'

Rising to a crouch, Raul wiped the old man's blood from his face, and then gestured towards the compound gates.

Reinforcements were coming.

Ducking back from his vantage spot, bullets were pinging into the cliffs all around Tomas, thumping into the trees and decimating the foliage surrounding him, like he was in his very own snow dome of debris.

His advantage was lost. The Order had reinforcements now, and they'd spotted his position. Taking another bullet from his pocket, he cowered back into the crevice that hid him from the yard. He was struggling to focus over the din though, and again he fumbled, dropping the bullet to the ground as a chunk of rock was blasted from the cliff face, smashing into his cheek as he ducked down to retrieve it.

The next thing Tom remembered, was waking up under a hail of masonry, tiny explosions riddling the cliff face above him.

The blood dripping across his face felt warm as he lay there, his world pulsating and debris pouring down all around him. The gunfire sounded distorted suddenly, echoing even more through the ringing in his ears. He tried to push himself up, but again the cliff exploded, tiny shards of rock flying in every direction, so he dropped back down and hunched up as small as he could, tucking his head under his arms as the cliff-face crumbled around him.

Tomas was pinned, the raid had failed, and Sinead was on her own.

Chapter 13

Order had been restored, and the lesser celebrated calm *after* the storm washed over the scene. The Order's reinforcements had dealt with the sniper, and the only sound now was the faint echo of the last shots, like firecrackers going off in the distance, laughing at their cowardice almost it seemed, in the face of adversity. The immediate danger was gone. Only the reinforcements interrupted the peace now.

'Who tha hell was dat?'

Pushing himself to his feet, Raul straightened his jacket, taking in the scene like the ghost of Blackbeard surveying the remnants of a boarding. He was a sight to behold indeed, covered head to toe in the splattered remains of the old man, and a demonic vision that suddenly seemed perfectly suited to his new role in life. His breathing had slowed and his composure returned, and he didn't seem at all shaken now, taking in the scene with a touch of dignity somehow about him. A satisfied air of tranquillity almost.

Stooping to retrieve his hat from the puddle of blood that it sat in, he wiped it on his jacket and then replaced it on his head, the dreadlocked guard still beside him, his sawn-offs still raised, scanning the slopes where the sniper had been.

'Are you shu they gone Rodney?'

The dreadlocked guard grunted in the affirmative, so after a moment, Digsy pushed himself back to his feet, first to one, and then to the next as he vaguely remembered being shown as a child, and peered out over the truck's bonnet.

All was still but for the rustling of the leaves. There was a pleasant hush about the scene almost. No more shooting or shouting. No more bullets ripping Raul's truck to shreds.

Only a trickle of blood seeped from the old man's corpse now. Two bloodied corpses lay face down in the dust at the far side of the warehouse, and the fat guard lay crumpled by the shed, but there was no one else around.

Digsy's jacket was splashed with blood, so he stepped over to the water barrel by the warehouse, shattering the layer of ice that had formed on the top, and that was when he saw her.

Cowering in the undergrowth near the shed, and barely perceptible through the foliage. She was well camouflaged, but Digsy could definitely see a woman crouched a few meters beyond the corpse of the fat guard. He quickly averted his eyes so as not to draw attention to her, but it was too late.

Sinead sat slumped in the undergrowth, her arms cradling her knees which cushioned her face. She'd completely forgotten her peril, and was lost now, immersed in her grief and oblivious to the world around her. Oblivious to the danger she was still in. The shooting had stopped, but she hadn't noticed. She couldn't believe it. It hadn't sunken in yet. Her Da was dead! Tears were in free fall at the shock of what she'd just witnessed. No one should have to see something like that. Sinead felt lost now, and alone. Was alone now, and she sobbed at the prospect of never seeing her Da's face again. If only she hadn't been so impatient. Tears were streaming down her cheeks, the vision of her Da leaping over the truck's bonnet replaying over and over in her mind. If only she'd listened to him and waited instead of getting too close, none of this would have happened!

Angry voices brought her back to the present though, so she wiped her tears away and looked back to the yard. One of the guards was coming towards her, dressed in black, tall, slender and agile like a ferret.

Her grief would have to wait.

Springing to her feet, she ran, across the open ground, pushing through the grass, and burst through the shrub-line between her and the fence, branches splintering and cutting into her as she pushed onwards, bringing fresh tears to her eyes.

Through the hole in the fence, through the bush, and the wrecker's yard she emerged into was full of places to hide.

There were hundreds of wrecked cars stacked three or four high all around her in rows aligned to the marsh. She heard the fence behind her rattle, so she headed left towards the mountain's foot, and ducked down the last row, panting and sweating, straining to hold back the tears, and edged onwards, trying every door as she did. None would open though, every one wedged, locked or mangled. She tripped and put her hand to the ground for balance, and held back a scream as a shard of glass drove into her skin.

Gently, she pulled it out.

The footsteps were louder now. Her pursuer had guessed correctly and was coming her way, so she shimmied backwards, facing back the way she'd come, and levelled the pistol she held with hardly the strength to do so. Her arms were trembling, blood dripping down to her elbows as the footsteps grew louder still, and then there he was.

The guard had stopped at the end of her row, and turned to face her, like he'd sensed her presence, and he stood there, grinning savagely down at Sinead, tall and slender, with greasy sun-bleached hair falling over his protruding features.

His grin disappeared as he noticed the pistol pointed at him though, and he lowered his rifle, his face twitching as he perused his vocabulary for the right deflamatory words.

Sinead had never killed anyone before. She'd never had to and didn't know if she could. The horrific act went against everything she stood for, everything her Da had taught her, and her heart raced at the thought of it, her arms trembling and oh so weak suddenly.

The guard raised a hand and took a step towards her.

'Stay der!' she snapped, crying and shaking again, unable to hold it back now, the gun barrel wobbling around like a sparkler before her.

Grinning as he saw the terrified look in Sinead's eyes though, the skinny guard stepped closer again, bringing his rifle back up with a wicked glint in his eye.

Chapter 14

No one else was around now, so Digsy dusted himself down and stretched out his limbs, rolling his neck in a painful finale. His head throbbed, and a cut traversed his brow from where the old man's boot had scuffed him.

He was lucky to be alive he knew though, with only a scrape on his knee and a scuff to show for it. Others hadn't been. Two of the attackers were down, and crows were already picking at the corpse of the fat guard, tugging at his clothes to get to the blubbery meat below.

Raul and Rodney had gone to search the cliffs and the woodland beneath it, where the sniper had been. They were out of sight now, so at the considerable risk of being branded a chauvinist for his efforts, Digsy set off in the opposite direction, towards the compound's perimeter fence where he'd seen the woman.

The skinny guard had gone in her direction, and Digsy was in no doubt as to the guard's intentions should he find her.

Reaching the fence, he saw nothing amiss. It stretched fifty metres to the left, as it did every day, and on the right reached a corner, cutting inwards to meet itself on the warehouse's north side forty metres further. The old car yard and the marsh were beyond that. That would be the woman's best escape, so that way he went.

Near the corner, where the fence cut inwards, he found a small hole at its foot, the wires recently cut and bent back in on themselves, and beyond that broken branches betrayed her route, so he followed and came to the wreckers yard, and as one might imagine, the scene was abound with mangled vehicles and burned-out wrecks, stacked in rows aligned to the marsh, some fallen between them, with brambles and grasses sprouting through their windows, doors and rust holes.

A muffled scream came from Digsy's left, so he took an air pistol from each pocket, and crept down the lines of cars, slowly passing row after row, double checking each one as he passed it by. He could hear sobbing now, growing louder and clearer, and the skinny guard finally came into view as he stepped up to the last row, ten metres down it, hemmed in by a cliff to his left and a wall of cars to his right. His back was to Digsy, and he was straddled atop the woman. He struck her and she cried out. He struck her again with instructions to stop crying, the ring on his index finger tearing into her cheek.

That wasn't on.

'Remove yerself from the lady, MATE.'

Digsy trained his air pistols down on the skinny guard, who started, and then slowly twisted to face Digsy, keeping the woman pinned as he did.

The guard appeared not in the slightest intimidated though. More irritated at the interruption than anything it seemed.

'Fak'n you again. Who d'you think you are mate?' rasped the skinny guard as he met Digsy's gaze, who stepped back a pace and raised his pistols up to the guard's face.

'I'm the man responsible for not shootin' you,' retorted Digsy. 'They were only after food. Get off her. **Now!**'

Grinning as if the idea were an absurd one, the guard shifted his weight as the woman wriggled beneath him. He slammed her arms down to stop her and she obliged with a whimper.

'Naaa mate. They killed Sumo mate.'

His gaze was fixed on Digsy's, pure evil its essence.

'Na mate. She's not getting away with that.'

Everything about the guard reeked of malice. He flicked the hair from his view, and then he lunged, throwing himself into Digsy, sending him sprawling backwards into the long grass behind him.

The ground was soft, but Digsy was startled, and the skinny guard was on him in an instant, lefts and rights pounding down in a barrage the likes of which Digsy hadn't thought the guard capable. His body armour absorbed it well though, and he struck back with his right knee, thrusting it up with all he could muster into the skinny guard's side.

Down he went.

A thorn cut into Digsy's wrist as he struggled to his feet. He cringed and his arm buckled slightly, and the guard was up before him again. The guard looked to the rifle he'd cast aside, as did Digsy. Digsy was closer to it than the guard was though, and the guard looked nervous suddenly, looking to the rifle and then back to Digsy, inching closer as Digsy did likewise. The guard chose to go for Digsy in the end though, not the rifle, but he'd been slowed, and Digsy saw the blow coming. Grasping the guard's leg as it swung in at him, Digsy twisted, and the guard crashed onto his back with a grunt. He landed next to the rifle though, and grabbed it, so Digsy slammed his boot into the skinny guard's face, sending him sprawling backwards in a manner not dissimilar to that on which he'd embarked Digsy moments before.

What strength remained suddenly drained from Digsy's limbs. They felt like jelly suddenly, and he dropped to his knees, falling forwards onto his palms and struggling for breath now. He felt numb for a moment, but that soon passed and the pain took its place.

The cut above his eye was bleeding again. A solitary drip stained the dirt below him, so he pushed himself back to his knees and dabbed his brow with his sleeve. There was only a little blood, though it felt like more.

The day was clear now. The sun had burnt the haze off, and again the trees were alive with birdsong, pigeons cooing and twittering sparrows hopping from tree to tree in an effort to lighten the mood that was tainting the scene.

No sound came from the skinny guard, and he wasn't moving either, which didn't bode well. The Order wouldn't take kindly to Digsy maybe killing one of their own he knew. Quite the contrary.

His mind flicked back to the raid. Was it simply a food raid? Who were the raiders? One of them was pushing herself to her feet a few meters from him.

Standing tentatively, painfully, he stooped to pick the guard's rifle from the ground.

'Tank you.'

No one else was there, so Digsy presumed he was the intended recipient of said utterings, and he looked towards the woman, still catching his breath as she peered nervously over at him.

Of average height, she was emaciated, cuts and scrapes on her arms, and a big one traversing her cheek. Her dirty blonde hair hung down her back, knotted and tangled and covered most of her face. She wore a sleeveless denim jacket, a red shirt beneath it, and black jeans, both tattered and filthy. Beneath the filth and malnourishment though, he saw a kind, honest face, scared and sad, but proud. Big piercing eyes, watery and bloodshot above a thimble of a nose.

She looked afraid of Digsy.

'Are you okay? Are you hurt?' he ventured after a few moments' awkward silence.

'No, I'm grand, tanks. We were just after food, me and mi Da...'

Breaking off her explanatory sentence, tears once again welled in her eyes, so Digsy reached to place a comforting hand on her shoulder, but she flinched away and he pulled it back. Cowering back, she grasped a rock from the ground, stepping back from him with the rock held high behind her. There was a real fear in her eyes, and Digsy held his hands high.

'Don't worry, please.' he offered. 'I was only trading with'em. I'm Digsy.'

He stepped back from her again, and the woman seemed to calm somewhat at that. Her shoulders dropped and she lowered the rock slightly, though still held it ready. The sun was high in the sky now, and Digsy could feel the heat on his back, his t shirt starting to stick to it between his shoulders.

'You should go,' he said after a moment. 'There'll be more guards along soon.'

'But...'

The fear in the woman's eyes had gone suddenly. She dropped the rock and gazed pleadingly at Digsy. The man stood before Sinead had been with The Order's guards moments before, at the warehouse. She recognized him, but then he had saved her life she reasoned.

Digsy could see her eyes well up, but he had to be resolute. Evidently, she needed his help, but The Order would have his head if he was caught helping her, and he'd perish without The Order's supplies.

'If they see this mess, they'll kill us both...' said he.

He wanted to help her but what could he do.

'Go now.'

Angry voices sounded in the distance.

'If you can reach the gorge, I'll meet you by the bridge later. Around dusk.'

He handed her the rifle and then stepped over to the bow the guard had dropped, picking it up, and slung it over his shoulder.

'Okay, tanks. I'm Sinead.'

Turning with an appreciatory smile, she brushed a natural dreadlock from eye to ear before stooping and disappearing down the line of wrecked cars.

Chapter 15

'Red bro, come 'ere.'

Raul was apoplectic still, but hid it well in the knowledge that Red and the other guards were still very impressionable. His jacket was a mess, covered in gore and sticky. It was his favourite jacket too, and that annoyed him more than the raid had. Who would have the nerve to attack The Order? To steal from them and kill one of theirs? As yet, the sniper hadn't been found. Rodney was still looking for him, but Raul had given up and gone to inspect his truck instead. It was ruined too. His pride and joy had been ravaged. It was riddled with bullet holes all down the driver's side. All of the windows were shattered and the front right tyre was burst, but remarkably, the engine still turned over when he started it, and spluttered valiantly into life.

'Yes baws?'

Clearly still excited at having been in a gun fight, Red saluted Raul as he approached, catching his breath, and awaited instruction. The man was a cretin, but he was loyal, and he stayed obediently as Raul cut the engine again, stepping out, then he removed the jack from the boot, placing it on the ground beneath the truck and started pumping.

'Where is yo mate? The skinny fella?'

The jack was in place under the chassis, so Raul stood and swept his arm towards it, directing Red to take his place.

'Errr, I don't know boss. I thought he wuz wid'chew.'

Worry was clear on Red's face suddenly. His friend was missing, but he obediently crouched and started pumping nevertheless.

'Ain't you seen 'im boss?'

The tyre was an inch off the ground now, so ignoring Red, Raul took the spare from the boot and dropped it next to the burst one. He wasn't in the mood for questions, so he beckoned Red up and then shoved him to the side.

'Never mine'dat, hill be fine…'

Of more concern to Raul, was Digsy's whereabouts. He too had vanished, and if Raul didn't have him followed this time, it might be months until he got another chance to find Digsy's cave. No way could he put up with Her Ladyship's whining for that long.

A hawk screeched high above them. A wisp of white floated across the sun. Raul had to find that cave.

'I godda job for you Red bro. Ninja work,' he added.

That should be enough to get Red excited he knew, and it was. His eyes widened and he perked up suddenly, eager as a beaver on dam building day.

Raul then instructed him to find Digsy, and to follow him. No more, no less, and definitely not to approach him. 'Yes baws,' replied Red conspiratorially.

The breeze caught a pile of dead leaves and sent them circling across the packed earth, like a mini tornado as it waltzed across the compound.

'We need to fine'is cave. Repot back to me when you fine it.'

With another salute, Red trotted off, Raul finished changing the truck's tyre, and then went to join Rodney, who was searching the marsh for whomever it was that attacked the warehouse.

Chapter 16

Sinead's surroundings were naught but a mangled blur of despair, distorted by tears and the pain of loss in her heart. The pain of the worst day of her life. She was battered and bruised, and her will to go on was fading by the second. Tripping on a tree root, she crashed to the ground, but felt not the pain, muted as it was by the agony of the day. Her Da was dead! She'd seen his head explode, and couldn't shake the image of it from hers. Dobbin and Boob too, both of them, dead, and she had no idea at all what had happened to Tomas.

It was all her fault!

Steeling herself, and wiping the tears from her eyes, she assessed her surroundings. She was in the car yard still, which sat on a plateau overlooking the marsh, and that was her only way out. The only way to reach the safety of the foothills beyond it. Directly to her left, the mountain rose steeply, so the only way to the marsh was down the two steep banks to her right. The road through the marsh dissected the two banks though, and The Order's guards were looking for her further down it.

Sinead was thirty feet above the marsh now, and had a clear view over it, its waters twinkling in the sun and inviting her onwards.

She could see the guy in the pirate suit stepping from the orange truck half way along the road, steam rising violently from the truck's bonnet, the driver's side riddled with bullet holes like a massive piece of honeycomb. From it, the road curved back towards Sinead, and she could see two more guards lurking along it, parading its edge and poking their rifles into the bushes, and clearly searching for her, but stopping short of stepping into the marsh.

That was Sinead's only way out, and it was a formidable obstacle she mused, her resolve ebbing and flowing with her every thought. There would be guards searching the car yard behind her soon though. She had to move.

Slowly, she eased her way over the bank, and into the thick tangle of foliage lining it, and lowered herself, but she started to slide, and had to dig her heels in, watching as the mound of dirt building up beneath them fell agonisingly away, and then she slipped, twigs and thorns tearing at her clothes, until she slid to a comfortable stop in the thick tussock at the bottom.

Surely she'd been seen. Her heart raced. How could she not have been? All was quiet around her though. There were no gunshots. No shouting. Nothing but the happy chirp of the Fan-tail she could see zipping about across the road, hopping at light speed through the air it seemed.

Only the road separated Sinead from the bank down to the marsh now. It seemed so small and yet so wide an obstacle. The roadblock was at the crest of the road not far to her right, but the guards from it were still searching for her to the left. Hugging the verge of the road was Sinead's best bet she decided after a moment, as she didn't like her chances in the marsh, so she eased her way on, keeping as low as she could, when a twig snapped behind her and she froze, cutting short her breath.

Someone was behind her.

Slowly, she turned her head, her eyes darting this way and that, and then she was wrenched backwards, her scream stifled as an arm wrapped itself around her, pulling her back to its owner. Dropping the rifle, she struggled with everything she had, swinging her elbows and fighting for her very life.

But to no avail.

Her strength was drained and her fight likewise.

Sinead had nothing left.

Chapter 17

The compound was deserted on Digsy's return. Only the solitary guard that Raul had instructed to oversee the transaction remained. His moustache was red and thick, and cut down his cheeks almost at right angles down to his jawline. Camouflage embroiled him, expensive hunting clothes, but filthy, multiple tears hidden by the fabric's chaotic pattern. Raul and Rodney had gone in search of the attackers the guard told Digsy, down towards the marsh, so Digsy unloaded the moonshine, and once the merchandise had been swapped, Digsy now all but stocked up for the winter, he cleaned himself up, the two said their farewells, and with tears of sorrow and heavy hearts, went their separate ways.

Idling the truck back down the road towards the roadblock, Digsy pondered the proceedings. It had been an interesting morning, and a far cry from what he'd expected. Despite the unpleasantries though, he deemed his mission to have been a successful one. The trade had been completed. Now he had most of the supplies he needed, and had acquired a bow with a quiver of arrows to boot.

The girl though, Sinead. That had been an unforeseen hitch. Who was she and had she escaped?

He could see The Order's guards searching the car yard to the left where he'd left her, and others, Raul included, doing likewise a hundred metres further down the road into the marsh.

She'd be lucky to escape Digsy knew, but he'd wait for her by the bridge as promised regardless. Could he have helped her? Could he have done more? He knew that he could have of course, and that he probably should have too, but encroaching feelings of guilt aside, he turned right at the roadblock, away from the unfolding scene, and down the hill into town.

Now he could get more supplies.

The road into town was a straight one, north to south down a gradual slope through the outskirts, stretching into the distance before disappearing amongst the mass of rubble that filled the valley there. It looked like Godzilla had relieved himself on it and not flushed.

Mud, debris and grime lined the entire way now, the mountains framing the suburb like a giant compacter waiting to crush it. The road, which ran down the eastern flank of the valley, ominously close to the mountain there, was riddled with cracks, some of which spewed water which flowed down its sides into the creek further down its course. The buildings lining it there were mostly in ruins. Many on the western side however, those further from the peaks, still lived and breathed. Most bore scars of some description, but there was life there. Chickens and goats scurried around in makeshift pens and smoke rose through holes in the roofs of the unified three-storey blocks.

Few people were around though. Only those not able to work for The Order. The dregs of society. The old, the diseased and the disabled, skin and bone, sitting in doorways whittling, gazing aimlessly into space, or haggling with the vendors of ramshackle stalls that were dotted along the road, trading whatever they'd found for whatever was on offer.

Roadkill mostly.

The town had only boasted a thousand residents since the rest had perished or fled, and as the town centre was off limits to the piteous under The Order's reign, this innocuous strip of land had become New Queenstown's slum. Hundreds of people hoarded in the dishevelled buildings that lined the valley now, every kind of grime imaginable subject to the laws of entropy there, emitting a truly rotten stench that clung to the ether.

Two men struggled in the mud as Digsy rolled by, watched by a dozen more, each one vying for blood and cheering them on as a burly fellow behind them leant protectively on a cart full of dead vermin, watching on with an air of interest, and cheering as the larger of the brawlers had his head helped into the mud. Another shouted 'Five rats and a squirrel!' and the gathered roared.

On Digsy rolled, still idling the engine so as not to draw attention, but to save on his precious moonshine too. The driver side window had been shattered in the raid, so he dragged his cuff along its base, the thick leather easily clearing the shards of glass that were still poking up from it. It was much colder without the window he noted, so he turned the heater up to full, the hot air an instant relief to his hands as he did.

The road swung to the left just before it reached the town centre, curving around the foot of Queenstown hill, and the valley spilled out to a gradual descent towards the lake here. Behind it, the slopes were strewn with toppled tower-blocks and lavish homes which had crumbled down the mountain, forming a thick wall of debris which lined the road. Of the flat land to the right of the road though, most of the buildings were mostly intact here, and the taller buildings dominating the town centre could just be seen beyond them.

Just before the town centre, another guard stood at another roadblock, which didn't inspire confidence in Digsy, but as he drew closer, he recognised the sizeable frame to be Mo's. Mo was tantamount to a roadblock in himself. At just over six foot, he paled in comparison to the guards at the warehouse, but with legs like oak trees supporting a sturdy frame, he was an imposing figure indeed.

Mo, on recognising Digsy's truck, resumed his position on his car bonnet, which in turn resumed its position on the ground.

'Wha'chup to bro?' sang the gentle giant as Digsy pulled to a stop beside him, grinning at the welcoming smile on Mo's friendly but wise face. His eyes were half closed, as they always were, and yet they still somehow shone. Looking as satisfied as ever, and with starvation never an issue for this resourceful fellow, Mo was always a pleasant encounter.

'Mo my good man. Oh y'know, getting shot at. That sorta thing.'

Mo nodded knowingly.

'True bro, I heard sum noise. Was it a raid?'

Concern became his face as he noticed the blood splattered across Digsy's jacket.

'You okay there bro?' he asked with a frown, drawing a glance from Digsy down to it.

His jacket was splattered with flecks all down the right side, which he'd washed at the warehouse, but he'd evidently missed some, so he spat on it and wiped it again, and then proceeded to enlighten Mo as to what happened at the warehouse half an hour earlier.

'True bro, that sucks ay.'

Mo's face remained placid, but there was a sad note to his voice now.

'Oh well, it's a hard life we lead, ay bro.'

Shaking his head, he stepped from the car's bonnet again, leaning into the window and into the glovebox, for in the glovebox, was his muse. Mo was a peaceful soul at heart you see, and not being a fan of The Order's archaic brand of order, he did as little as he could to appease his employers, always seizing the occasion to relax. He was always one to turn the other cheek when occasion occasioned, and he certainly didn't seem too concerned at the news of his colleague's demise.

Leaning back from the car, he lit the smoke that was now sat in his lips, inhaling deeply, and once the pipe of peace had been passed, Digsy begged his leave.

The sun had moved further to the west now, closer to the peaks there than the ones to the east.

There was no time to waste.

It was a short roll through the town centre to the lake, and one couldn't help but be taken by the unsubtle change that betook the streets suddenly. They were clean and bustling, happy and at ease. A Mariachi sat leaning against a crooked lamp, weapon of choice poised for action, yet none came but the thrusts and parries of the stick in his mouth as he chewed it. Vendors vendored from thriving shopfronts, children played with fancy toys and birds sang in the trees, swooping between the domineering buildings that lined the streets— mostly still intact, mostly box-shaped, and mostly still towering up five storeys.

No sunlight graced the ground here though, indeed the gloom was constant, but a different feel hung in the ether here. Lamps hung from every building and flickered as he passed. It felt almost cosy, almost quaint. The people were clean and full, and the mood was one of positivity. The rotting stench of decay didn't penetrate the air here. Rather a collage of more pleasant aromas, and he picked each one out as he passed them by. Here and there were stalls roasting various nuts and potatoes wrapped in blackened foil, others serving mulled wine and ale, wood pigeon, rabbit or ferret, or whatever the day brought. All of it a huge contrast to the roadkill on offer only a few hundred meters to the north.

The buildings gave way to an open expanse as Digsy approached the lake, and he pulled to a stop before the marketplace. A score of fish stalls, punters all busy bartering and haggling sat before him. The market square was half the size of a football pitch, with a huge willow, naked and drooping sat near its centre.

Behind the market, a low stone wall curved to the left, tapering back into the lake where it met the shore behind it. To the right it met the dock, where he could see the TSS Earnslaw—slender, long and elegant, and now The Order's HQ, poking out from behind the old casino that sat on stilts above the lake to its right. It was a quaint little spot, and lending an envious backdrop to it all, sat the twin peaks of Walter and Cecil—an ever-watching presence, bulbous, reliable and true.

Larry the fish merchant was who Digsy sought. He'd been in the trade since the old days, and he ran the biggest rig in town. He knew all the best spots, knew all the news, and Digsy knew he could get him a lot more than fish if he needed.

A loud fellow, Digsy found Larry easily, tall and slender, his head strangely small with grey hair sprouting from the sides.

Wiping his hand on his apron, Larry offered Digsy his hand, which Digsy politely declined.

Something wasn't quite right though.

It wasn't Larry's normal slimy attempt at a smile that greeted Digsy today. Larry was distracted, his bottom lip butting up into the top and his brow was furrowed. He was looking over Digsy's shoulder, which was directly occupied by a somewhat forceful hand.

'Howdy limey cock sucker!'

Hanging from the aforementioned hand, Red stood with his back to the adjoining fish stall, blocking the punters' way, and ignoring their pleas as they huffed and shuffled around him, refraining from further abuse though, as they noticed the arm band and the rifle he carried.

'Guess who I dun found?' Red went on after a moment, twisting the wiry strands sprouting haphazardly from his chin. He didn't appear entirely certain as to the answer himself though. There was a hush around them, and a score or so townsfolk stopped mid barter to watch the unfolding drama. Digsy was running out of patience.

'I don't know Red. Jesus was it? Or God maybe? How about the Buddha that lies within?'

The retort wasn't appreciated on Red's part though, and the butt of his rifle swiftly found its mark in Digsy's stomach, who crouched double with a groan as shoppers all around him gasped in unison.

'No, heathen…' Replied Red.

'It was a reee-torii-cul question… I dun found you boy!' He sounded so happy with himself, and snorted a little as he sniggered, stepping back, he flicked the safety on the rifle and lifted the barrel up to Digsy's face.

'Baws wants to see you boy. Now!'

Chapter 18

Sinead felt so weak in Tom's arms, writhing and battling to begin with, and totally oblivious as to the arm's owner. Tomas hadn't wanted to alarm her of course. Far from it. Indeed he felt terrible for having done so, but he couldn't risk their location being compromised, so he held her tightly until she stopped struggling, and resigned to her fate, she quickly obliged.

The bushes and tussock they cowered amongst hid them from all but above now, so he loosened his hold after a moment, and looked back up the hill behind them, making sure no one had seen them, his hand tight over Sinead's mouth still though.

All was clear.

'Shhhhh, lieben. You are okay, it is me.'

He felt her go limp and lowered his hand, loosening his grip further as he scanned the surroundings.

His voice sent waves of relief flooding through Sinead, and she turned to embrace him.

'Tomas, tank sweet Jesus!' she sobbed. 'I taut yis were dead.'

'Nein lieben, not yet. You are okay?'

She slumped down beside him, and Tomas pulled her towards him, her head buried in his chest now.

'I tink so,' she whispered finally.

'Mi Da's dead. The bastards killed 'im.'

Smiling a sad smile, Tom kissed her on the forehead. He was unsure what to say suddenly. Seeing his friend's head explode had saddened Tomas to the core, and what Sinead was going through he could only imagine, so he stayed quiet and held her tighter, when he heard muffled speech coming from the direction Sinead had just come from.

Slowly he turned, putting a finger to his lips as he looked back up the slope to its source. Two of The Order's guards were stood at the edge of the wrecker's yard now, on the precipice of the slope that Sinead had just come down. He could just make them out through the bushes. They stood there unmoved with a good view over the whole marsh, so he pushed Sinead down and followed, curling up to make themselves look as small as they possibly could.

'Sshhh, lieben. Ve must be qviet.'

Chapter 19

Having been ushered through the market, the rifle prodding him in the back every few steps as Red heckled him onwards, Digsy was herded towards the wharf, and the TSS Earnslaw, and after a wee shove he found himself aboard.

Before him the ship's funnel stood tall, bold and proud, rising up behind the semi-circular bridge that watched over her bow. She looked older up close, and more decrepit. The once red and white paintwork was faded and flaking, and the woodwork brittle, but those were her only woes upon which to dwell. The narrow walkway extended both sides of Digsy. To his right, he could see the wharf beyond her stern, lined with dishevelled structures and stretching along the lake's edge into the distance. To the left, the hull tapered gracefully inwards to a point at her bow, the town creeping up Queenstown Hill like a giant pin cushion of mangled steel beyond it.

The entrance to the ship's lounge was in that direction, and there he was shoved.

On approaching the door, Red grabbed Digsy by the arm, and then knocked twice. The door opened after a moment, and then, without warning, he shoved Digsy through, who staggered forward and crashed into the opposite wall inside, which being of a solid constitution, broke his flight nicely, and he crumpled to the floor in a daze.

A moment was required on Digsy's part at that point. Happy he was not. He wasn't a violent man by nature, but he'd taken a few hits that morning, so he composed himself, stretching out the shoulder that'd taken the brunt of the impact, and then like a dog out of a cage, he sprang, slamming his fist into Red's jaw. The blow was a hard one, and Red hadn't seen it coming. His head crashed back into the wall behind him and he crumpled to the floor with a whimper.

Before Digsy could act further though, huge arms smothered him and he was down to his knees, the arms crushing, pressing down on him, squeezing the breath from his lungs. The weight pushing down on Digsy was immense. He couldn't breathe. He really couldn't breathe. He tried to say so but he couldn't. It felt like the life was being hugged out of him, his eyes striving for a life free of Digsy, his ribs trying to embed themselves deeper. He couldn't think for the blood trying to break from his every vein. He tried to slam his head back into his opponent's face, but met only chest. He was fading fast. Panic was nigh. He struggled with all he had, lashing out wildly as stars began to amass in his vision, his fight fading, vision blurring and strength draining, and one would be forgiven dear reader, for being pessimistic in your presumptions to-wit Digsy's longevity, when as if by magic, the voice of an angel sang out…**'E-fak'n-naff'!'**

Praise be.

The vice-like grip was loosened and beautiful air rushed back into Digsy's lungs, like a thousand tasteless cigarettes smoked at once. He slumped forward, gasping for breath, but his arms gave way and his head hit the floor with a thump.

There he lay, sucking in as much air as his ravaged lungs would allow.

Chapter 20

How long Sinead and Tomas had been hiding in the undergrowth was unclear, but the air was much colder in its shadow, and Tom could feel Sinead shivering as they lay there, awaiting their chance to escape. All that stood between them and the marsh was the road that cut through it now, but the road was open, offering no cover from the guards that were still searching for them further down it.

The chatter from the guards at the top of the bank behind them started to recede after a while, and finally vanished, so Tomas tapped Sinead on the shoulder, pointing towards the other side of the road, and then to his eyes with forked fingers. Signalling for her to wait, he inched forward, staying crouched in the bush-line, and then with one last look around, he pushed out of the shrub and onto the road.

His head told him to go to ground, but instinct cried, *Run!* so acting on the latter, he set out, pouncing into the bushes that lined the top of the bank beyond it. He waited for what seemed like an age for the sound of gunfire, sure it would come, but by the grace of Gandalf it didn't. The guards remained oblivious to Tom's passing it seemed.

Shuffling forwards, further into the undergrowth and out of sight, he mopped his brow with his sleeve. He felt tired and weak suddenly. His heart was beating faster than he'd ever known, and the stress of it all was bringing him out in a sweat.

Get a grip, Tom!

He suddenly felt the fortitude that'd never failed him failing. He felt like a mere recruit again, like he'd somehow regressed twenty years, his nerves honing his senses to precision as the fear he remembered from his younger days dug its claws back into him.

But why?

Action wasn't a new phenomenon to Tomas. Indeed, he was battle hardened, and proud of his steel-like nerves. This time it was different he knew though. This time he was older. Older and slower he was finding, much to his chagrin, and he had Sinead to protect too.

Looking back to her, a look of relief mixed with fear he met in her eyes, and he raised his palm to her, instructing her to wait.

'Vait for my signal,' he whispered, and she nodded back with a nervous smile.

It was only ten metres or so down to the marsh from Tom's position now, so he inched himself over the slope's precipice, grabbing the sturdiest branch he could find, and started to slowly lower himself over the edge, when he heard someone shouting behind him and a shot rang out.

Chapter 21

The ship's lounge was ominously silent, the distant hum of bustle, and the gentle lapping of the waves against its hull all that Digsy could hear. His breath was coming back to him, his ribs no longer sore, and he found himself lying face down on a wooden floor. The floor was well polished he noticed. Cared for even, and recently too from the faint smell of varnish he could smell still permeating the room. He could see dirty, scuffed boots surrounding him as he pushed himself up, which grew legs and torsos with arms and hands that were holding guns which were pointed at him, the faces atop them all grinning savagely down.

Pushing himself to a knee, he gingerly stood and brushed himself down, tender and aching all over still, and took in the scene.

The ornate lounge he found himself in was the size of a tennis court, but narrower, crammed with a mismatched mix of antique furniture—mahogany, teak, walnut and oak, short and tall, ornate and plain, blocking most of the light, and giving an Aladdin's cave look to the somewhat cramped room. Four of The Order's guards lounged around it, including Red, who was sprawled out on the floor by the door still.

A white-topped lady, whom Digsy presumed to be Her Ladyship—The Order's head honcho—was sat behind a desk to the rear. She wore a well-pressed scarlet suit with her hair tied up and bobbed behind her, and elliptical glasses through which her eyes appeared huge, and she watched Digsy with tickled interest as he assessed the surroundings he'd found himself in. At just under five foot, and in her late nineties at least he presumed, Her Ladyship somehow oozed evil, and Digsy could only imagine the atrocities she'd committed over the years.

'Well fak'n well. So you're fak'n Digsy, are ya?'

Her voice was nasal, whiny and condescending, with a conceit negating any hopes that Digsy had left for the remainder of the day's prospects.

'Charmed,' was all he could splutter in reply, struggling for air still as he was.

'I've heard a lot about you…' Her Ladyship continued, fixing her hair in the mirror she held before returning her attention to him.

'And not all good, I must say.'

She tapped the table opposite her with the mirror, and then placed it down on it, and before Digsy could express his penchant for standing, the guard behind him shoved him toward the table and giant hands pressed him into the seat.

'I'm not sure what you're referrin' to…'

Adjusting himself, he leaned back into the tattered leather, lifting his eyes to meet hers. Her Ladyship grinned back at him and he averted his gaze, nervous suddenly under the sinister aura she emitted.

'I'm a legitimate businessman.'

She let out the start of a laugh like she'd heard it all before, and then stood, pacing for a moment, as if appraising the rag tag group of halfwits that were supposedly protecting her, then she turned back to him with a new venom in her eyes, and hissed…

'My Ladyship.'

Digsy understood the statement not. She sounded like a hyena with a boomerang lodged in its throat.

'Ma'am?' he asked.

'You mate, call me My fak'n Ladyship.'

She leaned intently in at Digsy, the guards towering behind her, and clearly alert to the potential of bother, and evidently anxious to partake, fidgeting with their eyes wide, raring to beat Digsy to a pulp it seemed.

It could have been going worse though.

As yet, no one had mentioned the raid or the skinny guard. He'd been expecting that to come up straight away. Presumably Red would have informed Her Ladyship had he not been unconscious, and Digsy was happy not to have to answer any questions as to his entirely innocent role in the matter.

Her Ladyship pondered as she watched Digsy gulp, and then nod, her eyes narrowing as she decided to take a different approach. Sitting down again, she leaned back in the chair and put a hand to her chin, forming an L around it with her finger and thumb, the other to her elbow, sizing Digsy up like she was deciding his fate for him.

'Your grog's… errr… not too bad there matey…' she went on after a moment. 'It soothes a few ills around here.' This said with a more amiable air as Her Ladyship broached the matter at hand—the matter of Digsy's moonshine, which he well knew he held most of the cards in. The Order needed his moonshine. He was their only supplier. They relied upon his services, and would do until such a time as they could make their own fuel, or find his cave. Her Ladyship was clearly aware of this too though, and also of the fact that Digsy in turn relied on their supplies, so he stayed quiet and let her do the speaking.

'Thing is mate…' she obliged, and then paused, looking out through the window for a ponderous moment, watching as a flag outside started to flutter under a new breeze.

'Ain't there always a fak'n thing ay?'

Again she paused, shaking her head, and then cackled as if to herself, ever amused at life's little games.

'Well, the fak'n thing is mate, it'd be faaar fak'n easier for ya to make the fak'n grog here in town mate. And ya fak'n know it.'

Folding her arms at her chest, she waited for a response. None came though. It was silent in the lounge now, and somewhat tense, until one of the guards coughed as if to prompt her onwards.

'How about ya work for us Digsy mate?' she did so with a touch or irritation in her voice suddenly. 'And I won't fak'n ask again.'

At which point a groan came from by the door, where Red mumbled incoherently, still laid out flat, but conscious now.

'Yes Digsy mate, you were fak'n sayin'?'

An amused grin crept onto Her Ladyship's face as she watched Digsy fidget and shuffle in his chair. The last thing he needed was a conscious and vengeful Red, particularly given the current company, so he picked his words hurriedly.

'Under normal circumstances, that would be lovely.'

His gaze reverted back from Red, who was trying to push himself up.

'But I can't right now, I'm a busy man, y'know.'

Her Ladyship had clearly expected that. Her elbows were on the table, and she was leaning in at Digsy now, her hands cusped before her and her frown ever more pronounced.

'In that fak'n case...' she spat with more than a note of frustration, leaning back again and taking the glasses from her face. Her eyes looked tiny suddenly, and somehow more evil. Folding the arms back, she slid the glasses into her breast pocket.

'We'll need more of your fak'n grog mate. Fak'n double, for the time being at least,' she added, clearly alluding in Digsy's mind to the fact that his services weren't as indispensable as he'd possibly imagined them to be.

He started to voice his concerns regarding the seasonal restrictions to his chosen trade, but she cut him off again,

'Make it fak'n here then mate...' spat she.

'Otherwise, I'll expect another batch in a fak'n month. Now fak off!'

Chapter 22

The bullet pinged off the road behind Tomas, so he pounced forward over the bank and into the undergrowth, dropping the rifle as he grasped desperately at the foliage surrounding. The ground gave way as he scrambled to find a footing though, and down he slid, his feet cutting channels through the loose dirt, branches clawing, thorns digging into his hands as bullets zipped past him, decimating the greenery around him.

He kept his balance though, and as he reached the bank's foot, he grabbed the rifle that'd come to rest beside him, pushing through the bush and then splashed into the icy water.

Instantly the cold shocked Tomas. His muscles contracted, and his entirety was tense suddenly, and painfully weak, his breaths shallow for a moment and coming up short. Ignoring it was impossible, surviving for long in such conditions likewise he knew, so he drew in a deep breath when he was able, and pushed further into the marsh, cringing as he pulled a thorn from his arm and a drop of blood plopped into the water.

The guards were searching the top of the bank where they'd spotted him now, just across the road from Sinead. Their voices were clear, urgent and alert, but clearly unaware as to where she or Tom were. Tomas was well hidden. A rusty beam poked up from the water beside him, and indeed, the remnants of the stilted suburb that formerly sat above the marsh were evident all around him, metal and rotting woodwork entwined with the foliage that was thick here. Marsh grass surrounded and towered above Tom, the water up to his chest, black like oil and gleaming now in the waning sun. Before him, the marsh stretched out for a hundred metres to the mountain's foot, and to his left stretched twice that, hugging the road before reaching the higher ground beyond it, where it morphed into the foothills, and Tom's only exit.

Away from Sinead too though.

Away from his love. Tom wanted to run, to lose himself in the tangle of wetlands and escape, but he couldn't leave Sinead behind. He couldn't leave her in the hands of The Order. Had they found her, or was she safely hidden? She wasn't the escape and evade type he knew. She'd been mollycoddled by her father and she wasn't cut out for it.

He looked up the bank he'd just come down, the one he'd have to surmount to get back up to her, and then sighed a resigned sigh. No chance. The Order's troops were searching that area now. There was no way he could get back to Sinead without being seen.

Only the sun's hat poked up above the mountain tops to the west now, the setting rays casting a blanket of warmth over the basin like a force-field, trapping in, and accentuating the gloom below. The mountains seemed more menacing suddenly, dark and looming as the sun sank behind the highest, casting a golden halo around it.

Sinead dared not breathe.

Two guards were stood just across the road from her. They were making there way over the bank, down to the marsh, but the guards in the car yard behind her were back too now. They were stood at the top of the bank behind her again, looking out over her position. She was confident she was out of sight, nestled beneath shadow and foliage as she was, and she was sure the guards hadn't spotted her, but she was afraid for Tomas, and unsure if the guards had found him.

The shooting had stopped now.

Had Tom been shot, or escaped?

Cramp was niggling her left leg, so she shifted her weight and stretched it out, feeling the muscle loosen as she did. Then she heard a truck starting up, and could see its lights streaming out into the dusk further down the road, and she lay waiting for what seemed like an age, yearning for a glimpse of Tomas, for some sound or indication that he was okay. There was nothing though. Nothing but the occasional grumbling of the guards that were searching for them.

Their voices were louder suddenly though, and much clearer. Looking back up the bank towards them, Sinead could see one of the guards clearly now.

He was dangerously close, and making his way down the bank towards her.

Edging his way back into the quickly encroaching gloom, carefully feeling his way through the slime, Tomas was submerged up to his neck now, his boots clearing the debris that would otherwise cut his feet to shreds.

Goosebumps riddled his arms, and he was so cold. His fingers felt hot though, so he flexed them in an effort to get the blood flowing properly.

Basking rays of glorious light still blazed over the western peaks, lending the setting a certain radiance, but it would soon be dark. Was this a good thing or not? It would certainly help Tomas escape, but how would he find Sinead? How would he negotiate the tangled webbing of the marsh if he couldn't see it? He was tired now, soaked and freezing.

A cone of white light suddenly cut horizontally into the dusk, an engine roared to life, and a minute later, the orange truck pulled up on the road not far to Tom's right. The fire barrel there lit it up, and he saw the pirate and the dreadlocked guard step from it.

Pushing through the water, away from the guards as quietly as he could, only his head above water now, Tomas heard someone whistling behind him, near to where he'd left Sinead, and then someone shouting. The light was fading quickly, but the twilight betrayed a silhouette on the bank behind Sinead's position. One of the guards was making his way down it towards her, so without a second thought, Tom levelled the rifle and squeezed the trigger.

The shot reverberated the valley and the form dropped, a dark spray cascading into the gloom.

The clap of the gunshot was the first Sinead had heard for a while, and it lingered, masking any noise that the guard approaching her made. He had to be metres from her now, but then a strange noise followed the shot. A tumbling, scrambling, crunching sound. Branches cracked, dirt and stones tumbled down the bank, slamming into Sinead or coming to rest all around her. The eve was silent but for this one confusing sound. She felt like a trapped rat. Felt a fear that she'd felt too many times already that day. Closing her eyes, she expected the worst, and her fears were realised when something crashed down on top of her, slamming her face into the earth and suppressing her terrified scream.

Sinead dared not move.

A hush filled the twilight suddenly, her heart pounding though, and deafening to her ears. Sinead was mortified, breathless and panicked. She knew it was the guard that'd crashed down on her. Heat still radiated from his corpse, which lay across her back, pinning her from left leg to right shoulder, blood dripping across her neck and forming a puddle on the ground that was approaching her mouth. She gulped short, panicked breaths, manoeuvring to ease the burden that was crushing her, but the torso covered hers entirely. The weight of it was squeezing the air from her lungs.

She panicked. Other guards would be coming, and they would find her. Her shakes would give her away she knew, but the panic was crippling. She held her breath and the shakes subsided, but she seemed to flatten further.

A second guard was crossing the road towards her now. Sinead could hear him, and then he was stood right before her. She could feel the puddle of blood at her lips now. All had gone terribly dark.

'You okay, mate?' the guard enquired of the corpse atop Sinead, prodding his dead friend with his rifle, and the body twitched, squeezing a jet of warm blood across Sinead's face. He prodded the corpse again when an answer wasn't forthcoming.

'Steveo mate, you okay, mate?'

Still the corpse didn't reply though, so the guard leaned in closer, his hand to the dead man's neck, and so close that Sinead could smell the smoke on his fingers above the stench of the dead guard atop her.

The night was still now, and peaceful finally. Just the way Raul liked them. They took his mind off the days so he could forget about the shit he had to endure through them.

On cloudless nights, after the kids had gone to bed and the streets had emptied, Raul loved nothing more than gazing out at the endless brilliance of the universe above him from the comfort of his rooftop couch. The countless specks of ancient light blanketing the blackness took his mind off the daily turmoil, and helped him relax. He recognised some of the constellations. They gave him a comforting feeling. A constant in this crazy world, and a whole realm of possibilities. He could let his mind wander, and escape, voyaging amongst the stars he remembered from the movies as a child.

Not right now he couldn't though. Raul had no time to gaze at the magnificence of the night above him now. No time to ponder life in all its wondrous glory and where it all went wrong now. Now he had to find whomever it was trying to evade them in the marsh. He would make them pay by jove, stars sparking into life one by one as he removed his hat lest he lose it in the marsh.

The fire barrel Raul crouched behind was nice and warm against the harsh nip of the night, and he didn't want to move. The heat was so comforting, and even though it wasn't the most suitable of shields, he hesitated, soaking up the moment's precious warmth—the one comfort he could keep to himself and didn't have to give to Her Ladyship.

There was something almost sacred about it.

Move he must though.

An orange flash came from the marsh as he did so, and a bullet smashed through the rusted metal inches from his head, the barrel swaying as it punched through, sparks launched into the darkness and prancing around above him as a second bullet quickly followed. Hopping back, Raul staggered and almost fell, but threw his hands back in time and scrambled for the cover of the marsh's edge.

Adjusting his sword-belt, to-wit never inviting castration again, he crept down the marsh line. Amidst the night he could see Rodney, crouched a few metres from him, and clearly raring to go now, so Raul nodded and Rodney inched forward, both his sawn-offs out before him.

Nothing could be seen beyond the reach of the fire barrels, so he signalled to Rodney to throw a flare, to-wit, Rodney again obliged. He ripped the chord and the flare blazed into life, turning the dreadlocked giant and all around him a brilliant blazing red. Holding it at arm's length, Rodney gazed into its core, as if being drawn into it, and then he drew back his arm and launched it into the marsh.

Its residue lingered after it'd passed, leaving a smoky red arc fading in the dusk, and the marsh came alive suddenly with the shadows of flora twisting and dancing midst the red deluge.

That was twenty metres to Tom's right, and life suddenly sprang back into the night, smoke mingling with the foliage midst a glow that somehow summed up the night to Tom's mind, enhancing the dread that was all that he could see left before him now.

It did serve to highlight his pursuer though. Tomas could just make out the dreadlocked guard in the dying light of the flare, so he shifted his aim and fired, but the guard ducked as he did, and Tom scrambled back as a bullet whipped into the water before him.

Another shot quickly followed, and then another from a different weapon, water splashing up all around Tomas suddenly, the marsh rippling like a wave pool as he tripped and fell back into it. He had to move. He had to get away, but then something else splashed into the water, a couple of meters to his right. Something heavy, like a rock, but more metallic somehow. The sound was a frightening one. There was no mistaking it though, so Tom threw himself back, but he was too slow, and he was launched unaware and into the darkness, deafened, numb, and entirely oblivious.

The blast echoed like a roar from the heavens. The valley walls seemed to shake, and Raul rejoiced at the explosion. When in doubt, lob a grenade he'd always told Rodney, and a warm feeling welled in him at his teaching's success. The sight of the body flying into the blackness sent waves of delight washing through his very being. He could finally relax, and he holstered his Magnum and looked up to the stars in thanks.

'**Rodders, ya mad bastaard!**' he yelled in exultation, pointing in the direction he'd seen the body fly.

'**Good throw bro. Now go get 'im.**'

Chapter 23

The sun was behind the western peaks by the time Digsy had traded what he needed to, getting everything on his list except a gun, and the town was cast in gloom. The summits of Walter and Cecil on the far side of the lake though, still shone like twin halos, shining like beacons to ward off the encroaching night's perils. They looked like enormous glowing breasts thought Digsy as he set off to go and rescue the damsel as he'd promised he would, their reflections shimmering in the glassy waters of the lake beneath them. Four glowing breasts! Surely this was an omen.

But would Sinead wait for him if she did escape?

Had she actually agreed to do so, and did she even need his help?

It was a big risk to take Digsy knew, but as he turned onto the long straight leading from the town centre up to the roadblock, a quick chat with Mo on the way out, he determined to at least see if she was there.

The road leading back up to the marsh was now just a long void, lined with firelight shimmering sporadically along its length. Barren was the way, just a few stragglers trudging from it, disappearing into the buildings to the left whilst there was still light enough to do so. Dim lights flickered to life as he passed them by, the moon lighting the edge of a bulbous front that was nipping at the western range now, slowly rolling over and engulfing it like whipped cream on chocolate cake.

A hundred metres from the roadblock, Digsy spotted what appeared to be a hullabaloo there, so he pulled to the side of the road for a closer look. He could just make out a commotion in the dim firelight surrounding the roadblock. There were several figures there, one being pushed around, heckled and poked.

Stepping into the street, he focused his binoculars.

The roadblock sat at the pinnacle of the road before it dropped again to the marsh. Circling it, the fire barrels lit it up like a pyre, and Digsy could clearly make out four or five people stood there within them. He recognised a couple of them. Raul stood out like a priest at a porn shoot with his pirate hat topping off his silhouette. A second guard, a woman it appeared, stood cloaked and hidden beside him, and the dreadlocked guard, Rodney, was all too recognisable. He was towering over a cowering form in-between them. Leaning forwards, his dreadlocks leading his head, he yanked the form back up by the hair. She screamed, and Digsy's hopes for his damsel evaporated with the air that he breathed.

Sinead looked deflated and beaten, and almost limp in Rodney's grip. He shoved her and she fell towards Raul, but Raul stepped aside and she crashed into the car behind him, crumpling to the ground.

It was a sorry sight.

Raul and his cronies certainly looked like they were enjoying themselves, teasing and tormenting Sinead, and heckling her mercilessly, but there was another there too, cowering by the car. A kick to the ribs and he too crumpled, his fatigues ripped and filthy, he lay still where he fell.

Digsy couldn't believe what he was seeing. It was like a scene from a movie that he might be forced to be the unwitting hero in—a scene from a thousand endings where the hero valiantly risks life and limb to save the stricken princess—a daunting prospect that Digsy suddenly felt utterly in awe of. He wasn't the hero. Far from it, and he never could be, this much he knew for certain being the enlightened cur that he always had been.

Nevertheless, on he went, the headlights low, the engine no louder than the breeze under moonshine it ran off, and he stopped the truck unnoticed before the turmoil.

'Twas an upsetting scene.

As a cat will torment a cornered mouse, so Digsy's old friend was tormenting Sinead, taunting her as she begged and flinched, covered in cuts and grime, and clearly shaken, but intact it seemed. Her head was down, all kinds of fluids congealing in a puddle beneath her. She cried out, her arms up before her as Raul feigned attack with the butt of his 44 Magnum, smashing it into the car by her head instead.

'Fook dis bro.'

Raul seemed out of breath at his exertions, puffing and panting and resting his hands on his knees.

'Throw dem off the cleef,' he went on as his breath allowed, turning after a moment, and walking away from Sinead with a nonchalant strut.

A flash of hope remained it seemed, as strange as that might sound. The throwing of lesser offenders off the cliff you see, was seen as a sort of divine hand within The Order's ranks. Those that had done wrong, but not necessarily enough to warrant instant death, were graced the slim chance of surviving the fall, as that particular cliff was directly above the Shotover river.

The cliff was near the bridge before the intersection to Digsy's cave, near to where he'd told Sinead to meet him, and it didn't sound like Raul would be going with them.

It was a good place for an ambush.

He blew the truck's horn, the sound amplified somehow by the night and resounding like a foghorn across the sea.

All eyes turned to Digsy, and his smile quickly vanished.

'Evenin…'

His voice came out croaky and timid, and he strained to keep the nerves from it as he slipped his hand to the air-pistol on the seat beside him.

No one replied though, and everyone glared. Palpable, malignant glares, particularly Raul's, who stepped closer to see who it was doing the interrupting in the low light outside the barrel's reach. The weight of all those eyes on him was terrifying to Digsy. It appeared to be some kind of demonic ritual that he'd happened upon, cloaked figures gathered in a ring of fire in the dead of night.

He could feel the beat of his heart vibrating through the truck's frame, and feel the guns and ill-feelings that were being directed at him.

'Errr, Raul mate. Can I get through please?' he stammered as Raul's gaze found him. 'It's getting on. I need to get goin.'

Drawing his 44 from its holster again, Raul kept his eyes down, gazing at it adoringly, and then flicked the barrel out, spinning it ponderously as he stared down its length. He nodded his assent after a moment though, and ushered his minions out from Digsy's way, only looking up as he flicked the gun's barrel back into place and pointed it at Digsy.

'Watch yoself Digsy...' said he, with the hint of malice that Digsy was sadly growing used to. 'Der's bad folk out der bro. I'll see you soon.'

Forcing a smile, Digsy nodded his thanks, the barricade was cleared, and Digsy rolled on, glancing towards Sinead and ignoring the taunts that followed him from the guards. Sinead looked so battered, so distraught. She needed him and he was driving away.

How could she know that he still planned to save her? How could he actually do so? and why did he feel it his duty to? These and other questions hounded Digsy as he passed through the marshland and up into the foothills, the truck's lights showing the way across the ravaged asphalt, snaking up and into the darkness as the light from the roadblock faded behind him.

Two minutes later, just before the first bridge over the gorge, he slowed and pulled off the road.

The cliff was just down the track to his right.

Grabbing the bow he'd acquired from the skinny guard, and slipping his air pistols into his pockets, he made sure the truck was hidden, and then set off towards the cliff. The ground was crunchy underfoot here, and a thin layer of permafrost already covered the spots that were hidden from the sun at this time of year. The going was tricky in the sparse moonlight. Digsy moved slowly, and half way down the track he came to what remained of the house that had been hewn from the rock there. Beyond it, its lawn dropped down fifty metres to the trail which led to the cliff in question.

On Digsy went, tentatively making his way through the undergrowth, with only the moonlight guiding him, each step a nerve-racking step closer to whatever ghastly folly fate held in store for him. The bow was across his back. He had an air pistol in each pocket, and an unnerving sense of doom pervading his every thought.

Two minutes later, he heard the dull roar of the river cutting through the gorge not far ahead of him, and as the trail ended, the gorge emerged as if from nowhere, and the entire valley came to life as the clouds parted, the moon lighting up the mountains all around him lending a contradictory warmth to the breath-taking night vista.

Only a few meters before Digsy, the gorge dropped away vertically– a huge void cutting through the landscape, pitch black but for the river sparkling at its base. Across the gorge, on the opposite cliff, he could see a couple of houses cowering amongst the trees there, with the dimmest of lights shining within them, and smoke rising from them, churning up from their chimneys before dissipating into the night.

It was a sight to humble the vainest of men, but there was no time to enjoy it.

The rock from which the executions took place sat pancaked before Digsy, and was well lit by the moon now, almost effervescent it seemed, its flat surface hanging out over the gorge, soaking up the moon's rays and shining ominously, as if awaiting its next victim.

This would be where it all went down he suddenly realised as the gravity of the situation he'd gotten himself into dawned on him.

This could be his end.

And to that end, a rudimentary plan quickly came to Digsy. The gist being: as The Order's guards approach the cliff with Sinead, he'd emerge from the shadows, sneak up behind them, and then fill them full of air pistol pellets. They would then hopefully fall over the cliff, he would rescue said damsel, and all would hail Digsy.

What could go wrong?

Bloody everything, returned the last remnant of common sense that his moonshine hadn't yet infiltrated. It was quite the task he quickly realised, a real fear growing in him as he checked the clips, buttoned his jacket up to the top and hunkered down in the shadows.

The clouds closed in and the shadows returned. Concealed, he waited.

Chapter 24

Sinead could feel the vehicle slow as the lay of the road worsened, and although blindfolded, she had a rough idea where they were. There were only a few places they could be on this road—the dirt road that runs off it down to the cliffs, most likely. After their capture and subsequent thrashings, she and Tomas had been bundled into the truck, under no illusion as to their destination. She'd heard the pirate guy say so—the cliff. The place was notorious for the bodies that oft graced the shores of the river beneath it. Indeed a delight for the carnivores that'd become rampant in New Zealand, but a grim reminder of The Order's benevolence for those blessed with the need for only two legs on which to walk.

Sinead had heard of maybe ten different bodies found there over the last year or so, but also heard reassuring stories of survival too. A few at least, although never directly from the horse's mouth.

The truck stopped and a door opened, and Sinead was dragged to the right, her legs dropping from beneath her as they left the truck's seat and she crumpled down to the ground.

The ground was cold here, and frosted she could tell as she crunched down into it, and the chill went through her instantly. A dim, flickering glow from the torches the guards held was all she could see through the blindfold, the only sound their mumbled ramblings and the howl of the breeze through the trees.

It was freezing, and Sinead's hands were numb, but they were tied behind her so she couldn't warm them.

Frost crunched underfoot, and suddenly the blindfold was ripped from her, bringing a tear to her eye as her hair was wrenched forwards with it. Everything was dark still though. It took a moment for her eyes to adjust, but when they did, the cloaked figure stood before Sinead seemed not of this world. Something biblical. Something horrific, tall, ghostly and menacing.

The black cloak the guard wore clung to her curves and draped down to her ankles. The hood was up, and cast most of her face in shadow, but Sinead could see a scar on her cheek in the light of the torch she held, framing, and somehow enlarging her hateful eyes.

She looked so feral. So evil.

All she lacked was a scythe.

She didn't look to be all that old, but cropped by a tangled mess of greying dark hair as she was, the sight took Sinead back to Halloween as a child.

'Watch this one, boys…'

The woman grinned down at Sinead, and spoke with a tone that sent a shiver down her spine.

'And play nicely, won't you, I'll check ahead.'

Crouching down beside Sinead, the guard kissed her on the cheek, so tenderly that Sinead could hardly feel it, and then she stood again, crunching off into the shadows.

Her footsteps grew quiet, and soon there was no sound but for the wind, and the rustling of leaves as it swept through them. There was nothing at all from Tomas. No movement nor sound. He was curled up on the ground not far from Sinead, unconscious it appeared, but breathing still. The guards that'd been carrying Tomas though, were approaching Sinead now, wicked grins and evil eyes as they crunched through the frost towards her.

Ten meters sat between them.

An owl hooted like a novelty starters pistol, and up she leapt, slipping and sliding and mindless of the terrain that lay invisible all around her. She could sense her freedom. She could taste it almost, until a hand grasped her collar and she was yanked back again. She tried to pull away but the grip was too strong. Try as she might she couldn't pull herself free. Fingers dug into her neck and clamped down. She swiped out but met only air. She battled and writhed, but her feet slipped out from under her and she dropped to the ground with a whimper.

'Leave us be yis bastards.'

Sadly though, to no avail were our damsel's mewings. Indeed, they seemed only to spur the fiends on. The bigger of the two pulled her towards him, his moustache tickling her, the acrid deluge seeping from his lips nauseating, and he yanked her back up in hysterics, when a yelp came from the second guard, who was launched to the side with a wail. Tripping over a rock, he crashed head first into a boulder beside him, and the crunch of his skull was chilling. There was a brief moment's pause. A startled lull. The guard holding Sinead loosened his grip, turning, but his jaw was craned back as Tom's fist slammed into it and they both fell to the ground in a heap of flailing limbs.

The moonlight was patchy. Two torches lay burning at their feet, hissing and spitting as the flames caught the frosted grasses they wrestled in. Their faces were in shadow still, and Sinead couldn't tell one from the other. Couldn't tell Tom from the guard. She couldn't make out anything through the night. It was all so confusing.

A rustling sound came from behind her, so she turned, scanning the shadows, her senses tingling and alert to everything now, but blind to it too.

Shadows danced in every direction midst the silver and orange hues of the moonlit torches. The frost glowed orange and twinkled like nebulae midst the void of space. Everything seemed to be moving, everything coming at Sinead.

An army of Satan's hordes had her surrounded it seemed.

Tomas blocked the blow that was coming down at him, and brought his elbow up into the guard's chin, knocking him backwards with a whimper. From there, it was child's play. He grabbed the guard and locked his arms in position, pushing down and squeezing. He could feel the guard's strength waning as he grasped desperately at Tom's arms, striving to loosen them, striving to free himself, but he couldn't, and Tom leaned in further, swiftly putting the moustached guard to sleep.

All was dark around Tomas now, but for the ground where the torches lay, one of them crackling suddenly as the gust picked up and almost blew it out. Nothing else could be seen. Not a star in the sky, nor a rock on the ground. Even now though, Tomas felt the buzz over the pain that he knew would soon be racking him. Even after the beatings he'd endured through the day, he still felt the thrill of the take down, the rush he remembered with relish from his youth as the moustached guard withered below him. The guard was limp in Tom's arms now, so he dropped him, and then pulled the bindings he'd managed to loosen from his wrists, dropping them to the ground.

'Get off me!'

The voice came from the shadows. It was Sinead, but where was she?

He picked up a torch and held it out before him, but it didn't help. All he could see was it, flickering about before his eyes. He swung it around but found the same in every direction. It was all so confusing, all so dark. Left seemed like right and up like down.

'Help Tom!'

A giggle came from somewhere close by, but he couldn't tell from where, until he saw something moving in the shadows and stepped closer, and then there was Sinead. She was held in place by the dreadlocked guard that Tom now knew as Rodney, who was smiling down expectantly at Tomas, their duel inevitable it seemed.

'I don't suppose ve could talk about zis?' ventured Tomas with a nervous chortle, stretching his arms out and rolling his neck in readiness, but Rodney shook his head and shoved Sinead to the ground.

The omens weren't in Tom's favour it seemed. Rodney was a worrying prospect, but Tom felt weak suddenly, and conscious of his own fragility too. He wasn't sure he had anything left in him. Not the strength, the energy nor the spirit. Ideas were at a premium, cunning plans likewise, so Tomas improvised, hurling the torch he held at Rodney as hard as he could. It spiralled towards him through the night, flickering wildly as it did, but Rodney merely ducked to the side and giggled.

The gleam in his eyes told a thousand tales. No quarter would be given here, and it all happened rather quickly from there.

Had Tomas blinked, he would have missed it. Had he hesitated, he would have died.

Rodney lunged in, but Tom was alert to it, and he deftly ducked to the side, catching Rodney off balance, and he slammed his boot into Rodney's calf, bringing him to a knee with a pained roar.

That had worked better than Tom had expected. He was encouraged, and feeling confident suddenly. Victory was within reach, but Rodney was pushing himself back up, so summoning what he could from the wreck the day had made him, Tomas slammed his fist down into Rodney's jaw, and cried out at the pain of the impact, staggering backwards in disbelief.

Crunch!

A sickness instantly welled up inside Tomas. He felt the blood draining from his face and rushing to his hand. Rodney's face was like rock, and Tom cradled his throbbing hand, the victory he'd for a second envisioned slipping away with the strength in it.

The blow had done naught to slow Rodney though. The man was a machine, and he pushed himself back up again, shaking off Tom's blow like it were a tap.

'My turn bro.'

That didn't bode well. Slamming his fist into his opposite palm, Rodney turned back to face Tomas. He hesitated for a second though, rubbing his jaw with a snigger, so Tom stepped forward in one last desperate effort, and launched his boot up at Rodney's manhood, striking for victory, launching for life, but alas he was too slow, and Sinead screamed as Rodney stepped to the side and slammed his massive fist into Tom's head.

Chapter 25

It was getting very cold now, the southerly picking up and adding to the bitterness that was quickly settling in. Digsy was growing impatient. He'd been crouching in the shadows for a while now, and his legs were starting to ache, his bad knee throbbing and his fingertips tingling, but then a scream suddenly bounced between the peaks, distorting it into a ghostly howl which echoed all around him.

It had to be Sinead.

Stealing from behind the bush, he made his way back down the track, but a hundred feet from the clearing, he heard the sound of frost crunching underfoot, and saw a cloaked figure easing through the darkness in the distance, so he dropped silently and lay as flat as he could at the trail's edge, blending in to the darkness as the figure approached, its breathing audible now, and only metres from him.

He closed his eyes lest they reflect the moonlight. The footsteps stopped a few metres to his right. He heard a fumbling sound, then the spark of a lighter. Opening his eyes again, the cigarette glowed lucid against the dark backdrop of the night, illuminating its owner—a cloaked figure, tall and curvaceous, taking a moment out, and so close Digsy could hear the crackle of the tobacco as the flames engulfed it.

If the clouds were to break, he would be seen. Should he sniff, he would be heard. The rapturous pounding of his overly exerted ticker might even play too loud for the cold night air.

The guard took another pull on the cigarette, attempting to blow smoke rings, but then another scream cut through the night. Muttering something inaudible, the guard flicked the cigarette over Digsy's head and ran back to investigate.

Staying low, Digsy pushed himself to his feet and followed, hugging the trail's edge with his air pistols drawn.

'Just shoot him, ay Roddy.'

Holden had only just come around, and he was still a bit dazed, subconsciously stroking his moustache as he gazed down at the German knelt before him. The cheeky git had almost choked Holden, and then had the nerve to put him to sleep. Holden had had enough of Tomas now, and he wasn't in the mood for messing around.

'Not here though mate. Do it over there,' he said, pointing into the darkness.

'Dump the prick in the bushes mate. No one'll find 'im there.'

Sinead screamed and scratched as she watched Rodney dragging Tomas away, but then the moustached guard returned his attention to her.

'Dumb wench, not so clever now, are ya?' quizzed he, coughing up as much phlegm as he could and gifting it to Sinead's face.

She didn't get the chance to thank him though.

'Hold your horses Holden!'

The voice came before the crunch of her footsteps, and then the cloaked guard that had disappeared minutes before emerged from the shadows, her stride confident and her voice true, crunching casually towards them.

'I told you to play nice.'

With a grumble, the moustached guard dragged Sinead to her feet again, ramming his rifle into her back, and she was shoved onwards, stumbling, tripping and terrified, unbelieving as to what was about to happen, and utterly terrified.

Sinead had never been executed before, and the thought of it suddenly scared the bejesus out of her.

Everything was dark, everything hidden. All Sinead could see was the foliage fluttering in the torchlight before her, their path overgrown and narrow, and only visible a couple of meters ahead of them.

She barely had the strength to stand, but the butt of the rifle forced her on anyway.

She wasn't struggling now though, and seemed resigned to her fate if anything it seemed to Digsy. She'd lost her jacket, and what remained of her clothing was ripped and muddied, a deep cut from her knee to her shin clearly visible through the tear in her jeans.

Following at a distance, Digsy crouched in the shadows, stepping as silently as he could through the veil of frost that covered everything. He could hear the guards speaking, but no more over the crunch of their footsteps.

This was it.

Digsy's heart was doing the conga, his moment growing closer, clouding the visions of a horrible death that were rattling around in his head. He was ready to go now, almost eager to go, and he wouldn't have to wait long.

The track suddenly gave way to the clifftop, the guards emerged into the moonlight, and the rock from which so many souls had flown was suddenly lit up beyond them, ovular and flat almost, the size of a small car.

They were a few metres shy of it.

'Up you get.'

The guard took a knife from her cloak and cut the bindings at Sinead's wrists, and then shoved her forwards, propelling her into the side of the rock, and she fell onto its surface with a whimper.

This is it, thought Digsy, his hands to his pistols as he strained to remember Dr Jones's winning approach to similarly enticing situations.

Well, dis is it, sniffed Sinead, rubbing her wrists where the bindings had been as she looked down to the abyss before her. She was immersed in herself and oblivious to all else around her now. The platform she stood on was frosted and slippery, and soaked up the moonlight, dominating her vision, like she was stood on an ice moon.

She would see her death coming she knew. Not much of it. Just a drop into the abyss, but she'd know about it.

The roar of the river filled the night now, and she tried to look at anything but it, but it glistened at its peaks as the clouds again broke like fireflies floating in the blackness. It looked so pretty, like fairy lights strung across the vast gorge she now stood over, twinkling in an apparent effort to ease her pain.

A shot rang out in the distance.

A second followed a few seconds later. The clouds again closed.

'Looks like your mate made it to the Pearly gates before ya love,' chortled the moustached guard, and Sinead's heart sank further than she ever thought possible.

Tomas was dead.

Everyone close to her was dead now, and Sinead felt empty suddenly, but not weak. Quite the contrary actually, and she lashed out at the guard behind her, knocking the rifle from her grip as the guard recoiled with a startled yelp.

The night was dark again, the wind up, and the clouds were racing by overhead like a conveyer of used cotton wool balls. Sinead heard the guard's rifle clatter to the rock, so she did the same thing again, swiping out at the guard, who slipped back and then reached out, grabbing Sinead by the arm for balance; when in a surprising twist, there was a strange clicking sound, like a woodpecker hammering a tree, and the guard with the moustache screamed, dropping to his knees with his hands to his face.

Click-click Aaaarrrrgghhh!

An agonized howl cut through the night as the pellets drove into the moustached guard's face. Digsy's air-pistols were empty, and the guard was screaming, down on his knees with his hands to his face, so Digsy hurled the pistols one at a time at the guard's head, and there he crumpled.

That'd been the easy part though.

All was dark now. The moustached guard had dropped his torch, and the ground beside the platform was all that Digsy could see. Atop it, Sinead and the cloaked guard were almost invisible. Two interlocked shadows almost as one, waltzing and grappling, and impossible to distinguish. Pulling the bow from his shoulder, Digsy reached back for an arrow, notching it on the bowstring as he tried to pick out his targets through the gloom. All he could make out though, were two silhouettes writhing around at the cliffs' edge, the torches crackling and hissing, lighting them sporadically suddenly as the breeze picked up and blew the flames towards them.

They screeched and shrieked, spat and clawed, Digsy's arms quivering now as he strafed the arrow between them, searching for just a glimpse of familiarity, he was desperate to intervene.

But then one of them dropped with a whimper and the other one drew a pistol from her robe, levelling it at Digsy.

Not before he'd found his target though.

There was no time to think. Digsy's moment had come. His stars were aligned and his heart raced as time seemed to slow to a crawl. The guard's movements were almost robotic they were so slow, and the bow-string felt so heavy suddenly. With an effort, Digsy pulled it to its limit as the pistol centred on him, but then, with conspiratorial timing, the clouds again parted, bathing the scene in a mystical radiance, and the tantalising scene before Digsy was revealed.

Chapter 26

Stopping short, Digsy was stunned suddenly, confused and utterly bewildered. Gazing down the arrow to the cloaked figure beyond it, he couldn't believe his eyes. His arms were quivering uncontrollably. He was dumbstruck. Straining to make sense of the vision that was stood right in front of him. Confusion was rife. Rampant even. He couldn't shoot the guard now. Not now he'd seen the face glaring back at him. The heavens had revealed his dreams and worst nightmare all at once. The scar under the eye was new, and the general evilness she emanated, but Digsy saw it in an instant—Those pouty lips that he loved so. Her adorable crooked nose and her long flowing mane, once blacker than the night itself, but now a tangled, sooty grey. She looked so different, so evil, but it couldn't be anyone else.

He'd presumed her lost and yet now there she was. The light of his life. Mary.

What the hell!

His face contorted like an epileptic trout on a trampoline. He didn't know whether to laugh or to cry, to sing out loud or to scream. His wife was alive, standing right in front of him, grinning like a mad woman and pointing a gun at him!

Sadly though, the recognition wasn't mutual on Mary's part, and as Digsy lowered the arrow, loosening the bow's string and gazing at the love he'd presumed long since lost, the cloaked guard that he now knew as his wife Mary, having found her target, squeezed the trigger.

His mind whirling, Digsy staggered back, unsteady on his feet suddenly, a searing pain in his left shoulder and a sudden chill to his core. He looked to his shoulder and put his hand to it, warm blood trickling through his fingers and down his arm, and he swallowed, clenching his fists as he looked to his amore.

'Mary…' he pleaded, his voice quivering as he looked into her eyes. 'It's me sweetheart. Mary?'

It made no sense. The indifference in Mary's eyes betrayed no emotion whatsoever. She had no idea who he was it seemed. She too looked confused now, but a grin was creeping onto her face.

She watched him with interest.

'Mary, come on babe. Please baby,' he blubbered.

Digsy was starting to feel light-headed now, and woozy, and his legs were failing him. He raised his open hand to Mary, the other holding his wound, and forced a painful step forward.

'Mary luv. I don't feel great. Come on luv, let's go home.'

'Who's Mary?' enquired Mary, thrown by the unexpected display of amore from this strangest of strangers, and she studied him, perplexed and slightly amused by this most baffling of creatures. Who was this that spoke like he knew her? Pursing her lips, entirely stumped, she analysed his features, searching for familiarity, but she could find none. He looked so pathetic, a blubbering broken mess as he bled and begged before her. She poked her rifle at him with a scowl, making the scar across her cheek sharpen at the nose and duel with the bag under her eye.

She couldn't help but feel slightly sorry for Digsy suddenly though. He was a pitiful sight, but that was just a weakness she knew, and Raul had warned her. No sympathy he'd preached. The scum would slit your throat in an instant given the chance, so having reached a decision as to her next move, Mary raised the gun to Digsy once more.

There was a brief flash. Digsy saw that, and then a detached feeling became him, and he felt the strength draining from his core. A strange sensation indeed, like a combination of all the drugs he'd ever taken suddenly came back to haunt him at once. His world slowed down and his senses numbed. He felt light-headed suddenly, stars dancing across his eyes, but worryingly warm too now, and he staggered back again, unaware of doing so, and he must have tripped, because then a sudden lightness took him. His world seemed to invert. He felt a falling sensation, not the hard impact he'd expected, air rushing past him, and then something smashed into him, a hard impact yet cushioned, engulfing him in a shroud that took his breath away instantly.

A different world welcomed Digsy at that point.

A peaceful yet turbulent world.

He couldn't breathe though. His lungs screamed for air and he panicked. He needed to breathe and of this he was certain, but he couldn't, and he could feel himself growing weaker and weaker by the second. He could feel the river dragging him along too now. Digsy's fight was gone though. He didn't have the strength any more, nor the will suddenly. He knew he was done for, and as a vision of Mary as he once knew her danced into his mind, laughing and joking and happy-go-lucky as he remembered her, Digsy's world turned to black around him.

Chapter 27

The moonlight remained true as Sinead eased herself up, and then crouched, leaning on the stone platform before her. The wind was light now, but bitter, and she was shivering violently. Her head was pounding, and she could feel the blood dripping down her cheek from the gash she could feel at her temple. Then she remembered her scuffle with the cloaked guard. That explained the blood, but she hadn't quite followed the goings on from there.

Moments before, when she'd come around, Digsy had suddenly been there, the bow he held trained on the cloaked guard, and the guard's pistol on him. Sinead's head had been ablaze, and the scene a muddle of confusion. From what she'd gathered though, Digsy knew the cloaked guard from the old days. He'd called her Mary. She obviously meant something to him, and he hadn't been able to shoot her, an affliction sadly not shared on Mary's part.

Where was he?

The torches were fading now, struggling for breath and damp, perfect circles around them where they'd melted the frost they sat in.

Atop the platform stood the cloaked guard she'd heard Digsy call Mary, a few metres from Sinead. Her back was to Sinead, and she was stood near the cliff's edge, peering over into the gorge with her rifle trained down.

Nobody else was around. Just herself and Mary. Then she heard a groan though, barely audible over the meek whistle of the breeze, and glanced over to see the guard with the moustache coming around, splayed out on the ground beyond the platform with his hands to his face. That made three, but where was Digsy?

A glistening on the platform caught Sinead's eye, the moonlight shimmering through the blood pooled upon it. Sinead had heard the gunshot. At least she'd presumed it was a gunshot, and she could only assume that Digsy had been shot and fallen from the cliff. The anguish of so much loss suddenly boiled up inside her, and an evil plan sprang into her mind.

All it would take was a push.

That thought hadn't occurred to Sinead though. Sinead had a less subtle plan in mind. She stood tall, glaring defiantly at the back of this *Mary*, and then, like a woman possessed, she charged, and with no regard for the consequences, launched herself shoulder first at Mary, who'd heard her indiscreet charge, and with impeccable timing stepped to the side.

There was no way Sinead could stop herself. First, she was charging, then she was pouncing, and then she was upside-down and plummeting downwards into the void, screaming an utterly pointless scream as the glistening river hurtled up towards her.

It was over in a second.

Hitting the water felt like hitting a wall of metal buckets filled with water. Her orientation was gone, and her breath too. She had no idea which way was up, or which way down. No idea where her salvation lay. The water quickly slowed her though, and her fingers grazed a rock on the riverbed, so she pushed herself from it, driving upwards as the last air she had bubbled from her; and finally she surfaced, spitting the icy water back into the night with a strange sense of rebirth that invigorated her instantly.

Bejesus yes!

She'd made it. She'd survived the fall!

Steadying herself, she looked around, and the scene almost took her breath away again. It looked like she was floating in a tide of molten silver. The world was black but for the river glistening and rippling at her chin, and she was momentarily taken aback by its beauty. She could feel its pull too though. She knew it could be deadly, and the current was strong, so she kicked out, and finally felt the rocky ground beneath her.

Heaving herself onto the shore, she dropped exhausted to her knees.

The noise was almost deafening at the foot of the gorge, the roar of the river and the wind whistling through it like a jet plane going by overhead. It was much colder than up on the clifftop too, and Sinead was in tatters. She was so tired. She'd been battered and bruised, kicked and beaten, her Da had been killed and she'd almost just drowned; but she knew she had to find the strength for just a little longer, and she knew now that she could.

Turning to look back up from where she'd fallen, the vertical cliff face towered up on the far side of the river before her. How had she survived that fall? How had she missed the rocks poking up from the river all along its foot?

Bang!

A shot rang out from the clifftop, zipping from a rock metres from Sinead, and she looked up to see Mary stood at the cliff's edge, peering over it, and tiny against the backdrop of the night now.

'Where are you? Come to Mummy,'

Her voice was distorted by the wind, and ghoulish, another speculative shot zipping from the rocks, but much closer this time. She had to move. She had to find some cover. There was none to be seen though. Nothing but shadows all around her.

That only left the river.

Another shot clattered from a rock as she tried to judge the river's strength, but then she thought she saw something moving in the water. Without light it was hard to tell for sure, so she stepped back into the shallows for a closer look.

It hadn't been her imagination.

On closer inspection, there was definitely something odd about the cluster of the rocks she could see poking up from the water near the foot of the cliff. Something not quite right about them. They had a familiar form. Certain contours. They looked to be twitching too, and she was certain rocks didn't twitch.

Chapter 28

Jimi sang of ploughmen as Digsy tried to figure out what it was that was strange about the day. There was definitely something a bit off he could tell, but he couldn't quite put his finger on it, so he turned up the volume, sank back into the soft leather, and sipped an oh-so-satisfying sip, a warm fuzziness permeating as he tried to remember how he'd got there.

A shiver traced his spine as he took his first ever sip of his first ever homebrewed moonshine. It tasted good, if not a little noxious, and he imagined an army of bacteria fleeing under the fiery tsunami's approach, cleansing everything but his liver he liked to tell himself, though he suspected it may not be true.

Mmmmm.

A taste of paradise, and he started to think of different ways in which he could spice up his future efforts—a touch of mint here possibly, a spot of ground special leaf there. The possibilities were endless.

If only his still were bigger!

Lighting the smoke that was cradled in his lips, he inhaled. A moment passed, and then the room started to wobble, but he'd expected that. That was normal, and indeed one of the perks some might argue, and to be thoroughly embraced. His head soon acclimatised though, and he held the glass up before him, studying its contents with pride, swishing it around before his eyes and drowning in his own vanity. To create one's own nectar, thought he, is to be one step closer to heaven.

He looked to the plant he'd been lovingly tending by the window, and smiled.

Two steps.

Indeed it was a satisfying feeling, and Digsy was enjoying wallowing in it, but then something akin to a bomb suddenly went off inside his head.

It was a disturbing sensation. Digsy's world turned dark and his limbs to jelly. He was so cold all of a sudden, and he was struggling for breath, the room warping around him now, random flashes of white midst the blackness as Hendrix sang on in the background; but his words were skewed, the music warped and out of time.

'Diiiggssyyy!'

Jimi's voice appeared to have turned into a woman's. Nope, it was Mary's voice he quickly realized, not Jimi's, but it was warped too. Her face looked to distort as she walked into the room, so he rubbed his eyes and looked again. It appeared she was drifting away from him now, and getting smaller all the time. Wait, no, he was the one doing the drifting.

What the deuce!

Absolute darkness enveloped Digsy then, yet he felt naught but a serene lightness, like he was floating, drifting helplessly in a sea of emptiness. Had he taken anything he wondered? This was all very strange if not. The room he was in moments before had vanished, and Mary along with it.

How bizarre.

The world around Digsy began to fade then, and all was chaotic suddenly, everything moving and rushing around him. His breath failed him and he panicked. He had no footing suddenly. No control of himself at all.

All became clear to Digsy at that point though. He knew he was in the river suddenly, and he knew that he'd been shot, but a strange kind of peace became Digsy then. A serene sense of departing, which didn't bother him at all. All he wanted was to sleep, but Sinead grabbed his trailing arm before it followed the rest him under and pulled with everything she had.

Her every fibre strained as the river pulled back, but somehow she found the strength, cradling Digsy with one arm as she grasped desperately for the shoreline with the other. Slowly she dragged him to safety, and then dropped down to the rocks with a groan.

Awake suddenly, a vision appeared through the darkness before Digsy. It was a face he could tell. A blurred face. An upside-down blurred face, but a kind one. It wasn't Mary's face though, and he couldn't make it out properly. He was freezing.

Is this dying?

Everything hurt. Everything ached, but he was no longer it the river it seemed, which was something. He could feel the rocks digging into his back, so he rolled onto his side, coughing the last of the water up, and then screamed, rolling back again.

Then the face again. It was above his, talking and busy, but he couldn't see what with. Without the face though, there was nothing. His vision clouded then, and the face disappeared. Things getting darker…

'Mary? Ma…'

Digsy was unconscious again, so Sinead removed his body armour, and saw the bullet holes passing right through it—one to his left shoulder, and one to the side of his stomach. He was unresponsive too, so she slapped him across the face, as if that would stifle the flow of blood that was seeping from him, and instructed him not to die on her.

Another shot pinged from a rock metres from them. Sinead's nerves were in tatters now, but she had to come up with a plan she knew. A way to save Digsy and escape, but she wasn't in the best way herself. Soaked to the core as she was, Sinead too was freezing, and she sobbed as she realized she could do little to help Digsy. A gunshot was simply beyond her. Neither of them would survive the night if they stayed in the gorge she knew, but she couldn't leave him to die after he'd saved her life either…twice.

Letting out an exasperated cry, she looked to the heavens for an answer. That startled Digsy, and then there she was again – the woman with the face. The kind face, the one thing that seemed to be on his side through these most troubling of times. She gazed into his eyes with sorrow in hers. He tried to speak, but he only managed a gurgle. He tried to smile too, but instead he screamed.

Holding his hand, a tear dropping onto his wound, she looked helplessly down at him. It was dark but getting darker. The woman's face blurred again and Digsy panicked. He didn't want to die. Not yet. Not like this.

This must be it though.

Then he heard a buzzing sound, getting louder and closer, the pain as he looked too much for him though.

It sounded like a boat, and Sinead heard it too, filling the gorge with a buzz a swarm of bees would be proud of. She couldn't tell from where it came, or from how far, but it had to be close.

We're saved! she rejoiced.

Hang on a minute! screamed a more cautionary voice that she'd heard a lot more of lately. And she was right too, the voice so she was. Who good could possibly be in that boat? Thinking quickly, she bent Digsy's legs back at the knee, making him appear more rock-esque to the casual observer, and then placed a few small rocks strategically around him to complete the illusion.

The buzzing grew louder. It was definitely coming from up-river, and it was much closer now, so she ducked behind a boulder a few meters back from the shore.

The night was clear now, and the wind picking up again. The river reflected the moonlight back up the gorge walls, and they shimmered almost as much as the river did. Sinead could see the boat not far down it, twenty metres from her, its silvery wake floating like an upside-down pyramid behind it.

There was no time to move Digsy now. Game over. They would just have to rely on dumb luck now, which hadn't been much of an acquaintance of Sinead's, ironically enough since surviving the apocalypse.

Picking up two rocks, one in each hand, she readied herself, the buzzing growing louder still, and then suddenly stopping as the engine chugged to a halt not far from her. They had to be close. If she chanced a look she would be seen. Another shot came from the cliff, but missed laughably this time. Closer to the boat if anything.

She heard a splash of water, and then someone wading through it, approaching the shore and dragging the tin craft behind them.

The buzzing had stopped, and Digsy imagined he'd imagined it, but he could still hear the river, and found the sound comforting suddenly.

Where was the woman? He knew it hadn't been Mary now. That had been a dream, but where was she?

A voice came to him then. A man's voice. That didn't bode well. Digsy didn't have the strength to care anymore though. There was nothing he could do about it anyway, what with him dying and all.

A shot from the cliffs drowned the voice out and the bullet ricocheted wildly from a rock.

Sinead was pinned, and if Digsy kept twitching like that, the game would be up. She struggled to control her own shakes, the footsteps crunching onto the pebbled shore, and clenched harder onto the rocks that she held, ready to lash out as soon as they reached the boulder she was hiding behind.

So close now.

Another shot, and then she heard the voice again. It wasn't clear over the river, but the voice seemed familiar to her suddenly. She recognised it, but she couldn't tell for certain. A shot pinged into the tin craft and she flinched again, the rocks in her hands dragging her arms to the ground suddenly, her limbs themselves like weights hanging from her.

The voice was dear to her she realised, but she'd heard the gunshot.

'Sinead, are you zer?'

The voice was much louder this time, and more urgent, the shot in reply much closer to its target, skimming from the rocks and into the bank behind Sinead, yet her heart washed with joy as she realised the friend she'd thought killed earlier was still alive.

'Tom!' she cried. 'Tom? Is dat you Tom? I taut yis were dead,'

'Tsank ze lord…' came the relieved and somewhat strained response as Tom hobbled into view, stumbling on the rocks as he stepped around the boulder and into view. 'Ja, it is me…' he continued somewhat deflatedly.

'I have come to save ze day.'

Chapter 29

The rhythmic warbling of a Tui was the first thing to welcome Digsy back to the world, and yet welcome it he did not. It was about as welcome as a West Ham fan in Wimbledon, and a world away from the peaceful start to the day he normally embraced.

His head was pounding, and he felt strange in mind, body and spirit all at once, like his synapses weren't firing properly, not conjoining or reading from the same script, and not an entirely unfamiliar sensation to him, he had to admit, but disconcerting nevertheless.

The ground felt hard beneath him and a gentle breeze tickled his face, which wasn't what he normally expected on waking, so he decided that opening his eyes was the best way to solve this most perplexing of riddles. He was outside he saw as did so. In a bush it appeared, the leaves swaying inches from his eyes, their skeletons like x-rays, sunlight radiating through them in a patchwork of brilliant pastels.

How strange.

Digsy had only ever woken up in a bush once before, and he wasn't expecting it.

What happened? He couldn't remember to begin with. Everything was a bit of a blur, and his memories hazy, but then flashbacks of the night before suddenly flashed back in a hail of dismay, and his face dropped like an Italian footballer.

The day had gone well, and then… the earthquake!

Mary!

He scrambled to his feet, writhing through the foliage as he called out for her, his eyes darting this way and that, but there was no sign of her. Digsy was manic, searching like a man possessed, up and down, left and right, in and out of all kinds of nastiness. His mind whirled as he tried to remember what had happened, when he'd last seen her and where they'd been, vague glimpses of memories bouncing around his head like a Kangaroo on crack.

He was frantic. Seconds later he was manic again, until a tear crowned his eye, distorting the morbid scene that lay before him.

He went to wipe it away, but hesitated. It was preferable to the horrific reality beyond it at least.

And that was indeed true dear reader, for the scene that Digsy witnessed then was jaw-dropping. The once quaint alpine suburb was unrecognisable. There were no people. No birdsong. No life at all. The mountains surrounding were a different shape, and the entire suburb had been flattened by the cliffs surrounding it. Debris of all sorts covered everything. Nothing resembled what it was. Nothing was where it should be.

Few houses remained intact. Huge boulders and rocks were scattered everywhere, mixed up with various pieces of various household pieces, and pools of water and human waste from burst pipes seeped down newly formed cracks in the road, spewed out of others, or sat as bogs of filth under clouds of flies.

It smelled of death.

All was quiet too. Eerily so, and the smoke still rising from dying embers hung midst the pines that still stood, clinging to the scorched limbs like spider webs.

The strange haze that'd welcomed Digsy to the day suddenly returned, clouding his vision, so he rubbed his eyes to clear it, trying to get a clearer perspective on the dire situation he'd awoken to. He had to focus. He had to find Mary, but then the world started to sway around him again. He thought it was another quake to begin with, but everything was blurry too now suddenly. Everything was wavering and surreal, the birds singing in the trees too loud for Digsy's ears, the breeze a veritable hurricane blasting around him. All of his senses seemed amplified as he cowered back to avoid them.

117

And then there was Mary. Her face was suddenly before his, scowling at Digsy, laughing at him, and then all of a sudden crying hysterically.

She was talking to him now, though he couldn't hear her words. Telling him off for something it appeared. She pointed upwards and Digsy's gaze followed her finger. A boulder was hurtling down from the cliff towards them, rushing down to crush them where they stood. He tried to shove Mary from its path, but his hands went right through her and he fell to the ground instead. He turned to brace for the impact…but the boulder had vanished.

Then Mary was standing over him. She was laughing. She raised a gun to him and stuck it right in his face, the barrel millimetres from his eye as he watched on in bewilderment. There was a bang, and a flash, and then stars, thousands of them dancing across Digsy's eyes as horns began to sprout from Mary's head, and then hair from her chin which Digsy didn't think suited her at all.

Then a flash again, and a brilliant light eclipsed all else. A shrill whistling stunned Digsy, and then suddenly, everything had changed.

Digsy worked very hard at that point not to freak out, which was very hard work indeed. It definitely felt like a freak-out moment, but he resisted the urge and didn't. The surreal haze was gone, and things seemed normal again in a way that Digsy couldn't quite comprehend, but different too somehow. Not the normal "normal" that normal folk normally deemed normal, but an abnormal normal.

A new normal.

He was lying on his back now, on a soft flat surface, bright light stinging his eyelids and a burning sensation coming from his stomach.

His whole body ached and his mind was numb. What happened?

He strained to remember but his head wouldn't cooperate. Nothing seemed to work properly. He couldn't think straight, couldn't move and couldn't understand. Moments passed, chaotic visions flashing through his mind, his head a kaleidoscope of blurred, taunting apparitions. Opening his eyes, he saw unfamiliar grey walls surrounding him, and then slammed them closed again when the light got too much to bear.

Where was he?

Memories of Mary and the last time he saw her again came to mind, haunting and taunting him as he tried to make sense of what he knew now was just a dream. He felt dumb and light headed, nauseous and bewildered. The pain around his middle was intense, but the confusion more so. His head was a shambles, indeed everything was. He had no idea what was going on. No idea where he was.

The air felt warm, but he was cold, stiff and rigid, his entirety throbbing and tender, and even more so when he tried to move. He wanted desperately to get up, but he knew that he couldn't. Striving to remember something, anything that could jog his memory, he shifted his weight, trying to alleviate the pain that was swelling from his core.

The light stung his eyes as he opened them again, so he gave up for the moment.

Growing impatient, he tried again, and again his eyes burned, but gradually the light became more bearable, and the first thing he saw as his relentless blinking slowed, was his emaciated form stretched out on the bed before him.

He was pasty and wiry, his ribs sticking out like snow ploughs under the bandage around his mid, stains seeping around a wound to the right of his stomach where most of the pain was focused. A patchwork quilt covered his lower regions. He instinctively tried his legs, and much to his relief, they worked.

Slowly he took in his surroundings.

The single point of light was a small window high on the opposite wall. He was on a single bed, in what looked to be the middle of a kitchen. Hundreds of cracks and hairline fractures riddled the tiles surrounding the worktops. Empty medicinal bottles were stacked on a shelf, and soiled bandages hung strewn over the lip of the bin in the corner.

Memories, good, bad and ugly began to seep into Digsy's mind. He tried to put them in some kind of order. He remembered the cliff top. The girl – Sinead. He'd tried to rescue her, then…

Visions of the turbulent night smashed through his mind, a blurred tapestry of screenshots, hopping into his mind and then vanishing, but Mary's face was in amongst them too now. *That can't be right.*

Slowly, Digsy put the pieces together though.

The woman at the cliff… the cloaked one with a scar on her face… she'd looked like someone… I recognised her… noooo… It couldn't have been… It was though.

Well slap me with a chicken and call me toots! Digsy's wife was still alive.

He'd thought her dead for the last six years, and yet there she was.

The intricacies of their encounter—if the reader will kindly let their mind regress—being less than favourable to our Digsy, were all but forgotten to him at that point, and in his joy he forgot the pain, forgot the anguish and forgot the murderous specifics of their joyful reunion, and his heart cried:

She's alive! Mary's alive!

All of his senses were kicking in now. – The glorious smell of food. The sounds of nature from afar. The vile, acrid taste rotting in his mouth. The something attached to the end of his wee fella. He pondered for a moment, curious as to this most intimate of new sensations, and slowly, painfully, he lifted the sheet so he could identify the perpetrator, wincing as he pulled the plastic tube from his manhood and wiped the tear from his eye.

Yup.

He was a complete wreck, but definitely alive.

Chapter 30

18th September 2050

Footsteps sounded from beyond the room, hollow, hurried and light-footed. The door to Digsy's left opened with a creak, and in walked Sinead, with her head down, carrying what looked like a bag of sheets. She walked straight past him and placed the bag on the table, removing its contents and then placed them beside it.

She looked different, and much healthier. Her skin was rosy, and she moved with a bounce that said she enjoyed life now, and it'd been good to her.

'Hi,' Digsy ventured rather croakily, and Sinead let out a squeal of surprise, her hand to her breast as she turned to face him. She looked radiant, and memories again flooded Digsy as he pictured her as they'd met on the day of the raid: pasty, sunken and beaten. She'd recovered well.

Her hair was cut to her shoulders, washed and brushed into a silky golden cape. She wore an orange vest with her sleeveless denim over it, and she radiated vitality, in total contrast to the wretch he'd taken pity on who knows how long ago. She gazed at him in disbelief.

'H…hi,' she stammered after a few seconds. 'I, we taut y's were done for. How yis feelin'?'

She looked nervous, but she held his gaze, her hair drooping over her left eye, lending a coy appearance.

'Like death warmed up,' Digsy replied with a forced smile, shifting his weight.

'In a bad way for a while so yis were.'

Pulling an off-white sheet from the bag, she kept her gaze to the side. 'Shot twice, bullets went right tru, luckily for you. Nursey fixed y's up nicely.'

Digsy tried to push himself up onto his elbows, but a bolt of pain rushed through his shoulder and he slumped back down in frustration. Sinead walked back into his vision and put her hand on his shoulder.

'Don't worry…' assured she. '|Past the worst of it so y's are. Be right as rain soon.'

'M… Mary…' he stammered.

'Was that yer one dat shot y's?' she interrupted.

But it was a question she regretted asking.

Memories Digsy would rather have suppressed suddenly flooded back into him, his mind again exploding in confusion as the vision of Mary pointing a gun at him suddenly sprang into his mind. His fists had clenched despite the pain, and he was glaring at Sinead now, with wrath in his eyes.

Shot me? What the hell is she talking about?! but his memories spoke otherwise.

'Liar!' he snapped, sending a deluge of saliva careering down his chin, and inviting inquisitive footsteps from outside, echoing deeply through the hollow floor as they approached.

Again the door creaked open, and Sinead, relieved at the interruption, turned to greet Nursey as her florally abound mass bowled through the door, stooped at an angle her knees appeared unable to support.

'Is everything okay my dea… oh my, you're awek!' she boomed, evidently shocked at Digsy's lack of demise.

Nursey was a big woman of Pacific Island origin, and in her late fifties, was still abound with vigour and an obvious lust for life. As she ambled towards Digsy, the floorboards beneath her seemed to bend and creak as her corpulent form passed over.

'How are you, my boy?' she beamed, displaying the hugest mouth of sparkling teeth Digsy had ever seen.

'Would you look at yourself, ha-ha-ha. You gone made a mess of yourself, ha-ha!' said she on seeing the bib of saliva Digsy had embroiled himself with.

Nursey looked ecstatic at Digsy's helpless state, and he gazed back up at her, unaware of the terror his face betrayed. Grabbing another rag from the bag, Sinead then proceeded to clean up the aforementioned mess, much to Digsy's dismay and Nursey's apparent delight.

Digsy couldn't believe what he was hearing, what his memory reminded him of, and what he knew now had happened. Mary had shot him…twice! And he let out an involuntary moan, whimpering as the pain of moaning got too much.

Nursey picked a small tub from the table beside him and offered him its contents.

'Ere boy, dis will'elp.'

He took the innocuous pill and washed it down with the water from the cup Sinead held to his mouth, the act of swallowing alone like he was being stabbed in the throat with an ice pick. The full extent of grim reality had now revealed its ugly self to Digsy though, and he fell into a drug-induced slumber, paying no attention to the attentions of his carers, and drifted off into a deep, but very much alive sleep.

Chapter 31

Her Ladyship stomped around the Earnslaw's lounge like a rampaging squirrel, stopping short of kicking or throwing anything though, lest she damage the collection of antique furniture that she'd pilfered over the last few years, or indeed, herself. A guard hurried to the window outside at the disturbance, and promptly retreated as she snarled at him.

She needed those plans. The Order were desperately short on fuel now. Only half of her fleet were on the road, and she'd lost her chef somehow. Lost her moonshine supply. The festering cretin, Digsy, had just upped and disappeared, the jumped up little turd.

The frustration too much for her, she drew up before Red, glowering up through his poor excuse for a goatee and into his beady, nervous eyes, and then slammed her knee into the place in which no knee should ever be slammed. He bent double with a groan, crouching and whimpering as she glared down at him with a satisfied smile.

Pathetic.

She jerked her head up to the right next, grinning wildly at Rodney now, who winced and averted his gaze, towering above her with his head almost touching the ceiling, the tip of his dreadlocks hanging a foot above Her Ladyship's head.

Feeling powerful in the moment, she shifted closer to him. He cringed and shuffled his feet uncomfortably, dropping his gaze as the door creaked open with the roll of the lake.

Rodney was a truly daunting proposition at times, but at others, he was a six-foot-seven mouse of a man she mused, eyeing him tauntingly now, and revelling in it. That was only to his elders of course. Rodney respected his elders, and indeed seemed to harbour an irrational fear of them. Her

Ladyship liked that, and had a soft spot for his easily manipulated ways.

His dreadlocks swayed as he shuffled uncomfortably, keeping his eyes to the floor.

His shirt was double XL, but it still looked too small for him, and Her Ladyship found herself momentarily distracted, and appraising him more acutely than she normally would do. With a shiver, she shook her head and switched her attention to Raul, who looked straight ahead, failing to conceal his terror.

'But yooouu…'

She stepped closer to him, and he too shuffled uneasily.

'I can blame fak'n you.'

She stood inches from him, looking up past the bedraggled beard to the fear his plump face betrayed.

Pitiful.

It was plain to see that Raul had let himself go of late. Two months of growth grew thick and fast and covered his surplus chins. The boots he once kept spotlessly clean were now stained and caked in mud up to the shins, and the tear down his left lapel hung awkwardly, flapping as he moved like a thirsty dog's tongue.

Fair enough, it'd been a tough few months, but standards had to be maintained for dignity's sake she thought, feigning a knee to Raul's midsection as he flinched accordingly.

Sniggering to herself, she turned and went to the table, picking up a box of matches. It was a cold night, and cloudy, and what light remained was fading quickly, shrinking the world perceptibly around them. She lit two of the oil lamps behind her.

'This is your last fak'n chance Sargent.'

She turned back to Raul and extinguished the match with a flick of her wrist.

'You caught the fak'n German mate, sneaky back stabbin' little prick, so credit where credit's fak'n due mate, but ya fak'n lost'im again, didn't ya?

Pausing for a moment, she allowed Raul a moment in turn to respond. Raul knew Her Ladyship blamed him for Tom's escape, and therefore her not having the plans yet. He should have tortured the plans from the German, and then executed him himself, should have pushed him from the cliff himself, but he hadn't. Tom had sucker punched Rodney and escaped, so he stayed quiet and allowed her to continue.

'He knows where the fak'n plans are. He knows who's fak'n got'em, and I'm not a monster, but we've still got his fak'n daughter…'

And a right pain in the arse she was proving. Her Ladyship didn't intend to harm the girl of course, but she had her limits, and she wasn't going to let sentimentality get in the way.

'So bring me those fak'n plans, or it's **your** fak'n kids that'll fak'n pay Raul mate. You fak'n hear me?'

The quivering of Raul's bottom lip was answer enough for her.

She threw the teacup she'd picked up mid rant at him, the china shattering off his elbow and scattering on the floor in a symphony of clinks as he hurried for the door.

Finally, thought she. *A bit of bit of peace and quiet*, and she sighed, happy to finally be alone, until she turned to find Red and Rodney still cowering in the corner like the perpetually guilty half-wits they were.

Disappointment became her.

'Well, what the fak do you two fak'n faks want?' she almost whispered.

'Faaak… off.'

Chapter 32

Digsy spent the remainder of the winter holed up in the camp he'd somehow found himself in—a scattering of small stone bungalows in a clearing a hundred metres up the bank from the river. It was closed in on all sides by a thick hedge that marked the camp's perimeter, and was a pleasant spot, and Digsy had to admit, far more habitable than the cave he was for some reason beginning to miss so much.

His road to recovery had been a long one, week after week of pain and struggle, unable to move, and hostage to his injuries in a camp that he knew nothing about. He'd been rescued from the river Sinead had told him, months ago, and brought back to their camp on the night of the raid. Daily he cursed his luck for leading him to such a situation, but then his musings would remind him, that he was yet alive, he did indeed save the girl, and if things had worked out differently, he wouldn't have found his Mary.

Mary.

She was out there somewhere, he was sure of it, and although he still wasn't certain that his visions weren't just a cruel illusion, he yet remained hopeful that her improbable resurrection was indeed real. Indeed, most of his days, before he was able to walk again, were spent planning just how he'd go about winning his murderous betrothed back. Plans which would have to remain dormant for a while he knew, until he was fit enough to tackle such a task.

The camp had been there for two years, mostly made up of folk that had fled New Queenstown from The Order. Digsy's input had proven invaluable amongst its twenty or so residents, and he soon became an influential figure in their small community. He'd shown them how to build a still so the doc could sterilise her instruments properly. Taught the kids how to rig a trap, how to catch a critter and how to tickle a fish. He was actually starting to enjoy the communal life he was so easily adopting. It was pleasant, very different to what he was used to and he felt at home, a part of something and he liked it.

Once he was able to, he jumped at any opportunity to help around the camp, if only to occupy his mind. He'd helped build a coop for the newly acquired chickens, and helped repair an interior wall, as well as other things that warranted no mentioning, like planning the new water channel that ran closer to the camp, thus providing easier access to fresh drinking water and such.

He cooked with them and ate with them, drank and laughed.

One evening in early spring, Tomas, who it seemed to Digsy had never liked him, even told him about some plans for an old power station when he was drunk. Apparently, the plans were a copy of the original plans for the old Hydro-plant that'd been built more than two hundred years before, up the creek a mile to the south of the old town. Tom had said he thought he could replicate the plans, but that The Order wanted them too. 'Ze current powers zat be haf no currents to power zer beings currently. Ze Order are looking for ze plans, so zey can repair ze power haus for zemselves. On ze Q-T, Digsy, ja?' he'd spluttered conspiratorially, his first finger held vertical before his lips.

'Sinead has zem... Shhhh.'

The plans had been passed down through the generations. Sinead's ancestor had helped design it, and her Da had meant to rebuild the plant himself, but then The Order arrived, and he hadn't factored being killed into the equation, so Sinead inherited them.

That was the only time Digsy and Tom had really spoken at length. Relations had seemed quite strained otherwise, like Tom had something against him. What that could be Digsy couldn't fathom as Sinead fussed incessantly over him.

24 October 2050

Spring had sprung, and it was warming up quickly, so Digsy decided the time was right to get his effects in order. His old life was calling him, and his wounds were healing nicely. He was feeling much better, if not a little tender still, so he crept out of the camp one morning before the sun had risen, and made his way west, back towards his cave.

Oh how he longed for the peace and solitude of his old existence again. A sense of normality, whether it be an improvement on his current lot or otherwise. He had to find out.

His journey was short and the way was pleasant, so he took his time, taking in all the wonders that nature had to offer. He watched ducklings patrol single file behind their proud protective mother, safe in the knowledge that they're far too cute to hurt.

He watched a hawk, so graceful and elegant, hovering above its prey a hundred feet up, and then all of a sudden dropping like a bullet, wings tucked back for aerodynamic magnificence, and then it soared back up from the undergrowth with a duckling caught in his talons, tufts of fluff floating back to the earth, and Digsy's theory on ducklings shattered.

The ease in which this operation was undertaken however, served only to remind Digsy how hard it would be for him to find his own food from now on, and how he would face that problem head on if he chose to leave the camp for good. Indeed, it was a distinctly pertinent problem, as he was no longer sure how things stood between himself and The Order. Whether he'd been recognised at the cliff top that night, or if Her Ladyship and Raul knew of his misdeeds towards them in general. Either way, life was going to be tough for a while.

The views improved as his path steadily rose, the gorge the path followed opening up as he followed it upriver, and the Matakauri that once dominated the land did so once again suddenly, growing across the trail like barbed wire. Each branch was home to hundreds of thorns an inch in length and as sharp at the tip as a knife. He struggled to follow the track in places, hacking through the densest growth to avoid a harrowing climb around the cliff face, or a leap across a wide chasm driving into the cliffs.

The gorge eventually swung off to the left, and then cut back on itself to intercept Digsy's path on the other side of the hill before him. Eventually he clambered to the hill's summit.

Not far down the slope on the other side, the dilapidated old Edith Cavell bridge sat across the narrow gorge that split the land in two there.

That was all that stood between Digsy and his cave now. The cave was an hour scramble up the mountain on the other side.

The ancient bridge had seen better days. The supports that curved inwards from the cliff were still true, but a large crack spanned the bridge half way across it, and cut down its side.

To the right of the bridge, the gorge ended abruptly, the river raging from a circular hole in the rock a few hundred metres up its course, weaving its way back towards the bridge where it was channelled into the gorge. The mountains loomed less there, their slopes slighter. Ruined homes spilled up them to the right, and the skeleton of a jet boat sat rusted and riddled with holes on the pebbled shore to the left. The sun caught what hadn't rusted on it, and sparkled like a lighthouse warning of danger.

The sun was directly over Digsy's head now, so he crouched in the shade of a tall eucalyptus, its bark stripped by possums, peeling and flaking away from the silvery wood beneath it.

Taking a piece of dried possum hind from the pouch in his bag, he slipped it into his mouth and chewed the tough meat with gusto, a warm feeling welling at the thought of finally reaching his cave again. It was an easy clamber from here, across the bridge and up, but not wanting to rush his course, he sat in the grass and admired the view before him.

The sun was high and lit up the valley, a tapestry of green and yellow intertwined with scattered ruins, radiating brightly in a dazzling display of nature's splendour, and happier thoughts danced into Digsy's mind, of leisurely walks through the hills and barbeques by the lake. They had been such pleasant times, and they seemed so long ago to Digsy now. He enjoyed remembering them, sometimes at least, but his reverie was interrupted by the clap of a rifle, sending flocks of birds screeching from the trees and Digsy to the ground.

He scrambled up behind the tree he'd been leaning against, sore at his side suddenly and trembling. A stitch had come loose. He'd felt it pop and barely managed to keep the scream inside, and he could feel the warmth of his blood rushing to the surface now, and seeping down his leg.

Listening for a moment, he kept his head down as the shot's echo faded, and slipped the pouch back into his bag. A second shot soon followed, whistling inches above his head and thudding into a tree behind him. Then a third, and a fourth, dirt and bark springing up all around him suddenly, and getting closer with every shot.

The hike had tired Digsy. He was fading fast. His cave wasn't far now, just across the bridge and up, but the bridge had never been guarded before.

His stomach was starting to tingle, and his wounds straining as he hunkered low in the grass, flinching with every shot that ripped it to shreds around him.

Another shot, but it missed by metres this time, so Digsy chanced a look. Someone was coming towards him through the trees. He started to back away, but that meant going uphill he realized, and exposing himself more, so he crouched back down again, searching frantically for an escape as the harsh scape seemed to close its doors around him.

Why hadn't he stolen a rifle before leaving the camp? He didn't even have his air pistols.

Steep but open ground lay to his left, and the decaying frame of a house nestled midst a scattering of birches lay twenty metres beyond it. To his right, a rocky buttress jutting out from the cliff blocked his way in that direction, and there was nowhere else to go.

He could think of no way out.

'Don't shoot!' he cried.

'I'm unarmed.'

Hunching down as low as he could, he scanned the surroundings for a way out, for decent cover, but there was none.

'What the hell you wawnt?'

The accent was unmistakable, and sadly for Digsy, belonged to the man who'd likely castrate himself to see Digsy's demise.

'This here is pri-vate property. No trespassin!

An unwelcome growl came from somewhere close by, deep and rumbling, and clearly a large dog. That was a terrifying sound to Digsy, so he picked up a rock beside him and hurled it at the cliff to his right, and then hauled himself up, sprinting for the house to the left as the ground at his heels exploded.

Across the open ground and into the tree line. The cover of the house was close and the pain excruciating, but on he charged, moving as fast as his injuries allowed. He was almost there too. Sheer will was leading the way. Bullets zipped by but on he charged, bounding over rocks and ducking under low hanging branches, and only a few tantalising metres to go, when he caught his foot on a tree root and down he went, rolling to a stop in the grass only a few meters before the house.

Needless to say, it was a painful fall, but hope abandoned Digsy at that point too. No hope of clemency in the face of this adversary.

Rolling on to his back with a grimace, he looked to the sky.

He heard laughter from nearby, and a *Yee Ha!* followed by a couple of whoops. The dog was barking excitedly now, but he could barely hear it above the chorus of guffaws resounding the valley.

The clouds morphed into Mary's face, and then Sinead's, and Digsy smiled. He'd been so close. *Fate really is a cruel mistress,* thought he as the Mary in the sky winked at him.

The footsteps closed in.

'Where are ya?' they enquired.

The shrill whistle of a man calling his dog sang out, and Digsy obediently turned his head towards it.

'I promise I won't bite.'

The dog was growling now, its handler struggling to restrain it, and it yelped as it tried to pull free and the chain around its neck dug in.

Becoming dog meat wasn't on Digsy's to do list. There was no way he could outrun a dog in his condition though. Where was it? It sounded close, and then a wizened head with broad shoulders and a beard appeared above the grass line before him.

'Ello treacle,' they said, 'Off ye trot Bessie.'

And off Bessie trotted.

Digsy scrambled back, the dog gargling now, excited and on the move. He couldn't see it, but he could see the grass it was ploughing through folding like dominos before it. It would be on him in seconds, but Digsy's back was to the timbers of the house now. He could back away no further.

He closed his eyes, expecting the worst, his arms instinctively up protecting his face, when another shot shook the valley and a second quickly followed, and all was quiet again suddenly.

The suspense was killing Digsy.

Was he dead?

It didn't seem so.

He opened his eyes and the guard was gone. As was the dog, just a bloodied mound of fur lying in the grass a meter before him now. The grasses were swaying in its wake, and blood was splattered across the foliage where the guard had been.

How very strange.

Another shot sang out, but from beyond the bridge this time, and the bullet slammed into the ply boards meters from Digsy, from where a further blast replied. It was all very confusing, and again Digsy found himself painfully uncertain as to his wellbeing, the line between this life and the next as clear to him as a Dutchman with a lisp.

Another shot from the building, and another one at it. Someone was inside, but no one seemed to be shooting at Digsy now.

'Digsy, it's me, Digsy. Are you okay?'

The enquiry came from within the house, the less than reassuring resonance like a choir of angels to Digsy's ears though. A camouflaged figure stepped through the gap where the door had been, crouched beside Digsy, and then morphed into Tomas.

'Cover your ears, Digsy.'

A car door slammed beyond the bridge, Digsy obeyed and Tomas fired again. They heard an engine growl into life, and the screech of tyres as the vehicle sped away, and then no more.

Only a couple of the stitches had broken at Digsy's side, though the pain was still intense, like a continuous salvo of paper cuts tearing into his skin. On closer inspection though, it wasn't too bad, so, pushing himself up, and having thanked Tomas for his help, keeping the coincidence of Toms having been there in the first place in his head, Digsy accepted Tom's offer of a chaperone back to his cave, and relief caressed his soul as the plateau they eventually clambered onto, revealed itself to be entirely undiscovered, and nicely overgrown in his absence.

No one had been here.

The Order hadn't found his cave.

With an effort, Digsy grabbed the rope and pulled himself up, gritting his teeth at the strain to his stomach. The air inside was muggy and foetid, like when he'd first seen it years before, and had a strange sheen that made it harder to see than he remembered. The shafts of light cutting down from the ceiling swarmed with insects, dust and moths, and glowed midst the blackness, shining down on the table which had been ransacked by possums he could tell. Such a strangely welcoming sight.

Digsy was home.

Tomas appeared behind him, gazing in disbelief at the filth that the torch illuminated.

'Vat is zis?' he laughed. 'You live here? Oh you are so very fanny. Vait until Sinead hea's of zis!'

Adding: 'I sink you haf much to do Digsy, ya. You are safe now, I vil leave you to it.'

And with that, Tomas disappeared down the entrance shaft.
'Bye Digsy. I love your place ya.'

Chapter 33

Holden wasn't concerned at the shoot-out that he'd heard in the distance, or at the reports of vagabonds roaming free in the hills and shooting his fellow guards. It had been a long day, and Holden's mind wasn't entirely where his employers might expect it to be.

He'd been torn away from his venison pie, just as he'd taken the first bite, and cajoled into labour. The Order had recently extended their territory north of New Queenstown, out to the bridge at Arthurs Point, and there'd been an attack there apparently, but at least Holden's was an easy job he'd reasoned, and he intended to make the most of it. Guard the bridge was what Raul had instructed of him, and that's exactly what he was doing.

The day was clear and the wind light, the river high and matching the shade of the sky above. Red and Rodney were scouring the mountain behind him, and others elsewhere for any sign of the intruders. That left Holden on his lonesome guarding the bridge, and he was as happy as he could be with his lot.

A bit of peace at last.

Leaning back against his pickup truck, he took a lighter from his pocket and lit the cigarette in his mouth, and his nerves instantly relaxed as he blew the remnants back to the ether, coughing and spluttering, and wiping the filth from both sides of his carefully manicured moustache.

Caressing the scar on his top lip as he did, angry thoughts captured Holden as his mind went back to that night at the cliff. The night he'd been shot in the face. Oh the pain, oh the anguish, oh his poor face, and oh how he'd make the vermin that did it to him pay he thought with vehemence; and oh how he'd enjoy it. The memory of the doc writhing around in his face, trying to remove the pellets with a pair of tweezers, was still vivid to Holden, even though it was months ago, and he'd had a generous helping of moonshine beforehand. It was bloody agony, and he clearly remembered Rodney and Mo holding him down as he tried to wring the doctor's neck for his endeavours.

Holden had indeed spent some time considering how he would exact his revenge when he finally got his hands on the louse that'd shot him, and he was quite surprised at his own ingenuity in formulating such heinous ploys.

He'd imagined hanging the culprit upside down from the bridge over the gorge, covering him in jam, or maybe even his own faeces he'd thought as his mind delved deeper and darker, and watching on in glee as the hawks and sand flies slowly stripped the maggot to the bone.

Or weighing him down in the river before the snowmelt, and again watching on as the river slowly rose and drowned the snivelling little arse-rag right before his eyes.

These were but a glimpse of the dazzling array of schemes Holden had envisioned over the last few months. Indeed he enjoyed exercising his mind in such a manner, and his mind was straying in that direction again, but then a Tui found its voice somewhere amongst the pines, the sweet warble echoing down the gorge, dulling the edge that had just announced itself on his day. With a smile, he strolled over to the bridge's railings, peering over them down to the rushing, brilliant turquoise waters below, drew in the last of his cigarette, and flicked it over the warped railings, watching as it spiralled down to the abyss.

Then he heard a noise from near the mountain's foot, a stone thrown from his position on the bridge – the crunching of foliage and branches snapping, so he reached for his rifle, scanning the treeline as he did. Nothing moved though, and after a few moments he relaxed again, assuming it was one of his own. Stroking his thumb and forefinger down his moustache again, he leaned down to the truck's wing mirror to double check that it still suited him. Then he heard something else. A gurgled scream cut short from somewhere behind the shrub-line, and then someone burst through it, charging straight at him.

****

'Well lookee here at this here!'

Red pulled himself up onto the plateau he'd happened upon, wiping his forehead on the back of his sleeve, and breathless now after climbing up the steep terrain to it. It was around midday and warming up quickly, even in the shade of the pines surrounding him. He and Rodney had been scouring the foothills, searching for whomever attacked the bridge earlier, and they were close to giving up hope, when Red found a small track leading up. Not obvious to the untrained eye, it was only the merest of tracks, but had definitely been used more than once.

Red had been given basic tracking training on the job in the old world, but he'd found it fascinating, and been on dozens of tracking weekends over the years, and was therefore sure he knew what he was looking at—a few too many cracked twigs here, compressed ground there and the like. Well, the track led to the plateau he stood on, and a very interesting looking cave indeed.

A scattering of pines sat evenly spaced around the plateau, which was about the size of a bus, the ground thick with bronzed pine needles with tufts of thick grass or rocks poking up here and there. To it's rear, the cliff rose steeply before Red, a hundred feet or more, and he crouched next to the overhang he'd noticed near the bottom of it. It definitely looked like there was an entrance of sorts beneath it. The ground was trampled too, and as he leaned in for a better look, a shot rang out in the distance, and he flinched, inadvertently standing and smashed his head into the overhang.

'Sunnuva biach!'

Crouching back down with his hands to his head, he bit his bottom lip, as if the pain of that would subdue the pain in his head.

The shot sounded like it had come from back down near the bridge, so he pushed himself back up, massaging the

138

crown of his head as he called for Rodney and set off to investigate.

***

The guard raised his rifle, Tom ducked to the left and the bullet zipped past him, tearing the fabric of his jacket as it did. Tom had been making his way down from Digsy's cave, and he'd almost made it back down to the bridge, when he'd spotted the guards. The first guard had been easy. He hadn't seen Tomas, and had died quietly, but then Tom had gotten sloppy.

Pushing through the growth that covered an old track running from the road down to the river, he cut off the path and into the undergrowth, a bullet zipping off a boulder to his right and thudding into a tree to his left. The bush was thick, but he pushed through it, and moments later burst through onto the smooth stones of the riverbank, scrambling for cover behind a boulder at its edge.

The river was high and gushed by behind Tom, cutting to the right, and then back to the left before disappearing under the bridge again. He could hear naught else above it, so he assessed his surroundings, looking for anything that could aid his escape. There was nothing though. Nothing but smooth grey rocks, the mountains looming all around him creating an amphitheatre for the gladiator Tom knew he was.

He was cornered. The river blocked the way behind him, and at least one guard was approaching through the bush.

Sliding his last bullet into the rifle, he peered back around the boulder, and then there he was, emerging from the undergrowth, the goon with the moustache you could swing off. His face was riddled with freshly healed scars and his rifle was at the ready.

Holden stepped from under the canopy, onto the river's shore, and instantly spotted the German, half-hidden behind a boulder at the river's edge, but his gun was already raised and pointing at him.

That was a terrifying moment for Holden. It didn't last long though. He saw the flash as he raised his own gun, then

139

a bullet ripped through his forehead and he dropped to the ground, the ashen stones around him instantly turned red as his head crashed onto them.

Crouching for a moment to catch his breath, Tom spotted the guard's ammo belt draped across his corpse, so he made his way over, staying low and reaching out, but then another shot resounded, pinging off a rock behind him.

'Well howdy there cock sucker.'

Red limped onto the shore with his rifle trained on Tomas, but Tomas was quick, and both barrels settled on the other.

'Lookee here who we dun gat here!' exclaimed Red on recognition of Her Ladyship's informant, panting a little, and glancing around nervously.

'I'll thought yous died at the cliff that night boy,' he went on in some confusion, frowning as he saw the moustached guard lying in a bloody heap on the rocks behind Tomas.

'Why did you shoot my partner, partner? And why you point'n that there gun at me? Looks like we dun got ourselves a Mexicain standoff,' he continued, somewhat answering himself, and looking puzzled now at the situation he'd found himself in.

'Not really,' replied Tom.

He squeezed the trigger and Red crashed back onto the rocks behind him, and there he remained.

The day was growing warmer still. Sweat dripped from Tom's armpits and his clothes clung to him. The day had been long, hiking, climbing and fighting, but Tom was energised, and was relishing the action that he'd missed so much. On he ran, hopping from rock to rock away from the bridge, following the river's path until he made it to the track that ran adjacent to it. He knew there to be a crossing of sorts further down it. Once across the river, the guards would never find him, so he sprang along the trail with all the urgency of an outspoken Englishman in Glasgow, adrenaline coursing through him as he spotted the crossing and made for it.

What Tom hadn't spotted however, was the large figure coming towards him through the trees to his left, so when a load akin to a small pony slammed into Tomas, it took him rather by surprise.

Crunch!

Down he went, rolling head over foot down the bank until he came to an abrupt stop in the bushes at the bottom.

Struggling to his feet, and only meters from the river again, Tom writhed himself free of the bramble he was entangled in, but Rodney was on him instantly. He drove his fist down at Tom's head, who ducked back in time to avoid it, slashing his arm on a thorn as he stumbled and fell to the ground.

Boot and fist came at Tomas, but he ducked and dived, avoiding them all as Rodney came at him like a jackhammer battering a road. Rodney was huge, and Tom knew he was no match for him should Rodney get his hands on him, and he clearly remembered their encounter at the cliff that night, but Rodney was slow, and Tom managed to avoid each assault that came predictably at him.

A big left swung in at Tom.

Ducking under it, he saw his chance, and he swiped his boot into Rodney's ankle, stealing it out from under him, and sent Rodney crashing to the ground with a groan.

Tomas wasn't finished there though. Oh no. Tom was incensed, and he slammed his boot down into Rodney's face and knocked him out cold.

Balancing himself on his trembling knees, Tomas gazed at the mangled face lying beneath him, more jubilant than he ever remembered feeling. What a rush!

'Zat is tveis I have beaten you now!' he glowered exultantly, holding two fingers up before the unconscious Rodney's face.

'Ha! Remember me do you? You big ugly bastard, ja? Ha!'

Tom felt untouchable all of a sudden, and he leant down and slapped Rodney hard across the cheek.

'Vakey-vakey.'

The grin welcoming Rodney spoke of a man who'd just spent a productive night with the Swedish ladies' netball team. Blood blocked the vision in his left eye, and the rifle pressing into his nose sent shivers of pain coursing through him, but he was okay Rodney knew, if not a mite shaken, and fully aware of what was happening now.

He could see the vengeance burning in the eyes of the man beyond the gun's barrel, and groaned a deserving groan as their eyes met.

Grinning back at him, Tom winked.

'You should haf killed me at ze cliff, Ja. You remember me now, don't you, Ja.'

And he did. Rodney's faculties quickly gathered as he recognised the face grinning down at him, spectacles bent and the glass in one eye cracked like a spider's web. It was the bloke Rodney was supposed to have executed that night at the cliff. Her Ladyship's informant. The bloke that had sucker-punched Rodney and run away.

Hope deserted Rodney at that point, as he thought of the revenge he himself would exact in such a situation. He tried to push himself up, but Tom's rifle kept him from doing so.

A decision had to be made Tom knew, but he didn't know if he could. Tom wasn't a murderer, but Rodney was a special case. Tom had never shot anyone in cold blood before, but exceptions had to be made. He had to escape, and this was a very bad man.

He looked down with sympathy into the eyes of his prey. Terror he saw in return. The terror of a man who believed wholeheartedly in something, but had fallen into a life abundant in regret. Tom's resolve hardened though, as he remembered the way they'd beaten Sinead that night. How tormented and terrified she'd been, and a rage welled within him as his trigger finger tensed.

His sympathy was no more.

He started to squeeze the trigger, ever so gently, when he heard the not so gentle sound of a similar mechanism yards to his right.

'Well, howdy there hun cock sucker!' chirped Red as Tom turned to greet him. 'I bet yous wish you dun shot me in the head, don't yous boy?'

Chapter 34

25 October 2050

The cold air on Digsy's face was the first of Mother Nature's mistresses to get their hands on him, and oh how he wished he was back at the camp again, the morning sun beaming in through the windows, the birds warbling and chirping away, inviting him onwards into the day. It was very early he could tell, the streaks of light from the ceiling like torches with dying batteries, and it was so cold in the cave. Cold and dismal. He'd forgotten how cold and miserable his cave could be. He was no longer used to it, and he coughed and winced as he drew in a deep breath, the air thick and stale and tickling his lungs.

Then came the pain.

Lifting the duvet, he looked down to the wound at his side, which stung terribly, but there was only a small stain seeping through the bandage. It seemed his makeshift repair the night before had done the job. He'd indulged in a few cheeky glasses of moonshine beforehand, which he'd hidden in the corner of the cave—purely for pain relief and to steady his hand of course. Once the Dutch courage had taken effect, he'd heated a knife over the fire, and held it across the wound while he'd screamed into a cloth for a few seconds. He'd then poured the bottle's remnants over the smouldering flesh and screamed a little more.

It was easily the most excruciating thing he'd ever experienced, and he threw up immediately after, proceeding then to pass out.

Throwing back the duvet, he eased himself up, and after a few ablutions to-wit his injury, he hung the pot he'd filled with fresh water from the tripod above the fire, and a few minutes later, as the army of tiny leaves fell unto its destiny, the blessed union was made. The cuppa warmed him instantly, and he could feel the nectar washing through him, sending its goodness to his every pore he imagined as he sipped it lovingly.

Something still wasn't right though. Digsy was stressed. The pain in his stomach wasn't helping, but his head was awash with emotions, plans and eventualities too, and this particular morning wasn't turning out to be the relaxing affair he normally cherished. He had so many things to do, so many problems to resolve that had all sprung from that one fateful day. He had to put them in some sort of order.

So much to do.

Light was streaming in through the roof holes now, the moths still bathing in it, the rest of the space gloomy still though, uninspiring and musty.

Scratching his unkempt head, his hair thick and bushy now, with a natural wave, he drained the last of the cup. Once drained, he then took a few deep breaths to clear his mind— some Buddhist thing he'd seen on TV-Tube years before. Apparently, some old bloke in Runcorn had done this many-a-time, and reached enlightenment so he had, accelerating his own reincarnation beyond comprehension, and then turned into a planet or some such. Eventually he'd gone on to be a God of all things.

Digsy quite liked the sound of being a planet, or God too he'd sometimes muse. Life as an infinite point of pure energy, connected to everything in existence would be pretty sweet he sometimes thought, and he'd picture himself hopping between realities, dancing with dimensions, righting wrongs and saving the universe.

He could definitely see it being a stressful position though, and he realised of course, that as God, he would be widely scorned, and even disregarded through his apparent absence. *Where were you when my son died?* the woman suddenly in Digsy's mind screamed. *Where were you when we needed you?* the masses cried in unison.

Digsy was getting stressed at the prospect of omnipotence already. As if being created in the first place wasn't enough!

All those bloody prayers to listen to, all those needy moaners would drive him nuts, and half of them were likely toss bags that didn't deserve divine assistance anyway. Trained monkeys would certainly be helpful went on this most productive train of thought.

Unable to clear his mind, he stood and paced the cave, on edge for some reason, and restless. His homecoming hadn't been the relief he'd hoped it would be, tarred as it was by injury and incident. It'd been a testing few months, and he needed to relax.

Music soothes the soul he remembered, resonating in harmony with one's mind and the planet, but the possums had wrecked his guitar.

Digsy needed some air. He couldn't think clearly. There was so much that he needed to do, and so donning his usual attire, lovingly repaired to a semblance of its former glory by Sinead, he picked up his particulars, and lowered himself back into the world.

Chapter 35

The day was young still, only a tender light streaming in through the window, but it was enough to wake Tomas from his slumber. He found himself strapped to a chair. A sturdy chair, and he was quite well strapped to it he'd deduced as he took in the sounds and smells around him. He was battered and bruised, but alert still, and blindfolded he'd concluded, given the lack of vision he'd awoken to.

Where the sturdy chair that he was well strapped to was, he knew not, as Red had blindfolded him after he'd caught him by the river. He could hear activity nearby, and the scraping of his chair echoing slightly off the stone walls of the building, and judging by the evidence so far, he concluded it wasn't a particularly favourable state of affairs in which he found himself.

He wasn't feeling too bad all things considered though, but his daughter. He hadn't seen her since Her Ladyship kidnapped her. That was months back now, and Tom could only take Her Ladyship's word for it that his daughter was still ok. His every waking moment, his every dream was filled with her face. That adorable face. Her Ladyship wouldn't hurt his daughter, he was sure, but she would kill Sinead if she discovered that she had the plans, without doubt.

Tom had been playing a dangerous game all along he knew. Playing one party against another will always invite certain risks. He'd had no choice though. On the one hand, he knew that Sinead had the plans, and he knew that on the other hand, Her Ladyship wanted them. To betray his friends though, to betray Sinead. How could he do that? Indeed, he'd agonised over the conundrum for days, and strained endlessly to come up with a way to keep both parties happy.

A door opened and footsteps approached, echoing slightly around the walls, and then stopped before him, the slightest of lights beaming through the blindfold until the door creaked shut again. Tom could see nothing more through the blindfold, and hear only heavy breathing as he sat awaiting introduction from the newcomer, breaths that were struggling to come to their owner he could tell, short, wheezy and strained.

Seconds passed before the blindfold was ripped from his face, and he was confronted by Red, grinning a greasy grin, twisting his new goatee and thinking almost aloud as his jaw rolled in unison with his mind.

Raising his hand, he stepped forth, allowing his gut to lead the way.

'Weeell howdy,' he started with as fake a front as one can possibly imagine.

'Sorry about the kidnapping and awl, and I hope we can forget aboud our…er…encounter by the river. We didn't mean yous no harm. Jus'stook ya for a critter is awl.'

Red offered Tom his hand, which Tom declined on account of being tied up, and offered to tie Red's balls to the Earnslaw's propeller for him if he'd like.

'Dumb Kraut.'

Cradling his chin in his hand, Red glared down at Tom as he reconsidered his approach. Evidently the one he'd adopted wasn't paying dividends, so he pondered for a moment, searching for a weak point in Tom's steely defences.

'Those plans weren't where you said they'd be boy. Now why would that there be?'

This was more the line of enquiry Tom had expected.

'I told you everysing I know…' he let out calmly.

'I gave you Digsy. Vat more do you vant from me?'

Pushing his tongue into his bottom lip, Red huffed, as if stumped at a quiz night question, and then went on…

'Well now, there is just one, iiitty-bitty little thaing I'm sure yous can… er… be of ay-sis-taince with,' burped he, happily embroiling Tom with a face full of olfactory splendour.

The door opened again and light streamed through it, blinding Tomas for a moment, and shrouding Red in a halo of gold. Then Tom heard footsteps on the floor boards, shallow and light, and a knot began to wind itself up in his stomach.

'Hello darlin'…'

Tomas knew exactly what was coming next.

'Come say hi to yow papa.'

The footsteps resumed, slowly though, and Red stepped to the side.

'Those genny plans…'

He grabbed the girl by the hand and dragged her forwards. The girl screamed and Tom cried out, lashing out suddenly, but he was still tied to the chair which crashed to the ground as he did.

'They worth a lot to us you know...' continued Red with an amused grin once Tom had stopped struggling. 'Make a man do terrible things to git that kinda power.'

The girl's face was hidden by a shock of filthy blonde hair. Her dress was ragged, she was clearly distraught and she started to cry. Being so close, but not being able to reach out and comfort his daughter was heart breaking to Tomas. Again he began to writhe, tugging as hard as he could at the bindings tying his arms to the back of the chair.

'Alles gut lieben. Alles gut.'

The words seemed so meaningless. So redundant. Red looked thoughtfully down at Tom, who's back was to him now, tied to the chair still, horizontal on the ground and drenched in sweat.

'We know you knows who's got'em boy, and the thaing is, we don't wants to hurt no one.'

He tried to look genuine, but quickly gave up, shoving the girl to the floor beside Tomas.

'But Her Ladyship's getting impatient,'

He crouched down before Tomas and grabbed the girl by the neck, dragging her closer, and held her right in front of Tom's eyes.

She saw Tomas then, and her face momentarily lit up, a child's joy adding a brief touch of warmth to the scene, until Red shoved her back again and she fell to the floor with a shriek.

'So I would heartily advise you to co-operate…' said he, leaning in so his face was inches from Tom's.

'For yow daughter's sake, **Boy!**'

Chapter 36

Sinead crouched and lowered the buckets hanging from their yoke to the ground, tired now after carrying them uphill from the river, the weight of them crushing her down as she slithered from under them and they slopped to the ground with a thud.

She could hear the river she'd just come from meandering still in the distance, chickens clucking and birds chirping, but apart from that, the day was quiet, warm and pleasant, only slender wisps of cloud tainting the otherwise azure blue brilliance above.

Picking herself back up, she picked up a plastic beaker and drove it into the bucket, chugging its contents with gusto as a warm breeze picked up and whistled around her.

Her hands to her hips, she took a moment, letting out an exhausted sigh. Sinead wasn't at all happy. She'd worked herself ragged looking after Digsy, and he'd disappeared somewhere just when she needed the help most. Tomas too!

Bleedin' men.

With the other recent intakes, and more hands around the camp now, Sinead had hoped things would get easier. There'd be more mouths to feed of course, but more hands to do the work too. They were all off on their own errands now though. She'd had to fetch the water, prepare the fish, chop the wood, as well as all the other jobs that her Da used to do, never mind her countless other chores that as ever went unnoticed. Tank bejesus she didn't have kids she thought as a vision of tiny blonde Digsys sprung into her mind.

At which point, her reverie was interrupted by a rather ordinary-looking fellow by the name of Baldman who'd strolled nonchalantly into view.

A new addition to the camp, they'd stumbled across him in the midst of another raid a month earlier. He'd lived in New Queenstown at the time. He was a labourer for The Order, but he desperately wanted out, and had aided their raid from within, supplying them with information on The Order's movements and such, and then requested asylum and moved into the camp.

He rounded the corner of Sinead's abode, apparently unaware as to her presence, and way off in a world of his own somewhere, and ambled across the overgrown lawn with his eyes to the ground.

Of average height and build, possibly in his mid-forties, and very normally attired, Baldman had no distinguishing features to speak of at all, other than, of course, his shiny bald head. Sinead coughed and Baldman jumped, fumbling over something she couldn't make out, before slipping it guiltily into his pocket.

'Mishus Murphy, how loovely,' he schmoozed, and Sinead raised an eyebrow, crossing her arms to her chest and allowed him to continue.

'I didn't exshpect you to be here Mishus Muurphy,' he did so somewhat nervously, his very normal eyes darting this way and that, taking in everything but Sinead.

There was something so strange about Baldman it seemed to her. Something not quite right. He'd always seemed so shifty, and Sinead hadn't trusted him from day one. Nursey had taken a shine to him though, taking him under her wing as if he were the prodigal son, and ignored Sinead's misgivings towards him, as well as those of the others.

Their eyes finally met as Baldman ran out of other things to look at. He looked so guilty suddenly, and he frowned, looking away again, first to the left, and then further to the left. Clearly up to something thought Sinead.

The faint sound of an engine came from near the settlement's entrance, beyond the hedgerow, and the screech of brakes, and then a gunshot rang out, and another, and then a high-pitched scream pierced the ether. Someone was attacking the camp. Baldman's eyes were wide suddenly. He went to speak, but Sinead grabbed him by the neck of his jacket, thrusting him back against the rough stone wall of her house behind him.

She held him there, her eyes blazing through his.

'What've y's been at yis baldy little bastard?'

She slammed him back again, amazed at her own strength as he snivelled and whimpered unashamedly.

'Did yis tell 'em where we are now did yis?'

The engines grew louder and so did the screams. A familiar voice came from beyond the hedgerow. A panicked female voice, timid and scared and screaming for Kaleb. Sinead stopped and listened, when another shot rang out and Mrs Jones from next door burst through the hedgerow, slamming face first into the grass with an impact stain forming on her back.

Without hesitation, Sinead slammed Baldman's head back into the wall and darted around the back of the house, slipping inside in the nick of time as a black armoured truck smashed through the hedge and bounced to a halt on the lawn.

Gunfire was sounding all around now. It had to be The Order. It had to be Baldman. Sinead's people stood no chance she knew. They were poorly armed and ill prepared, and half of the men were away.

Screams and shots echoed out as one followed the other again and again. It sounded like a massacre, so she ran to the hall, grabbed the rifle, and took the folder containing the plans that Tom had told her were important, shoving them into her trousers.

The front door slammed open.

Boom!

The shot blasted through the wall like it were paper, missing Sinead by millimetres, sending a thousand splinters flying this way and that, cutting into the walls and her alike. She heard the empty cartridge clatter to the floor and darted to the next room, ignoring the splinters in her arm, and closed the door behind her. Shots and screams were coming from every direction. Nowhere seemed safe. The door handle behind her rattled, so she ran to the bay door at the end of the room and stepped outside, ducking around the corner of the house, and then she turned back, levelling the rifle in the direction she'd come.

Her pursuer's footsteps grew closer, hollow on the wooden decking, and quick, so she backed around the corner of the house, rifle poised out before her, keeping a vigilant eye on the lawn surrounding.

'Here kitty-kitty.'

Back Sinead stepped, as quietly as she could as the footsteps grew closer. A shot rang out, followed by a scream, and then someone crying hysterically. No one else could be seen though. Her lawn was overgrown and empty to her left, her front door creaking open on its hinges to her right. She could see naught beyond the hedgerows, so she stopped to look through her kitchen window beside her, her finger tense on the trigger, and then jumped out of her skin as the window shattered and the gun barrel that'd punched through it settled on her.

Chapter 37

A warm breeze tickled Digsy's ankles as he lowered himself to the grass beneath the cave's entrance, wincing at the strain pulling at his stitches again, until his feet touched down and it eased slightly. Stepping from beneath the overhang, he stood.

A haze sat atop the slopes, masking all but the immediate surroundings, the morning sun lending an ominous edge to the day, an incandescence to the very air around him, and an all too familiar sense of foreboding ensnared Digsy.

The plateau he stood on still sat overgrown, as it had the day before, but it seemed more trampled now than it had been, and his mind started concocting all kinds of ideas as to whom the culprits might be. Tomas could have done it on leaving the day before he supposed. He was the most likely suspect, having ruled out killer zombies and the like, nosy git that Tom was, but it worried Digsy nevertheless. Looking around for other signs of intrusion, he was sure someone was watching him now as he scanned the tree line for movement.

Get out of my head! screamed his head to the paranoia loitering within it. He knew he was just playing tricks on himself again, but he couldn't help it. Something just felt wrong.

Right on cue, a shrill whistle came from behind him, so he turned and looked up the cliff face, and surely enough saw a shotgun there trained his way, balancing on a small man that he didn't recognise, who in turn was perched on a ridge in the cliff face, grinning down at him in glee.

'Hello Digsy bro.'

Again the voice came from behind Digsy. Turning to greet it, he saw Raul stepping from behind a tree at the plateau's edge, strolling slowly towards him, the plateau quickly filling with grinning henchmen emerging from every angle, their weapons all trained on Digsy.

'Raul, mate!' boomed he with a touch too much gusto, failing to mask his gut-wrenching disappointment at his cave having been discovered. His mind was wheeling, searching desperately for a way to avoid it being so.

'How's life?'

Raul didn't appear as excited at seeing his old chum as Digsy was pretending to be however. Indeed one might venture quite the opposite. He stopped inches from Digsy and glared intently at him, unnervingly silent and breathing heavily, his nostrils inflating like a raging bull's as the morning mist whipped around them.

The air was cold still in the shade, the sun still hidden behind the Remarkables to the east, with only it's top visible above them so far. The tops of the pines surrounding them though, shone bright, like hundreds of broken glow sticks poking up from the ground in a further effort to surround Digsy.

He folded his arms across his chest, and Raul grunted, which Digsy took for a reply, and then replied with a polite enquiry as to Digsy's health, to which Digsy replied in the positive.

'Where haf you bin?' Raul went on, stepping back and drawing his Katana with his eyes fixed on Digsy. The blade glinted provocatively as it caught the light, long and slender, and cut a graceful arc as he swooped it up, pointing its tip to Digsy's chest.

'We have bin lookin for you,' he stated matter-of-factly. 'We were expectin mo moonshine, a long time ago bro.'

A semi-circle of smirking guards surrounded Digsy, and the sheer cliff face loomed behind him. There was nowhere to run. Digsy had no idea whether Raul knew of his tinkering with the plot line or not—his rescuing Sinead at the clifftop, or his shooting the moustached guard to mention but a few minor indiscretions—but he knew Raul would surely crush his balls if he did, so he picked his words with care.

"I did myself an injustice in the hills a while back…' he offered lamely. 'I've bin recoverin.'

'Hmmmm,' parried Raul, his gaze shifting from Digsy to the plateau they stood on. Pondering for a second more, he seeming to shrug off the issue, and continued…

'So this is your cave ay?'

He stated this more than asked, nodding with an air of satisfaction as he took in the pleasant surroundings.

'This is whe you keep your sheet.'

'No, no, this is just temporary.'

Raul's eyebrow shot up and his lips puckered to the left. He looked to the cliff again, gazing up to its peak as Digsy gazed nervously down at the sword point resting at his chest.

'OK bro. We will see.'

Flicking the sword from Digsy's chest, he pointed it at the cave, to which two of the guards jogged past them to the cave's entrance. The first one shrank low and disappeared into the cliff face. It looked like the mountain had eaten him, and Digsy's heart sank. The game was indeed up. No longer could he sustain himself without his still, and they'd surely find it now.

The second set of legs vanished into the mountain face, as if a thread of snot sniffed back up into a huge stone nostril.

Chuckling to himself, Raul started strolling aimlessly, sword resting on his shoulder with a gay swagger to his gait now. He seemed to be soaking up the moment, savouring every second of watching Digsy squirm. Finally he stopped and turned back to him.

'Yu know anythin' boud any plans?'

A set of legs appeared from the cliff face, walked ten paces to the left, and were again vacuumed into the cliff—they'd found Digsy's still.

'No, mate, what type of plans? I'll keep an eye out.'

Raul grunted offhandedly. 'Never mind tha.'

Raising his blade again to Digsy, its tip hovering before his eyes, Raul held it there for a moment, before going on…

'Her Ladysheep wants to see you Digsy. She will mek you one final, veeeery generous offer, which you will accep bro.'

Chapter 38

'Gday Lav. Drop the rifle.'

Pulling his rifle back through the smashed window, the guard craned his head towards it and sneered as Sinead caught his eye. Stepping back, she let her rifle slip from her hand as she scanned the surroundings for an escape. A lawn cluttered with junk was all she could see though, old pallets, car tyres stacked four high, gardening tools and junk, all surrounded by a thick overgrown hedge with no way out. She could hear the guard's hurried footsteps as he ran to the front door and stepped out through it. His rifle was trained on Sinead now, his malice unquestionable. He was tall and slender, but lit from behind by the morning sun now, masking his face from her.

'Rememba me?'

As he stepped closer, his slimy grin and rat-like features came into focus, and Sinead recognised him instantly. Her heart skipped a beat, and her mind suddenly jumped back to the day of the raid. It was the fiend that'd attacked her that day. The skinny guard.

'Ding ding ay sheela...' croaked he. 'Round two lav.'

Shots were still sounding, but less now, and pleas of mercy that fell upon deaf ears. A light breeze tickled the scene. Sinead stepped away from the guard, who grinned sickeningly. Behind her, she could hear the other guard too now. He was on the veranda she could tell, just behind her.

'Where do you think you're going?'

The crunch of gun metal came from behind her, the guard's voice hollow, grainy and soulless, and the skinny guard before her raised his rifle as he stepped closer still. All Sinead could do was run, but she knew she'd never make it. The guards were too close, the skinny one speaking now, but she didn't hear his words. She felt so helpless, so small and so insignificant. A moment later though, just as hope had abandoned her, an as yet unknown party intervened.

Somebody screamed and then someone laughed, and then Sinead heard a gunshot, and she heard the guard behind her cry out and drop to the decking with a thud.

Turning from the skinny guard, she ran, but he'd lunged in at her, grabbing her by the arm, and he yanked her back in hysterics. Her arm felt like a dead weight suddenly. Like it'd been pulled from its socket. The skinny guard dragged her closer, his fingernails digging into her skin and drawing blood as she swiped out at him.

Luck was on Sinead's side though.

In his excitement, the skinny guard had forgotten about the aforementioned unknown party. Something moved to his right. The skinny guard hadn't noticed it though. He slapped Sinead across the cheek and she dropped to the grass, and then the unknown party charged at the skinny guard, slamming into him and launched him to the side with a startled yelp.

Who it was, Sinead had no idea.

The unknown fellow was up and going for the guard again, but the guard grabbed a spade that lay beside him, and swung it around, catching the man on the jaw as he pounced, and he went down with a howl.

It was a valiant effort, and the unknown fellow was tenacious if nothing else.

He was pushing himself up again, but the guard smashed his fist down into the man's face, sending him crashing back down in a hail of broken teeth. Sinead didn't know what to do, so she asked the guard to desist, to which he replied, 'I'll get back to you in a minute lav,' and he slammed the man back down again, rolling him onto his back with a 'Hmmm'.

Removing his jacket, he dropped it nonchalantly to the ground.

Sinead recognised the man on the floor now. It was Baldman. He looked like any battered man would normally look. Skinny rammed his boot into Baldman's gut, Sinead heard the crunch over the cry and she screamed. It went unheard though, or more likely ignored, and the skinny guard stood over Baldman, glowering down at him, huffing and wiping the drool from his chin.

Sinead knew she should run, but she couldn't. Her legs didn't want to comply. They'd decided they couldn't leave Baldman behind, even though they could do naught to help him, so she watched on, waiting for her turn and pointlessly pleading for mercy.

It took a moment for the guard to choose the most suitable tool for his next sortie. Crouching, he picked up a rock the size of his head, and then crashed it down onto Baldman's.

Sinead's blood chilled.

The skinny guard turned his gaze to her, so she turned, the life springing back into her legs, and ran. She heard the guard take off in pursuit only metres behind her. Into the trees lining the hill down to the river she ran. They had a boat tied up down there. If she could get to it she could escape. She didn't look back. She could hear the guard charging through the rough behind her. Not right behind her, but not far. She stumbled as she cut her way through the trees, losing valuable seconds, and the skinny guard closed in, crunching through the undergrowth and giggling hysterically. He was close. Sinead was tired and slowing, and he grasped at her, clutching at her collar, but came up short and roared in frustration as she writhed away from him.

She heard the guard stumble and fall, and found renewed strength, charging through the undergrowth, heedless of the thorns that were tearing her legs to shreds.

The river was visible through the trees now. A vivid turquoise behind a web of grey. Sinead looked back. The skinny guard was a way back now, and limping slightly. She could make it.

Bursting onto the shore, she headed for the shallows and carried on to the left. The sound of rocks crunching under foot betrayed her every step, but she cared not. The boat was tied up just around the bluff jutting into the river before her. She heard the guard limp onto the shore behind her as she splashed through the shallows, drenching her every inch, but she didn't look back again. She was only metres from the cove and her escape now, but as she rounded the bluff, she saw that the boat was gone.

The boat was gone and she was cornered.

So she picked up the biggest rock she could find, and moments later, slammed it into the skinny guard's face as he stepped into view. Down he went in a hail of teeth and blood, out cold instantly, spread eagled in the shallows with the water tickling his ears. Blood seeped from his mouth and a nasty gash traversed the side of his head.

Dropping to her knees, Sinead felt inhuman at that point. In a trance almost at what she'd just done. She was sickened at herself, and she wasn't sure what to do next—whether to hide or to flee, to help the guard or to make sure he was dead. The decision was soon taken from her though.

Another guard stepped around the bluff, stout and solid, but with friendly eyes and an honest face, chubby and warm, and a shotgun pointed at her.

The guard said hello and introduced himself as Mo, and through Mo was Sinead's only escape, so she dropped the rock she'd picked up and it splashed into the water beside her.

Mo turned out to be a pleasant enough sort of a bloke, ensuring Sinead that his intentions were harmless should she comply. He had a gentle aura about him too somehow. She knew he wouldn't harm her, and she even thought she saw him smile as his eyes met the skinny guard lying unconscious in the shallows beside her.

What strength Sinead had left was gone now, so she complied, and was escorted back to the camp where she was bundled into a truck.

Dark clouds rolled over Coronet Peak to the west, masking its summit in a blanket of gloomy grey, the air noticeably milder though as a storm brewed somewhere in the distance.

Gazing out through the truck's window, Sinead watched as the skinny guard was bundled into the back of the truck parked a few meters away. His face was a bloody mess she was pleased to see. She could see two bodies lying face down on her neighbour's lawn, and another by the front gate, and she could see Nursey too now. She was hunched up in the back of one of the other trucks, filling the entire space it appeared, but Nursey hadn't spotted her.

They hadn't stood a chance she sighed, watching as the guards heckled the prisoners and shoved them around like cattle for the slaughter.

So much bloodshed, again!

No one spoke as the convoy of trucks wound its way back towards New Queenstown. The glorious scenery passed by in a blur of despair, and Sinead gazed only through it, lost in her own reverie. Before she knew it, they'd passed through the town, the engine chugged to a halt, and she was dragged from the truck close to the crumbling memorial pillars on the lake front.

Before her sat the glassy waters of the town's bay, flanked by the dock which curved out to the right, and to the left by the peninsular that jutted into the lake, forming a horseshoe of sorts around the serene little bay.

Sinead was shoved in the opposite direction, and found herself faced with a small stone building. Humble in all but memory, the Lake Lodge of Ophir still stood testament to the mysterious few that built it all those years ago. The old lodge looked like a toy house but beige, and as Sinead was shoved towards it, it looked as though it may well be her home for the immediate future.

Boarded up holes where the windows had been allowed little light into the shell of an interior. It seemed much smaller inside too. Four naked stone walls surrounded her, small boarded up windows in two of them. There was a fireplace on the backwall, but no wood, a table with nothing on it, and a wooden bucket in the corner next to a small pile of hay.

Flies buzzed around nasty stains on the stone, buzzing around Sinead too now. Heavy rusted chains had been bolted to the back wall, the wrist cuffs hanging open and drooping almost to the ground, and maggots writhed on a tray of crumbs on the table, several feasting on a withered pigeon as they slowly picked it dry.

A mustiness permeated the room, tickling the back of Sinead's throat as a nausea brewed within her, and as she turned to question her captors, the solid oak door slammed shut before her, and she heard the ancient lock click into place.

Chapter 39

No more freedom for Digsy. No more brewing his precious moonshine without The Order's say so. The smile plastered across Raul's face had infuriated Digsy, and he'd watched on in horror as The Order's militia unceremoniously dismantled his still, hauling the pieces down from his cave and down the slope to their trucks.

Smug, self-satisfied wanker

Digsy had gone quietly, and was back in The Earnslaw's lounge now. Her Ladyship was sat behind the desk opposite him, and Digsy adjusted himself as she watched him with thin, stretched lips, drumming her fingers before her face as an amused look crept onto it.

Things were looking up for Her Ladyship suddenly. Having finally found Tomas again, his tip-off had paid dividends. The plans hadn't been at the camp as he'd said they would be, but he'd told her the whereabouts of Digsy's cave at least, and now she had Digsy and his equipment to boot. There'd be no need for The Order to trade for fuel soon, but she still needed his knowhow.

Digsy's stomach throbbed, but he forced a smile lest Her Ladyship acquire further ammunition with which to taunt him, and took in the room instead – the assorted furnishings with their finely carved intricacies, and yet Spartan too, they served as very good things to look at when avoiding probing eyes.

Her Ladyship studied Digsy. He noted how much people seemed to do that these days, and folded his arms across his chest. She smiled, her eyes fixed on his and he smiled back.

'So…' she started once the smiling was done with.

'We found your cave ay Digby.'

Her elbows were on the table and her hands were clasped before her face. She looked like a cat who'd found some particularly tasty cream.

'Looks like it, ma'am.'

She watched him shifting uncomfortably in his seat with interest. 'And it's Digsy by the way,'

The vein at Her Ladyship's temple throbbed.

'Fak'n Digsy ay!'

She stood and shoved the chair to the side, glaring down at him, and then turned and stormed off to the window, as if afraid of what she might do if she looked at him any longer.

'Well fak'n well, I do apologise, fak'n Digsy,' she rasped, the sarcasm so palpable you could spread it on your toast.

'That's alright, ma'am, you weren't to know,' he replied with a nervous chuckle.

Shooting him a menacing glance, which quickly morphed into a smile, Her Ladyship was amused at his audacity in the face of defeat, and turned back to the window to hide it, continuing…

'Game's up my old chook…'

She swung around, all business now, and stomped back to the table, slamming her palms down and rattling the cutlery upon it.

'We've got your still, and aaaall your fak'n equipment mate. You're outa fak'n business.'

She leaned in closer, looking for, trying to provoke a reaction, and smiled as Digsy kept his eyes down and she got none.

'I suppose I could just kill ya,' she went on after a moment. Digsy gulped.

'But that'd leave me without a chef now, wouldn'it?'

Her eyes were fixed on him. She was leaning in so close that he could smell the fish on her breath.

'I guess it would ma'am,' he readily agreed, his eyes fixed on the table.

'Hmmm,' she said.

'Here's a thought, Dipsy.'

She stood back up straight, looking down on him with a face that looked like it'd just come up with a brilliant plan, and hadn't at all been working towards this particular end for the last year or so.

'You could work for us mate, couldn't ya, fak'n Digsy?'

It was a rhetorical question Digsy knew. Her Ladyship would likely kill him if he refused, so he had no choice.

Shoulders dropping, he slumped back in the chair. The proposition had been expected on Digsy's part, only it was more of an ultimatum now that The Order had found his equipment. Her Ladyship had him by the unmentionables. Digsy had nothing left to trade without his moonshine. Nothing left to sustain his life. He was cornered, and he wanted to share his feelings to this regard most vigorously with Her Ladyship, 'I guess I could ma'am,' were the words that he wisely chose however, sighing a defeated sigh, resigned to his new lot in life…

Bitch of the Order.

'Good boy, Digsy. I knew you'd see sense.'

The room seemed to shrink around him.

This wasn't good.

He was doing what he swore to himself he never would. Selling out to the powers that be. Just another of The Order's pawns. Another cog in another corrupt, buckled wheel. Her Ladyship knew this, and couldn't keep the grin from her face.

'Know anything about any plans mate?' she went on, sitting back down in her chair, her elbows on its arms with her hands clasped at her chin, making a triangle with her fingers that rose to the tip of her nose.

'For a generator or some such?'

After Digsy had assured her that he knew not of the plans that he knew Sinead possessed to an apparently adequate degree, Her Ladyship huffed, adjusting her hair, and then continued to enlighten him as to his positive new role within their positive new society.

Once Digsy had been educated as to the intricacies involved in such a positively intricate endeavour, the prospect didn't look so gloomy after all. He would be well maintained he was assured. A good dwelling with running water and free food were at his disposal. He would have help, and all the tools he needed for his brewing, and most important of all, the freedom to come and go as he pleased, within reason.

He'd only need a couple of months to find Mary and arrange their escape by his reckoning. All Digsy had to do now, was sell his soul.

Chapter 40

28th October 2050

It was a mild evening, and dusk was falling when Sinead heard a vehicle chug to a halt outside the building she was imprisoned in. Chains clanked, footsteps approached, the door creaked open, and then someone was bundled in through it, crashing to the floor with a groan as the door slammed shut behind him.

Sinead hadn't been expecting company. The man remained sprawled out on the floor, and he was trembling. She wasn't quite sure what to do, so she crossed the space and crouched down beside the unknown fellow, her arm around his shoulder and sympathy in her heart.

He looked to be in a bad way from what she could tell in the low light of the room. His fatigues were torn and sullied, his hair sticking up three inches at random angles and held in place by the filth encasing it. He raised his head after a moment, and she saw that it was Tomas, and appropriately cried **'Tom!'**, ecstatic to see her old friend alive and safe, rubbing his shoulder and cupping a hand to his face.

'Tom, are y'alright, Tom?'

The worry was clear in her voice at the lack of his. He certainly didn't look very alright, more the exact opposite. He'd been given a fresh pounding by the looks of it, his eye swollen and his lip still raw. He pushed himself to a crouch and then turned to lean against the wall, remaining silent though.

Turning his head towards her after a moment, he opened his eyes, straining it seemed, to do so, blinking violently as if dazzled by the low light, and muttered:

'Iz zat you Sinead? Ah, Sinead, ze lovely Sinead. I am glad to see you are okay.'

He dropped his gaze, wincing and blinking as he took in the stark surroundings, and Sinead laughed with a rare tear of happiness welling in her eye.

'Same here, yis mad ting,' she sniffed. 'Look at yis,' she sighed, straightening his collar as she looked him over for injuries.

'I vil be okay, Sinead.'

She helped him to his feet but he fell back down again. She helped him again, this time onto the table.

'Vat about you Sinead? Are you okay? Vat haf zey done to you?'

Again Sinead laughed, clasping her hands to her breast, assuring Tom in kind that she too was fine, and enquired as to his antics over the last couple of days, and that of Digsy's. Tom duly regaled his somewhat tainted tale of their encounter at the bridge, Digsy's preposterous cave and Tom's subsequent capture, and they laughed and cried at the hilarity and heartache of it all.

He assured her that Digsy was indeed fine, and that The Order would never find his cave.

'How long d'y tink they'll keep us here now?' she asked after a while, more out of something to say than anything.

'Zat depends how long it takes zem to find vat zey ar looking for, I sink.'

His tone seemed almost conspiratorial to Sinead somehow though. It struck a strange chord with her, and her brow dropped at the candid answer.

'Right. An wot d'y tink dat might be now?'

Tomas knew he'd said the wrong thing, and he liked not this line of enquiry, but hid it well in the knowledge that his daughter's life was in his hands, keeping his composure to a degree with an instant air of contemplation about him. He felt terrible. He was betraying Sinead again, but what could he do?

Again, Tom noticed a trickle of doubt, even accusation in Sinead's gaze. Did she suspect him? It was hard to tell. He could see her eyes shifting and thinking things through, delving deeper into the ploy that he could see unwinding in her mind.

'Ich Weiss es nicht,' he replied off handedly, holding her gaze until it unnerved Sinead suddenly, and she looked away.

It was all so confusing. Tom sounded party to the goings on for a moment there, but she put the preposterous idea out of her head, turned to lean against the wall opposite him, and smiled as sincere a smile as she could muster. Tom smiled back in kind, and then cringed again, holding his arm as he brought his feet up on the table before him.

'Did dey ask y's about doze plans?' she asked after a while, and Tom replied in the affirmative, gazing into the corner of the gloomy little room with a sad smile.

'Ja, lieben. I told zem I know nassing of ze plans.'

He stuck his middle fingers up to the wall and laughed somewhat forcedly. 'Screw zem all ay, ha-ha-ha!'

His laugh startled Sinead, and then faded out to an awkward silence. She crouched to sit and lean, shifting around so the stone protruding from the bottom of the wall cushioned the small of her back.

'I hope you burned ze papers Sinead,' Tom continued, gazing dejectedly at her. 'Zey ar no gut to us ins here.'

Sinead had doubted Tomas for a while there, but he'd never do anything to hurt her she knew. She could see no reason not to trust him, so she grinned, unfastened the top button of her jeans, and slid her hand down, pulling out a plastic envelope containing plans and shook it before Tom's face.

'Noooo…' he exhaled with wonder in his eyes as he saw the plans shuffling around before him.

'Not bad ay. I taut deez might cum in handy, so…'

The amazed look on Tom's face morphed into one Sinead didn't recognise a moment later though. He was beaming suddenly, but he seemed overly exuberant for the situation to Sinead, looking to the papers and then away again, as if his eyes had been caught stealing them.

'Sinead, you ar ze cheeky frau ja!' he nodded, clearly impressed at her cunning. and she gazed at him quizzically.

His eyes were fixed on the plans like a man possessed now, and he leaned in towards them like they were pulling him in with an invisible lasso.

'Giv zem to me, Sinead, zey will be safer,' said he in a hushed but stern voice, holding out his hand as he slid from the table and approached her.

His tone had changed. It was a note harder now, with more of its inherent authoritative edge.

'Why, Tom?' she justly enquired.

'They'll be fine wid me here now.'

Kneeling before her, he placed a hand on her shoulder, his eyebrows raised with apparent warmth in his eyes.

'I cannot be zer for you all ze time…'

He looked down, suddenly embarrassed, and hesitated, before going on:

'Zey are less likely to… er… check down my pants.'

Raising his eyes back to meet Sinead's, his cheeks flushed. He couldn't hold her gaze, and again he laughed anxiously. He made a good point though, Sinead had to admit.

How could she possibly think such things of Tomas? Tom was pure gold. He'd been her best friend since they met that terrible day years before.

After a moment, she handed Tom the plans and apologised for her tone.

They spent the rest of the evening chatting over the old days and making plans for the new: how they might escape, what they would do to the bastards when they did, where they should live, how they would rescue Nursey and the others, and eventually fell into as sound-a-sleep as conditions would allow.

Tomas was already gone when Sinead awoke, and she dropped to her knees and cried out for him, for someone to save her. Anyone. She was sick of the constant pain and the torment, the suffering and the loss. She was sick of everything. She'd had enough and she wanted to go home.

She battered her hands against the thick timbers of the door, informing the guards outside of this, and slumped back down when they showed no interest.

Chapter 41

Over the next few days, Digsy grew more at ease in the new role Her Ladyship and The Order had so easily forced upon him. Hidden neatly away behind the scenes as he was, Digsy saw not the dark side of The Order, nor the misery they sowed. Not the beatings or starvation, nor the depredation and cruelty, but was instead kept busy and his mind occupied, immersed in his brewing and well looked after as he was.

He was under constant guard of course, but they remained mostly outside.

It wasn't long before his first batch of moonshine was ready, and it heartened Digsy, inspiring and enthusing him. Something to get his teeth stuck into and take his mind from the grind. A glorious taste of old, and 'twas glorious indeed, the pristine glacial waters doing more than enough to compensate for the frankly inadequate ingredients he had to play with. Masses of moonshine could be made with his new, bigger still. The Order's minions were delighted, and the powers that be more than satisfied with the paint-stripping results. Most of it was reserved for The Order's machines sadly, but once a few vats had been delivered to the medical centre, what remained was distributed liberally through ranks, and put to a more, shall we say, traditional use.

His new brewing shed was a veritable palace compared to the cave that he'd up until now plied his craft in. It was a spacious, two-levelled compound, tucked amongst the pines halfway down the peninsula that cradled the town's bay. An ice rink in the old world he recalled, and it proved ideal with its close proximity to the lake and the pump running between the two. In the centre of the warehouse, a furnace had been sunk into the concrete floor, and sat below the still he'd had The Order repair and improve. It rose ten feet up in a bold testament to the tenacity of drinkers everywhere now—a glorious life making life taker of copper, borne of the ashes of what it most likely had a tenuous hand in destroying he'd sometimes muse. Molly was its name. Molly the moonshine maker.

And oh how he loved her, oh how Digsy worshipped her. He alone could make her sing, and he alone could make her squeal. The precise measures and temperatures, the chemistry, the physics. How such simple ingredients can be transformed into something so different, something so powerful, blew Digsy's mind.

The Moonshine was invaluable, ergo, he was too. At least he presumed so, and he felt good about it. Secure for the first time in ages, and the freedom that came with not having to worry about food, or his own safety was a breath of fresh air.

He'd started enjoying sitting out between brews, sharing a cigarette and a glass of shine with his new apprentice Mart. They'd sit by the lake and gaze out in awe at the beauty and vastness of the turquoise waters and the mountains surrounding, so majestic, that the sight never failed to amaze him, and the constant haze of moonshine that coloured their days now, only heightened the sensory pleasure. They'd talk brewing and life, old times and new. How life had changed so much. How it was so much easier in the old days, and how Mart didn't know what he was talking about as he hadn't been born then. Good dude though he was, funny bugger, and constantly drunk under the genuine guise of quality control, yet attentive too, and keen to learn. Indeed too keen it seemed to Digsy at times, so he shrewdly kept some of the tricks of the trade to himself so as not to be the author of his own demise.

Things had been going well for Digsy so far, all things considered, and yet he still lamented himself for so easily succumbing to Her Ladyship and The Order. He despised their waskily ways, and yet here he was, sleeping in their bed, eating their food, and teaching them most of the tricks that he knew, that had up until now, ensured his longevity.

However he found himself though, was better than being dead. It was just a long-winded means to a very worthwhile end he assured himself whenever he found himself questioning his new role in life. This would be the easiest way for him to find Mary, and she had to be in New Queenstown somewhere.

Chapter 42

Days seemed to pass as Sinead sat contemplating her woeful situation, the sun rising and sinking as pitiful meals slid intermittently across the floor. It was dusk now, but on which day she knew not. Day had turned to night too many times for her to remember.

She'd passed the time by moving from one wall to the next, or by making little men or animals from the filthy, sullied strands of straw that made up her bed. Which was nice, but options had been quite limited otherwise, so she'd mostly just sat there, and then lay there, and on occasion tried to mix it up with a spot of crouching, or standing, but she'd had mixed results with those so far, and decided that sitting was the best course of action, until she had to sleep of course, when a touch more lying down seemed to reap the best results.

The prospect of a new life under The Order wasn't an alluring one for Sinead. She'd heard horrifying stories, and spoken to people who'd escaped their clutches, and the pictures they painted were nigh on Medieval: rats up your bum hole and all sorts. What they'd do to Sinead didn't bear thinking about, and she sat in the corner of the tiny cell with her head in her hands, her elbows on her knees and the thought of the loss she'd sustained replaying over and over in her mind.

It was all so unfair.

Things had been on the up slowly since that night at the cliff. She'd been too busy to dwell for long on the passing of her Da, which had cut her to the bone, but she'd struggled on. The camp had been prospering. They'd had food, water, new residents and muscle, and then, as the seasons will change, things had of course gone bollix up again, and she wept at the inevitability of it all. Of course it couldn't last. *Good things never do,* the devil on her shoulder poked.

And what of Tom and Digsy? it chided.

Where did they get to? it jibed.

Is it not too convenient that they should disappear, just before the raid on the village? it harangued.

NO, parried Sinead.

It is not.

Chapter 43

4 November 2050

Not long into his new life, the new day brought Digsy a friendly tap on the door, followed by an invitation to dine on deck with Her Ladyship, to which, being under obligation as Digsy was, he cordially obliged.

It was a warm eve, so he wore only a t-shirt and cargo shorts under his jacket, and the sun was already setting as he set out towards the Earnslaw where the soiree was to be held. A gloom was about the land as he strolled along the pebbled beach, hopping and crunching between the scattered bits of driftwood strewn along it.

What could the dinner invitation be about he wondered? Was Her Ladyship going to fire him? Or kill him even were the first thoughts that crossed Digsy's mind. Things had been going well so far, but had he outlived his usefulness already? Had he taught Mart too much?

The town appeared glum in the shade, crawling up the mountains before him and to his right, a thick blanket of smoke from hundreds of camp fires sitting above it, blocking the view of the summits entirely. The sky to his left above the lake however, was changing from blue to orange to pink, painting a collage of awesomeness in his moonshine-tainted eyes. The setting rays glistened off the lake's surface, sparkling on the crests of the tiny waves like tiny bulbs glinting on and off.

Beyond the beach he reached the market, which was mostly empty, just a few greedy seagulls pecking at the fish guts that gleamed in the twilight, and a few stragglers and dogs cleaning up what other filth remained. As the beach gave way to the boardwalk, he passed the old Masonic Lodge to his right, the armed guard at its door watching him as he did, and then he rounded the wharf and came parallel to the Earnslaw, where he noted the dinner table, with gleaming glasses and candles on over-the-top silver candlesticks flickering wildly in the breeze at her bow. He thought it odd, but nothing more of it, and having been directed towards the ship's bow, on he went.

The evening lent a sinister edge to the elegant, sweeping bulk of the ancient steamboat. The windows aboard were all dark, silhouetting his reflection as he passed them by. No light came from within. There were no signs of life anywhere. The narrow walkway was almost pitch black under its low ceiling, and Digsy held the guiderail to steady himself as the deck rolled gently under him. He carried on to the ship's bow to find the same. No signs of life anywhere. Only the table he'd seen from the shore was there, perched before the bridge, the candles still flickering, although there was no breeze, and offering the only light now but the waning sunset.

The door at the far side of the bridge opened suddenly, and Her Ladyship stepped through it, quickly followed by her retinue as they spilled out onto the deck, spacing themselves evenly around it, as if protecting the deck from the night.

'Digsy my boy, please, please. Do sit.'

Emerging from the shadows, she clapped her hands together, so devious and self-righteous as always, like she knew a lot that Digsy didn't, and intended to thoroughly make the most of it. She beamed at him with a smile blatantly lacking the good will it proposed, and he slumped down into the chair, awaiting the triumphant unveiling of her cunning ploy.

'Well now, fak'n Digsy...' she went on, pulling out the chair opposite him and sitting down, glaring at the guard nearest her, before adopting a business-like air, and facing Digsy with her hands clasped before her.

'I do hope you're settlin' in well mate, and just a small matter before we begin...'

She was almost straining to hold back a snigger it seemed.
'We're put'n on a spota... er... entertainment tomora.'

A wry grin came to her face and she paused, watching Digsy expectantly. He could tell she was relishing the moment, patiently awaiting his reaction at the somewhat underwhelming announcement, so he waited for her to embellish.

'I'd like to invite ya is all,' she obliged, but Digsy was struggling with her accent. She sounded like a cat choking on a harmonica, and he begged her pardon most humbly.

'Fak'n tomorrow mate!' she screamed, drawing nervous glances from the guards and a faint echo around the bay.

'You baboon faced fak'n cretin. In the fak'n square at fak'n midday. Alright!'

Her Ladyship looked annoyed, as if her ill thought out inquisition was getting her nowhere. Why, Digsy couldn't fathom. What was she rambling on about? What could the entertainment possibly be? Why did she invite him here to invite him somewhere else? And why was the table set up for a romantic dinner? Digsy didn't know what to make of it, so he nodded enthusiastically and smiled.

'Fak'n hopeless mate.'

Sighing a weary sigh, Her Ladyship pursed her lips as she studied him. She could tell Digsy had been testing his moonshine. He wore a slightly vacant expression, and slurred his words ever so slightly, which she assumed was normal to him now, as he had a lot of testing to do. Still though...

With a frown, and ever eager so get on with it, she stood and turned to her entourage, and then muttered something, to which one of them hurried back to the bridge.

Her fingers went to her temples, and she tapped them, and then shook her head in mock disgust at her own forgetfulness.

'Fak'n silly fak'n me.'

One of the guards, taking a torch from its brace, proceeded to light the lanterns hanging from the rigging, a warm glow suddenly about the scene, impenetrable to the darkness beyond them. Like the deck was all there was in the world.

'Pray fak'n forgive me Digsy mate, I almost fak'n forgot.'

Once again, the corners of Her Ladyship's mouth crept out, and she clapped her hands together, and then let out a triumphant cackle, beaming at Digsy now, desperate for a reaction, but certain she'd get one soon enough.

'May I fak'n present…'

She swiftly adopted a theatrical air, pointing with a twirl to the bridge.

'Behind door number fak'n one…'

A sickness welled in the pit of Digsy's stomach, and the guard that'd left moments before opened the door there.

'The beautiful…' Her Ladyship continued, straining to keep the glee from her voice.

'The one, the fak'n only…'

A figure, still in shadow, stepped through the bridge door and onto the deck, tall and broad, and yet elegant too. Her hood was up, and she was clad all in black, but Digsy knew exactly who it was. The chair scraped back as he stood, his pulse racing, his stomach churning as the cloaked figure stepped from the walkway and into the light.

Her Ladyship couldn't hold it in any longer.

'Iiiiiiit's Jaaanne. Ta daaaaaaaaaaaaaa!'

There was a moments pause, and then, realizing her error, Her Ladyship stopped herself short, cutting herself off, as she recalled that Digsy knew Jane by a different name, and tried again, like an orator rehearsing her lines.

'Nope, no. Fak'n sorry mate. It's not fak'n Jane at all is it mate? Silly fak'n me ay,' she chuckled.

'Iiiiiiit's Mmmmmmaary…Ta daaaaaaaa!'

And as if by magic, there she was.

Mary. The light of Digsy's life.

This was a moment that Digsy had prepared for more than once. Indeed he'd rehearsed it more times than he could remember. But it coming out of the blue like this had caught him off guard, and he froze, watching Mary approach like a ghost floating across the decking. His jaw dropped. He was stunned, confused and scared now. This was what Digsy wanted of course, what he'd wanted for years now, to see his beloved; but not like this, not surrounded by a horde of The Order's guards.

Mary stopped beside Her Ladyship. She looked so different, hard-faced and scowling like a petulant teenager.

Her hair was wild and flowed from under her hood, and she stood with her arms folded close to her, as if keeping anyone from stealing her intestines.

The cloak she wore was tied together with three buttons at the chest, and he could barely see her face behind the hood that flopped over it, but it was definitely Mary Digsy knew. The pert lips that look like blue whales headbutting. The slightly wonky nose under those dark eyes that you could get lost in if they weren't a smidgen too close together.

It was Mary alright.

She didn't appear to know what she was walking into either from the bemused look on her face. As much a pawn in Her Ladyship's game as he was.

An awkward moment passed without word.

'Is no one gonna fak'n speak then?'

Her Ladyship seemed underwhelmed. She'd evidently been expecting some form of drama, and clapped her hands together in an effort to spark some life into the scene, but once again, indulged in his own world as he was, all Digsy could focus on was Mary's face. That adorable face. He'd not seen it for an age. And even thought it to be no more, and yet there it was, right in front of his, complete with body and legs and everything.

Mary looked to Her Ladyship, a bemused look to her hardened face, clearly unsure as to what part she played in the proceedings, and clearly uncomfortable under the confusing gaze of Digsy. Agitated it seemed, but how could she not recognise him, he thought... again?

Her Ladyship gestured towards the table. Mary sighed and sat down opposite Digsy, oblivious to the leering wretches watching on in delight beyond her. She still looked gorgeous. A little mental maybe, but still gorgeous, and Digsy knew not what to say as she stared indifferently at him.

He looked into her eyes and then away again.

She looked so different. The scar... scars. His head was exploding with questions. What happened to her? Was she okay? How did she end up with The Order? Did she recognise him? But he was utterly bewildered, and utterly lost for words. Mary was clearly getting impatient, waiting for him to say something, and then looked away in disgust at his feeble efforts to do so.

It was definitely her though, that shot him that night on the cliff. Digsy knew that now, and he felt not the usual urge that he did for Mary suddenly. The longing that had crippled him for the last six years was suddenly gone. This Mary, it was her, but not her, and his mind was abuzz with confusion and denial at what was sat right in front of him.

He felt no connection with the Mary sat opposite him. He didn't know this Mary and it tormented him so. Why was this happening to him? To be reunited after so long apart, only to find the love that once burned mutually unrequited!

Mary looked away bored.

Another awkward moment passed, and even the gentle lapping of the waves against the ship's hull could be heard above the unease.

'Well that was fak'n waste of fak'n time, ay!'

Her Ladyship approached the table with the candle's glint in her eye, looking over the rim of her glasses, back and forth from one to the other, an equal share of disdain reserved for each, and then fixed her glare on Digsy, pursing her lips in an effort to keep the smile from them.

'I saw what I needed to Digsy old boy.' She gave him a reassuring slap, and then turned away to look nowhere in particular.

'See…' she went on. 'Mary here recognised ya from the cliff top, ooohhh, fak'n months back now. Do ya re-mem-ba that, do ya, Digsy?'

A pointed pause marked each syllable of the question. There was an unwelcoming edge to her words suddenly, looking down at Digsy with her hands clasped behind her and the fake smile gone.

'You gave us a bita botha mate.'

The night was almost black now, the oil lanterns flickering in the breeze that'd extinguished the candles, the deck shimmering as the lanterns bobbed with the lake's every breath. If Her Ladyship didn't look the part of the iron fisted dictator in the normal light, she did now, all orange and flickery. Indeed they all did, standing there flickering away in the torchlight. Digsy's bowels were loose. The game was up. Her Ladyship certainly had a flare for theatrics, but there was no denying it now. She clearly knew the part that Digsy had played. He'd been recognized at the cliff that night, and by Mary too of all people. By his wife! Mary had betrayed him.

A sinister grin crossed Her Ladyship's face as she watched Digsy squirm, and she allowed him a moment to compound his fear, before going on:

'Don't you fak'n worry though, mate. I just needed to see your face when Mary walked in. Make sure you are who I think you are, you pommie baastard!'

The thought of the old oppressor was almost too much for Her Ladyship, and she almost spat these last words out. Feeling the need to defend his homeland at that point, Digsy then explained, that, as reprehensible and often shameful as the empire's behaviour had often been all those years ago, the empire's shores had been threatened. Fortify she must. Tragically, the only way to beat her competitors, and therefore ensure survival, was through nefarious means, and had she not been a success, much of the rest of the world, may well have enjoyed that same tragic fate as the Aztecs, Incans and Mayans.

Unfortunately, Her Ladyship didn't concur. The vein in her brow started twitching. She collected herself though, clearing her throat, she shrugged the matter off, and continued:

'I think I'll leave you two to get… err… reacquainted. I can feel romance in the air mate, wink-wink,'

Overexaggerating a wink at each of them, she laughed.

'I'll see you in the square at midday Digsy. Don't you fak'n forget mate.'

And with that, she was off, leaving Digsy alone with Mary for the first time in six long years.

Chapter 44

The only light seeping into Sinead's cell was the slits of pale moonlight beaming in through the cracks in the window's shutter. The night was warm but miserable to Sinead. She didn't know how much more she could take, or how long she'd been there.

Day and night had seemed as one almost. She was tired, hungry and weak, and longing for just an hour to sit alone in the sunlight. Footsteps came from outside. She could just hear them above the water lapping the lake's edge not thirty metres away. They were coming towards her, so she grasped the window ledge, trying to pull herself up to look out through the gap in the boards, but she didn't have the strength, so she flopped back down again and crouched in the corner, waiting for whomever she could hear approaching.

She could hear voices too now, someone speaking to the guard outside, and the door creaked open moments later, a breeze of fresh air hitting her as something metallic was pushed across the floor, catching the moonlight as it slid to a halt before her.

It smelled good.

The door slammed shut again, so she dropped to her knees, feeling around on the floor until her hands found something wet and squidgy. It was too dark too see what it was, so she delved her hands in and opened her mouth —a particularly undignified way to devour venison with potatoes, veggies and gravy, I'll give you that, but it was nevertheless, one of the finest meals she'd ever had.

She licked her fingers until all she could taste was skin, and then lay down and drifted off, wondering what she'd done to deserve such a treat.

Chapter 45

November 5, 2050

The door by Digsy's head slammed shut and he woke with a start, the metallic reverb rampaging the tiny cabin like a huge gong. Grasping the pillow behind his head he placed it over it, loathed to face the day just yet. A sickness bubbled in his stomach, and his head was pounding, courtesy of the wine that he suddenly remembered drinking the previous night – a local Pinot Noir from what he recalled. A 2028. A delicate and fruity number, with an after taste of plumbs and the port from barrel it was stored in. Its bouquet still lingered and made a sour cocktail with the stale smoke Digsy could still taste. Removing the pillow, he sat up, scanning the room.

It was a ship's cabin that Digsy found himself in, the water's hollow caress against the hull echoing slightly, and the only sound bar the gulls he could hear cawing in the distance.

From the look of the clothes strewn around, it was his cabin that Digsy was in, but then he remembered he didn't have a cabin, so it couldn't have been, and he knew the second bit for certain, as he was the one that didn't not have one, and wasn't not in it, and of that he was certain too.

But whose was it?

A single light bulb swayed in the middle of the tiny space, one second lighting the clothes and the two empty bottles littering the floor around the fallen chair, the next the circular clock that hung between the door and the wardrobe to the left. Assorted colours hung in the wardrobe, dirty and damp by the musky smell permeating, and a pair of scuffed work boots were placed regimentally under the table in the corner, which was emptied and crooked, bent in at the fold along the middle.

Was it Mary's room? Had the old spark been reignited after all? The start of the previous night was still clear in Digsy's mind, but that was all. He'd been at the functional stage of drunkenness at that point, only having tested a few glasses of his moonshine, but when wine was added to the equation. Kablam! He was groggy and a touch confused. His head hurt and his mouth was dry.

Memories were hazy still, but the previous night had been somewhat of an anti-climax he quickly recalled. Mary still hadn't recognised him from the old world. She'd seen him at the cliff that night she'd said, and then recognized him again as Raul brought him in the day he was captured, but she'd never seen him before that.

She'd reached into her cloak, pulling out a cigarette. It'd bent into an arc, not quite splitting, so she'd straightened it, lit it on a candle, and then blew the smoke into Digsy's face indifferently, like it was a good substitute for a smile.

She'd spoken in boredom to begin with. She clearly wanted to be somewhere else, and made no pains to mask it, ignoring Digsy entirely after a while, not a trace of humour or irony at the situation that the author may have misconstrued as humorous and ironic at all.

She'd made it abundantly clear that she didn't know Digsy, and that she didn't want to know him. Furthermore she went on to state with utmost sincerity, she had no interest in their supposed past, and she didn't like him either, so please shut the flip up about it.

When it became evident to Mary that it was all utterly incomprehensible to Digsy though, she'd spelled it out for him, slightly impatiently, but with a new compassion in her eyes too.

She'd put both forefingers to her temples, tapping them gently.

'I lost my memory in the quakes.'

And that one sentence was a veritable epiphany to Digsy. His face had contorted. His breath had escaped him, but it had all suddenly made sense to him too. His life had at last made sense again. Mary had lost her memory on the night of the big quake, the night the boulder had split them apart six years earlier, and she remembered nothing at all before it!

'I'm sorry I don't know you, but I just don't, y'know,' she'd offered by way of consolation with a shrug of her shoulders.

Not long after that she'd wandered off, waiting until Digsy had gone to the gents to do so.

It hadn't gone as he'd hoped.

He brooded for a while in bed, his feet touching the cold steel at the end of it, the gentle swaying curdling his stomach, but he didn't want to move just yet, so he tried to distract himself by reading the quips and love notes that were carved into the ceiling above his bunk.

Red was here, and still is... look behind you was his favourite, and he forced himself not to look as much as he wanted to, consoling himself in the knowledge, that he was in bed, and the bed was surrounded by walls, so Red couldn't possibly be behind him.

Then he realised there was space under the bed. Red could be there. It could have been Red's room for all Digsy knew. The thought unnerved him, so he checked, and much to his relief, he wasn't.

'*Don't you fak'n forget, mate.*'

The words bounced into Digsy's mind suddenly, darkening his day in an instant. Her Ladyships words.

'*In the fak'n square, mate, at fak'n mid-day!*'

It was almost mid-day.

Chapter 46

There was a gloom about the day as Digsy emerged onto the main deck of the Earnslaw. The air was much warmer than normal, and the sky dark to the north, waves of ominous grey trundling past overhead, threatening, but not quite ready to dampen the day below just yet. No bird song welcomed Digsy this morning though. The only sounds were of bustle and activity, chatter and laughter, and quite lively it sounded too mused he, lowering the hatch behind him.

The marketplace sat below him where it always did, straddling the dock, only not bustling with trade as usual. Not the normal friendly natured haggling and jibing of commerce, nor the glimmer of the sun off the wet fish as they flopped and slopped here and there.

Bustle there was, but of a different sort entirely.

Armed guards stood four to balcony, staggered around the buildings that enclosed the square, and gazing out over it with their weapons trained lazily down. Most of the market tables had been stacked to make a wall around the stage which had been built at the square's centre, partially shaded by the huge willow that drooped lazily over it. Dozens of spectators were gathering around it, baskets of rotten fruits and vegetables being passed around the hordes of on-lookers that were starting to arrive.

A gap the height of a man separated the crowd from the stage around the barricade's circumference, with Mo, Red and a few other guards being all that stood between them—guns at the ready should anyone be foolish enough to try and break through.

Her Ladyship was stood on the stage with her back to the crowd, talking into the radio she held.

The square was quickly filling as rivers of people seeped in from the buildings surrounding it, filing in from the roads, walkways and wharfs where scores of houseboats were moored. They pushed in from every angle, the stench palpable to Digsy as he shoved his way through them, longing to be in the fresh air and space of the mountains again, away from the brooding mass of humanity that was quickly engulfing him. A feeling of claustrophobia was beginning to grip him, the space around him shrinking more with every step.

Time dragged as more and more people filled the square, the air of expectation growing in line with the crowd as everyone there exchanged theories on what they were there to see, what the stage was for. It sat six feet from the ground not far ahead of Digsy. He could see it through the hordes now, the supports holding it up a crisscrossed mess of salvaged timber, charred and splintered, and a maze of wonder for the pack of filthy kids that were playing beneath it. But what piqued Digsy's interest the most, was the willow limb stretching out horizontally above the stage, and the sack lying open beneath it, the end of a rope poking from its mouth. But for who?

Who were they going to hang?

Being a prime candidate for such an honour, Digsy began to worry, the last few months replaying over and over in his mind, more and more reasons The Order might want his head occurring to him with every beat of his heart. There were lots too. Maybe he **had** outlived his usefulness. Maybe he was for the noose after all, and he was trapped too should this be the case. There was no way he could escape, hemmed in by the crowd as he was.

He searched frantically for a way through them, but there was none. The people were packed in like mushrooms in a matchbox, an impregnable wall of sweat that a deodorant salesman would've relished.

Desperation was digging its claws into Digsy now, and his paranoia likewise. The crowd were boisterous suddenly and growing impatient, and moments passed as murmurs of disapproval began to rise, when an orange sphere suddenly cascaded into the sky, followed by a boom that rattled the very mountains around them. Their wait was over, and the people wheeled in anticipation of the delights to come. Jubilance filled the air, and a cheer went up, wanton and depraved as the accused was finally led onto the scene.

Flinching as a tomato scathed her shoulder, Sinead stumbled and fell into the elbow poking out before her, crying out as it jabbed into her eye. She was terrified and confused, hungry and drained, and had no idea at all what was going on. She'd been dragged from her prison and out towards the dock, where a crowd was gathered, evidently for her, and bundled along, her way lined by malevolent faces and her hopes fading more with every insult that came at her.

What was this all about?

Why was everyone being so mean?

There was no way through the mass of bodies, but somehow the dreadlocked guard directing her managed to forge a gap, easily creating space where none existed. He shoved her between the sweaty, lumbering obstacles, fingers and hands prodding and tormenting her as she winced and squirmed to avoid them. Insults were flying, and every face she saw glared lustily at Sinead, as if she were a lobster waiting to be picked out for the evening meal.

She could see the stage through the throng now, and said throng suddenly parted before her, every eye there settling on her.

Her Ladyship was stood at the top of the steps leading up to the stage, with her hands clasped behind her, beaming down at Sinead.

One of the guards picked up the sack and pulled a rope out, and then looked up to the tree limb hanging above him, then back to the rope again, and then he lofted it up and over, tying it up as another cheer arose from the crowd.

More prisoners were coming.

Sinead made no effort to move again after that, until she was dragged back up again, and up the steps to the stage like a rag doll.

The sky above the lake to the south was getting darker, but the sun yet glimpsed through the thin veil of grey hanging above them, spotlighting the ruins that littered the mountains surrounding them. They looked like aged hedgehogs thought Her Ladyship as she gazed out over the devastation she ruled over, their spines bent and warped, poking up in their thousands from every inch of ground it seemed.

Seeing the first prisoner had pleased Her Ladyship – It was the Irish woman that'd had the plans all along. Her Ladyship was looking forward to watching her hang. The crowd were like a pack of hungry dogs she was pleased to see, and she smiled, watching them heckle and jeer mercilessly as the prisoner passed. So many were hurling abuse now, and a malignant smile traversed Her Ladyship's face as she watched the wretched Sinead being dragged onto the stage, crashing face first onto it with a wail as the crowd whooped in delight.

It was all working out perfectly she beamed, double checking her pocket for the notes she'd made on her speech.

The wind had dropped, and a wood pigeon cooed knowingly as three more prisoners were shoved through the pack, bound and beaten, dragged up the steps and lined up next to Sinead; and well deserving of their fate in Her Ladyship's opinion.

'Marijuana?!!' she'd raged…

'Well I never!'

Two of the prisoners – one of them tall and the other one short, both slender though, and frankly an embarrassment to themselves in Her Ladyship's humble opinion – were unknown to her. The third though, she knew to be the large Tongan woman they called Nursey. There was no need for the guards to forge a path for her to cut through though. Nursey's bulk did the job for them, and she pushed easily through the wall of people separating her from the stage, trumping up the steps to it almost impatiently.

This approach wasn't so satisfying for Her Ladyship though. This one stood proud and bold, and not shaken at all by what was unfolding. She glared defiantly back at Her Ladyship, with an unnerving fire blazing in her eyes, so Her

Ladyship averted her own, uncomfortable all of a sudden, and turned back to address the crowd.

This is it, thought she, steeling herself as a light drizzle started to fall, an expectant hush became the square, and every eye there fell on her.

Chapter 47

The sky was darkening all around, and ominously so to the south. Her Ladyship took her notes from her pocket and stepped up to the pulpit, and then, clearing her throat, she drew in a deep breath, and began...

'Blessed residents of New Queenstown...' bold, loud, confident and brash, and full of the balls she wished she actually had dangling beneath her, and then she paused, expertly staggering her oration to allow the murmur to quell for her words.

A distant roll of thunder sounded and she looked to the sky with a frown, and then back to the crowd, a feeling of pride as she looked out over her subjects and they leered back in glee. Not concerned at the prospect of rain, only awaiting the words that would seal the fate of the wretches lined up behind her.

'Now, as you good people know...' she went on after a moment, her hands on the pulpit either side of her glass of water as the drizzle slowly started to refill it.

'We've worked fak'n hard to keep our beautiful town safe.'

A bobbing of heads ensued, which enthused her somewhat.

'An we're lucky to fak'n be here ay,' she chuckled as the people turned to each other acknowledging the fact.

'Clean water, clean air...' she pointed out.

'Whilst the rest of the world fak'n starves, we fak'n prospa!' She looked to her notes as the sea of heads nodded in unison.

'Could be worse ay,' she chuckled, and they agreed with her.

'The problem is...'

She took on a more sombre tone now, adopting a grave face as she turned to the line of prisoners behind her, directing the emphasis towards Nursey with an accusatory glare.

'We've been having one or two security issues lately.'

She locked her gaze on Nursey's insubordinate eyes, who returned the glare with a passion easily trumping it.

'Your grub's been stolen dear people. Your water too.'

She paused for a moment, allowing the lie to sink in.

'It fak'n pains me to fak'n say it. It truly fak'n does, but there are some here among us, good people, who'd steal the very food we feed our fak'n children!'

She put both of her hands to her heart and adopted a pained expression, closing her eyes and dropping her head, and then a sudden rage as her eyes bolted open, and she went on with a fury Furiously Furious Frank would have been proud of.

'Well I won't fak'n have it!'

She crashed both of her fists down onto the pulpit and rattled the glass on it.

'Who do they think they're fak'n deal'n with, ay?'

The crowd were gobbling up every bit of it, the line of people waiting to be hanged but a sideshow to Her Ladyship's theatrics now, and the people were gazing up at her transfixed.

Which was important to Her Ladyship. She needed the people on her side in this endeavour, as it was a controversial one, and felt a tingle crawl down her spine as the people obligingly bayed. As wolves hungry for blood they danced under her narration. Angry calls arose as the sea of faces grew more boisterous. She could see the fervour growing amongst them like a living being.

Like puppets on a string.

She waited a few moments, allowing the distaste to blossom as cries of denunciation captured the air.

'Who do they think they are?' and her personal favourite, **'Hang the bastards,'** sang from the crowd.

It was all working out beautifully, and she looked about her triumphantly, beaming out over her people with an inner warmth that softened the gloom that was swiftly enveloping the scene. She felt a sacred connection with each and every one of them, screeching for blood as they were like a pack of starving hyenas, and it warmed her so.

Taking a sip from the glass, she replaced it on the pulpit. The drizzle turned into a shower, and umbrellas started popping up all around.

'It was these wretches…'

She indicated the wretches in question lined up behind her with an outstretched finger, the mere thought of them sickening Her Ladyship to the pit of her stomach suddenly. Oh how she hated the vermin. *Why can't they just fak off,* she'd often muse whenever inflicted with one of the dirty bastards' presence.

'Who stole your food…'

The sight of the filth had grown too much for her, so she turned back to her people, the breeze chilling and whipping up, catching an umbrella that'd just gone up and launching it to the back of the square.

She'd hoped mentioning stolen food would tickle a few nerves, and surely enough, another angry call arose from the swell, and others quickly agreed, gasps escaping all around as people remembered the pie they'd made last week, but didn't remember eating.

Dance puppets, dance.

'Even murdered your fak'n neighbours!' she went on, inching her audience ever closer to the finale, and revelling in every sinister second of it.

The crowd were incensed, and fresh volleys of rotten fruit arced towards the stricken forms as they flinched and cowered to avoid them.

Her Ladyship held her hand up for silence.

'So…' she began again when the din allowed as the guards pulled the rowdy elements of the crowd into line.

'I ask you, good people of New Queenstown. What say ye…' She swung her hands up like a ballerina, flicking her wrists up and pointing out to the crowd. 'Be the fate…' Again she paused, loving every second of the attention she was wallowing in now. 'Of these vile creatures?'

An answer wasn't forthcoming though, which Her Ladyship hadn't expected, and found a mite irritating too, but the crowd still gazed expectantly up at her, so she decided to go off script at that point.

'We could stick 'em in prison...' she teased.

'But I don't believe **we**,' she emphasised this last word with another dramatic pause, 'should be responsible for their upkeep, what with fak'n food shortages being as they fak'n are.'

The more rotund people in the crowd murmured a general agreement, and she gently placed her palms back onto the pulpit, and looked out over the rims of her glasses to the faces gazing back at her.

'So, good people of New Queenstown. With your approval, these thieves, these fak'n traitors...'

Every soul there was itching to hear her next words. Even the birds had ceased to sing it seemed. The clouds had ceased to cloud.

Everyone there knew what the sentence would be, and so it was.

'Will hang,' she concluded, almost in a whisper, crossing her chest as the crowd roared its unanimous accord.

Abuse and insult tore into the whimpering damned as their fates were finally sealed. Sinead tried to sing a song in her head as her Da had taught her, but she couldn't hear herself past the roar that'd erupted, so she dropped her eyes instead, away from the evil eyes that were staring up at her, heckling her mercilessly.

Even the kids were at it, the little bastards.

A church bell chimed and echoed around the basin, deep and penetrating, and perfectly captured the moment. A child's laughter struck a bizarre light note, and the four prisoners were all dragged into place, four nooses hanging from the willow above them, the one to the left slightly higher where the tree limb curved up, and the prisoners were lined up beneath them.

The last of the nooses was slipped into place, and Her Ladyship stepped forward again, her hands up for quiet and then turned to the condemned.

'So, ye thieves, ye fak'n murderers.'

She looked over her glasses at the four pitiful specimens lined up before her. 'Have ya any last fak'n words?'

Silence followed, a thousand eyes skipping from Sinead to Nursey, from Nursey to Sinead, and to the other two that stood noosed and soiled beside them. One last pitiful comment, one last light note to brighten their day was all that the crowd wanted to hear.

No one obliged though. There were no pleas or cries for mercy. No sobbing or begging for clemency. Just shock embroiled the condemned it seemed.

'So be it.'

The disappointment was clear in Her Ladyship's voice. She stormed across to the lever that poked up from the stage's edge, the crowd cheering her on again, and clenched her hands around it, flexing and rolling her shoulders in readiness. A tyrannical rage oozed from her as she cackled and looked out to her people, like an actress playing to the crowd, raising her hand to her ear, overdramatising her movements and gently ushering the people towards the inevitable conclusion, and the crowd reacted in kind, locked up in the delightful spectacle, cheering and whooping at every turn.

Putting her finger to her lips after a moment, the hum ceased, and she took a handkerchief from her pocket, wiping away the moisture that was quickly settling on her brow, and then replaced it, well aware that her every move was being watched, and relishing every second of it.

Slowly, she extended her arm out in front of her, scanning the sea of faces gazing back at her, every one of them awash with joy, and drenched now, but not in the slightest concerned; and with a sinister smile and a wicked cackle, she turned her thumb to the ground, the crowd roared their approval, and she wrenched the lever towards her.

Chapter 48

Choked breaths, cracked bones and emptied bowels filled the ether as the trapdoor opened and the doomed wrenched to a final halt beneath the stage. An incredulous gasp followed, as if that particular end hadn't been expected, and an unnerving silence replaced it, only interrupted by the creaking of the willow limb as it strained under the bodies swinging below it. Her Ladyship sighed a wry smile and Digsy's mind raced, a rage rising within him which threatened to boil over.

How could Sinead be dead?

Surely it wasn't real. His eyes were closed, his fists clenched, his knees trembling and his mind swimming. How could this have happened? Sinead had done nothing. She was innocent, and yet they'd hung her anyway. Just to make a point it seemed. For entertainment even!

Her smiling face danced through Digsy's mind, and he shrouded himself in guilt. He'd let her die. He could have, no, he should have done something to stop them. Now he'd make the bastards pay.

He opened his eyes, and as expected, there before him were the limp forms of the recently deceased, swinging beneath the stage with the haunting remnants of their final breath still set on their faces.

But there were only two of them!

His eyes darted up, and his heart washed with joy as he saw Sinead still stood there, terrified and trembling beside Nursey, weeping uncontrollably and naught but a shivering wreck now after that little fright.

Alive though.

Sinead too had closed her eyes, certain that that would be the last she'd see of the world. She'd made her peace with her God, and she too heard the ghastly snap when she'd expected it to be her hanging limp below the stage. She was still alive though. She could tell that much, though her nerves were in tatters and she could feel the warmth of her urine running down the inside of her legs.

Craven faces still stared up at her, the trapdoor to her right open and the rope dropping through it taut and swinging slightly. Looking to her left, Sinead was flooded with a strange kind of joy, as she saw Nursey still next to her, slumped and broken though, tides of tears streaming down her cheeks, lost midst the damp covering everything now.

Her Ladyship was thriving on every overly dramatic second of it, and even now she sniggered to herself at the hilarity of her little ruse. Her gaze flipped from the swinging corpses to the two blubbering messes still standing noosed on the stage. The twin trap doors had been installed especially, and it'd worked a treat. To have reduced the likes of Nursey as she had was an achievement indeed.

She scanned the sea of faces for any signs of dissent, ready to nip it in the bud should she spot any.

The hush remained though, as the great unwashed gazed up at what they'd craved, what they'd come out in their masses to witness. A child started to cry, and mothers covered their young ones' eyes, protecting them from what they'd forced them to witness, and a murmur again welled after a moment.

'Well finish the bastards off ay!'

And another cried out in support, others joining in too, some in sympathy but mostly not, and all of a sudden the mob was baying for a fresh kill again.

Mission accomplished.

'Now…'

Her Ladyship held up her hands, and began lowering them again as the murmur lulled, joining them at her heart. 'I've gotta apologise to ya good people of New Queenstown. I've not been entirely honest with ya.'

This tangent had everyone's attention.

'We've had a traitor in our midst…'

The note of disappointment she'd added to her voice seemed to have done the trick, and a murmur arose as the people looked to each other as if they may be the treacherous ones, suspicious glances being cast at most everyone there now.

'This weasel thinks he can get eeeverything his own fak'n way,' she sneered. 'Give with one hand, and then take with the fak'n other.'

She shook her head incredulously and stepped back under the willow for shelter.

Digsy's mind was racing, his eyes searching for an escape as his fate seemed to close in around him. Surely Her Ladyship was referring to him.

'But I had to be fak'n sure good people...' Her Ladyship went on. 'Can't just go hanging people willy-nilly now can we? No good people, we can't,' she quickly added before anyone could connect the statement to the misdeeds of a minute ago.

'This efficient look'n fella here...'

She pointed at Tomas, who was stood by the stage with a guard on either side of him. She could see the blood drain from his face as he sank back into the wall of bodies behind him, but invisible hands shoved him forward and he fell into the stage, flopping to the swiftly softening mud. Something slammed into his rear and he writhed at the impact, boos and insults flying, but managed to struggle back to his feet.

'Has betrayed us all.'

The stage was behind Tomas now, and he pushed back against it, surrounded by impious eyes, glaring and inching closer as he kicked out to keep them at bay.

Tomas was stunned. How could this be happening? He'd done as Her Ladyship had asked. He'd gotten her the plans. He'd given her Digsy's cave, and he'd even given her the camp, but now it seemed he was for the noose too.

The crowd around him suddenly parted as Rodney pushed through them, grabbed Tomas and dragged him up onto the stage, the crowd heckling and jeering again, but they were getting rowdier now, and the guards surrounding the stage were struggling to keep the crowd from it.

'So… I say we put his loyalty to the test.'

Her Ladyship reached into her pocket and pulled out a tiny pistol—an old Walther PPK—and held it out to Tomas. His eyes betrayed not the fear or the pleading she'd expected though, but something different entirely, as if delving deep down into the depths of her soul to try and find just a shred of humanity in there somewhere. Smiling a wicked smile, she held the pistol out further, nodding her encouragement with her eyes fixed on Tom's.

'N… N… no,' stammered he.

'Y…Y… fak'n yes mate.'

Red nudged Tom and he reluctantly took the gun, the scale of Her Ladyship's treachery well and truly sinking in now. She cradled his fingers around it, patting his hand like a good boy, and stepped back, nodding towards Sinead in case he wasn't sure who he was to shoot.

Once more the mob grew silent as Tom stared at the tiny gun in his hand. He couldn't believe what was happening, how it was all turning out, or what he was being forced to do. He'd always wanted to fire one of these guns. Indeed he knew them well from the Bond movies his father had reluctantly allowed him to watch as a child, but he'd never imagined he'd get the chance in a situation as heinous as this.

How could Her Ladyship do this? Surely his daughter would be safe at least. Surely she wouldn't harm her.

He looked from the pistol in his hand to Her Ladyship, and then to Sinead.

He'd sentenced Sinead to death.

Again Red nudged him and he turned to face her, love and remorse bursting from his every pore, and yet she returned his gaze not with the hatred he'd expected, but with empathy, kindness and warmth, which cut him to the bone. He couldn't understand it. It made no sense. He wanted… no…he needed her to be angry with him.

'Zay haf my daughter, Sinead.'

'No fak'n speak'n!'

The breeze picked up again, the shower suddenly a downpour, and more tatty umbrellas sprung up one by one, joining the dots that were scattered across the square. All eyes were on Tomas though, and he could feel them all tearing into him, willing him to do the unthinkable as he strove for a way to avoid it. All he could focus on was the gun though.

He was to blame for all of it, and now this!

Brushing the wet from his brow, he took his glasses off and placed them in his shirt pocket. The silence was unnerving, every soul watching and lusting for an ungodly outcome, and then he raised the pistol to Sinead, his arm quivering as he blinked the tears away.

Nursey had stood silent until now, but she spoke out suddenly, shattering the tension.

'Tomas! Don'you be foolish boy...'

Every head turned towards her, and she stepped forward, but only as far as the noose would allow, the willow bending slightly behind her, and she screamed in frustration as it held her back.

Her Ladyship was in no mood for interruptions though. Not this day. Yanking the shotgun from Rodney's grip before Nursey could speak further, she levelled it at her head, and with a quick wink as she caught Nursey's eye, she squeezed the trigger.

Boom!

The crowd were stunned into silence as Nursey's head exploded, a torrent of claret as she slipped through the noose, thumping to her knees and then flopped to the stage with a squelch.

Sinead screamed. Blood pumped from Nursey's corpse like a faulty sprinkler, splashing everyone and everything around it. The stage was swimming with blood suddenly. People started pushing back as it dripped from the stage and pooled in the mud before them. Angry voices arose again, and suddenly dissent was threatening to break out. Her Ladyship was oblivious to it though. Shocked faces surrounded her, but she cared not. Nursey would serve as a lesson to any similarly inclined individuals she knew.

Reaching into her pocket, she pulled out a radio, winking to Sinead as she did, and as she spoke into it, the air echoed with the crunch of metal as the guards above trained their weapons down on the crowd below.

She raised her hands again for silence, to which the crowd still obeyed, albeit less enthusiastically now.

Adjusting her specs, she took a sip from the glass, watching the crowd over it as she did. The faces she had hooked moments before though, were looking about themselves dubiously now, casting critical eyes in her direction, startled by the archaic brutality and how far she'd gone.

Too much? she wondered, but only for a moment.

'Tom, mate, shoot your fak'n wench mate, or I'll shoot your fak'n kid,' she whispered, not wanting the knowledge of her deviousness to be widespread.

'Do it!' she snapped, slapping him across the cheek.

Tomas looked to the gun and then back to Sinead, disbelief in his eyes as he raised it up to her, the barrel trembling as he strove to pick out one of the many plans that were rattling around in his mind. Instead, he put his finger to the trigger and then caught Sinead's eye. She smiled at him and nodded, eyes red through despair, yet mouthing, 'It's okay, go on,' with utmost sincerity and love for the man who was to kill her.

'Yes Tom…' cut in Her Ladyship, 'Please, do go on.'

The rain slowed and the wind dropped slightly. Tom levelled the gun at Sinead's heart, breathing in til he could feel his lungs could take no more, every soul there captivated again, itching to see what would happen next.

It looked to Sinead like Tomas nodded at her then. Then she thought she saw him wink too, and then he'd turned before anyone knew what was happening and levelled the gun at Her Ladyship. Sinead screamed and the guards reacted, scrambling for the pistol or lunging at Tomas, but not quickly enough.

Her Ladyship had to be stopped, and Tomas was holding a gun, so he levelled it at Her Ladyship's face, and pulled the trigger.

Chapter 49

The only one not lunging at Tomas was Her Ladyship, safe in the knowledge that the pistol was empty, and the crowd howled in delight at the pantomime unfolding on the stage before them. Her face remained stolid as Tom's dropped, and he gazed down the snub-nosed barrel into Her Ladyship's conniving eyes, the conductor of the plot gleaming gleefully back at him, blind to the sense of distaste propagating around her.

'Not entirely unexpected Tommy boy, I must admit.'

Huge hands grabbed Tomas and bundled him down onto the stage.

'Now, in light of this... er... saddening turn of events,' Her Ladyship went on, turning back to face her people with a more solemn tone now, entirely manufactured, but appropriate in light of the situation thought she.

'We here at The New Wakatipu fak'n Order, will be seeking some...er...fak'n recompense.'

She looked to Tom and then to Sinead, shaking her head as if a disappointed parent.

'Such dissent cannot be allowed good people, lest our harmony wither like this bloke's cock.'

She pointed at Tom who was face down on the stage with Rodney's knee pressed into his back, and the crowd chuckled nervously.

'Mary darlin...' she called out.

'Would ya do me the honour?'

Looking to where Her Ladyship beckoned, Digsy saw Mary emerge at the front of the crowd, cloaked and hooded as per usual, with a machete tucked into her belt poking out from under the folds of her robe. Her eyes were wild, utterly focused on the evil she was to commit. Ignoring Digsy's pleas, she brushed past him, barging her way to the stage with a nonchalance that defied humanity.

Raul handed her his 44 Magnum.

It looked huge in Mary's hands, its polished barrel gleaming as she raised the steps to the stage and held it up to Sinead's head. With a sadistic smile, she pulled the pistol's hammer, and again an unnerving silence took the scene. Breaths were cut short in case they themselves could somehow be held responsible for the devilish doings.

Dogs stopped licking their balls.

No longer could Digsy sit idly by though. No longer could he allow such cruelty. It just wasn't cricket. Indeed, he'd thought that two minutes prior when it'd seemed Tom was about to shoot Sinead, but he'd been trapped in the horde and unable to do anything. Unable to get to the stage. Now he was at the front of the crowd though, and he stepped towards the barricade, kicking out at the guard who stepped into his path, and rammed his foot into the guard's knee, who dropped to the ground with a wail.

There was no going back now. Every eye was on Digsy. People pushed back from him, some from fear, but others to give him the space to go on. The stage was right before him now, so he vaulted through a gap in the barricade and charged up the steps, the guards surrounding caught unaware and hesitating, and he launched himself into Mary as another cheer erupted from the throng.

Crunch

Whoops of delight filled the air, and down they sprawled, flopping down to the stage in a heap of flailing limbs. Mary cushioned Digsy's fall though, knocking the wind from her, and he grasped for the gun she'd dropped, reaching out with one hand as he tried to keep her pinned with the other.

Boom!

He didn't get chance to act further though. A shotgun blast rattled the scene and Digsy was pulled abruptly back up, silencing the dissent in an instant.

'E...fak'n...naff!'

Her Ladyship levelled the shotgun at Digsy's head, willing him to act further so she could shoot him on the spot.

She was half tempted to just shoot him anyway, but then she thought that might be another step too far in the crowd's eyes, and she didn't want to upset them further.

The mob's favour was evaporating before her eyes. The people were cheering for Digsy now instead of her.

After a moment, though, she decided the mob's blessing wasn't integral to her masterplan after-all, and rasped...

'Rodney, line 'em up. We'll just fak'n shoot'em.'

Rain was coming down heavily again now. Boisterous calls arose from every angle, and a thick mist was rolling in from the lake. Digsy was dragged to his feet and lined up beside Sinead, who'd been freed from the noose and forced to her knees beside Tomas.

A new air was about the place suddenly. One which didn't bode well for Her Ladyship at all. The crowd were twitchy, and were liable to explode at any moment she knew. The guards above trained their rifles down as the ones below struggled to keep the mob from the stage, pushing people back as they tried to climb the barricade, people pulling at them as others pulled at them to stop them pulling at them. The crowd were divided, some shouting encouragement, and others in disgust, and Her Ladyship knew she'd lost their faith now.

She'd gone too far.

Grasping the Magnum from the stage, she stepped over Nursey's corpse, and over to the line of condemned that were knelt on the stage before her, eyeing them all one by one, as if it was their fault their executions hadn't gone to plan. The people jeered behind her, but she didn't care. The conscience she thought she'd dealt with years ago had startled her for a moment, and derailed her somewhat, but only one thing was in Her Ladyship's mind now.

What that was, was clear to everyone.

Columns of Cumulus seethed and churned behind her as she raised the Magnum's long barrel up to Digsy's head.

'Go on then sugar tits. Do it.' he taunted, much to Her Ladyship's abhorrence, so she cracked him around the head with the butt of the pistol and his face hit the stage with a thump.

The old bovine had him now, and that defiant voice urging Digsy ever onwards, was just a quiet whisper in the folds of his mind now.

Chapter 50

A few seconds later, and Digsy was still there, the rain beating down around him, diluting the pool of blood that he knelt in. Whether still being there was a good thing or not was debatable for Digsy, given his current predicament, every second a step closer to that final step, that final glimpse of the world. His head was down, and the moment stretched on for what felt like seconds to him. Was Her Ladyship simply toying with him? It was certainly her style he knew, to tease and torment whomever she pleased, like a little shit pulling the legs from an insect.

His head was ablaze, a fresh cut to the back of it.

'**Do it!**' someone yelled from the pack.

'**Finish 'em,**' others agreed.

The crowd were growing impatient again. Things weren't going to plan for Her Ladyship. Thunder rolled and people heckled, and then Digsy heard a scuffle to his right, just beyond the stage.

'**My Ladyship, look out!**'

She could hear a commotion suddenly, so she swung around, raising the Magnum, and saw the guard she knew as Mo charging up the steps towards her. He slammed into the guard there, sending him sprawling backwards into the pack, and then up the steps he came, bulldozing through his comrades like a cannonball through skittles. There was no time for Her Ladyship to react. Mo was quick for a big man. Grabbing her, he launched her into the willow's trunk and down she crumpled, dropping to the stage as another cheer went up from the throng.

This is it, thought Digsy. *There's no time for dilly-dallying now. No waiting for the opportune moment here. Indeed no, time is of the essence and one must strike whilst the iron's hot.*

Two guards rushed at Mo. He grabbed one by the neck, thrusting him backwards and kicked out at the second, who toppled back from the stage and landed in the crowd. Taking Sinead by the hand, Digsy pulled her to her feet and dragged her to the edge of the stage whilst Mo kept the other guards busy. They had to get lost in the crowd. Red had other ideas though. He was blocking the steps, and he thrust his rifle butt at Digsy, who ducked to avoid it, but stumbled and fell to the decking. The crowd were enthralled, energised and inspired at the unfoldings, cheering Digsy on and hurling abuse at The Order's guards now. Red came at him again, slamming the rifle down again and again, gasps and groans coming from every direction as the stage splintered beneath it. Red hadn't seen Sinead though, and he dropped with a whimper as she stepped up behind him and thrust her foot up between his legs.

'Run bro!'

Catching Digsy's eye, Mo blocked a blow from his right, grabbing the guard, and then launched him at the guard to his left. Mo seemed unstoppable, taking down anyone that came near him, and the guards on the balconies hesitated, unwilling to shoot one of their own it seemed. Next to try his luck however, was Rodney, and the two smashed together like two tanks colliding head on. It was like a clash of the titans, like mighty stag locked in a duel, neither giving way to the insatiable might of the other. People stopped to watch as the two warriors grappled. Mo blocked the knee that drove up at him, and then grabbed Rodney's leg, somehow lifting him from the stage, and sent him staggering backwards, but then a shot rang out and Mo grimaced, and a sudden panic took the scene. Unsteady on his feet all of a sudden, Mo wavered, and then he staggered to the side, flopping to the stage with a crunch.

The BFG was down.

Another shot came from a balcony, and people started to scatter, running for their lives this way and that, and trampling others in the process. There was no way out though. No way through the milling mass of madness. People scurried about like headless chickens here and there, fights breaking out as the guards on the balconies trained their rifles down on the unfolding riot below them.

The square was awash with confusion suddenly, elbows and fists flailing as people tried to escape, others going for the guards too now as the guards tried to pick one from the other and opened fire.

It was a blood bath. Shots and screams filled the air. People dropped all around, but cries of rally accompanied them. A sense of rebellion was quickly spreading. More and more people were going for the guards now, who pulled back to form a circle around the stage. It was turning into an uprising, and the throng smashed through the barricades to get to the guards, hacking back at whoever was hacking at them. Hordes of anger ripping into their oppressors like packs of starving dogs.

Pandemonium.

A Molotov cocktail flew into one of the surrounding buildings, and then another. Flames raced up the timbers and smoke poured into the square.

A blow scathed Digsy's jaw, so he turned and knocked the man out. Then a blade swung in at him. Digsy hadn't seen it though, so Sinead pushed him from its path and the blade slammed down between them. Ramming her foot into the assailant's stomach, he flopped down to the mud with a grunt.

Digsy shoved and kicked his way onwards, Sinead in his wake doing likewise, blows falling from here and there, from the guards and the mob alike, striving to get away from the melee that was engulfing everything now.

They were almost out too. The crowd thinned as they neared the square's edge, the building right before them ablaze, smoke streaming from its upper windows as the guards scurried from its balcony. The ground floor was clear though, so they made for it, and then there was Raul, his eyes fixed on Digsy with a fateful grin traversing his chubby face.

Mary felt invigorated, alive and untouchable. It was kicking off and she loved it. She wasn't sure this was the kind of thing she'd have enjoyed in her old life, but she was relishing every violent second of it now. Even the smoke streaming into the square from the buildings ablaze somehow soothed her.

Moments before, she'd been in the ring of guards around the stage, hacking for her life, and that had been fun. They'd repelled the initial assault and managed to push the mob back now though, and now it was a free for all.

Someone came at her from behind, so she smashed him across the face with the butt of her machete, and then picked her rifle up from the mud, put the barrel to the man's head, and pulled the trigger.

A fuzzy feeling flowed through Mary then. She felt warm inside, and tingly, and a shiver coursed through her as she wiped the blood from her cheek. Such fun, and oh how it warmed her. Fingers grasped at the rifle she held, pulling it from her, so she yanked back but the man was too strong. Catching his eye, he grinned at her, so she let go and he staggered backwards. Again she pulled her machete, and brought it down hard across the man's face. It cut through him like hot butter and he screamed, flopping to his knees in a deluge of rouge.

Mary felt no pity for the man knelt screaming before her. She wished she did. Wished she could find just a hint of compassion hidden deep within her somewhere, but she couldn't, and she drew the blade across the man's throat with a satisfied sigh.

The clash of blades filled the air, pained screams and war cries as one by one the people dropped. Brawls had broken out in every direction, the mud thick around their feet now, puddles of rain or blackened blood sitting in the craters that the slain kept on making. The hate burning in Raul's eyes was clear to see. Digsy could see its ferocity, its sincerity, and the passion that for some reason it burned with, so he directed Sinead away with instructions as to where to meet him, and then turned back to face him.

Taking his hat from his head, Raul placed it carefully on the stage beside Mo, who was still breathing Digsy could tell, but barely. The stage around him was swimming in blood, his own and Nursey's, pooling around them or dripping through the gaps in the decking. Some of the best blood humanity had to offer mused Digsy with a sudden heavy heart. The sight saddened him, and distracted him. His concentration lapsed, and a woman with a cleaver came at him from behind, swinging the cleaver in at his head. Ducking at the last, the cleaver swished past his ear, but then it came at him again. The woman was quick, and there was no time to avoid it, and all Digsy heard at that point, was a loud clash of metal as a second blade appeared from nowhere and intercepted the first. The woman screamed in frustration and looked to its owner, her eyes wide suddenly as the blade was thrust through her stomach and she slopped to the mud with a gurgle.

'You can thak me in 'ell Digsy…'

Raul pulled his sword back out and wiped it on the dying woman's coat.

'You are mine bro.'

Chapter 51

The square was much quieter than it had been only moments before. Not much could be seen through the smoke, and only the occasional shot from the balconies that weren't ablaze cut through the stifling, choked air. It was much warmer too, particularly around the square's periphery where Sinead was, being so close to the flames. Only a few people could be seen through the smog, which was thickening and starting to choke her. She could hear the grunting and wailing though, the cursing and screaming, as steel and wood clashed in a scene reminiscent of centuries gone by. The riot was more of a melee now. So many lay slain already, citizens and guards alike.

A handful of single combats had spread out around the square, rifle butts and blades replacing the guns and clashing all around her now. The Order's guards were fewer in number, as most of them had been pushed back through the buildings, but they were better equipped.

She scanned each clash for familiarity, looking for a glimpse of Tomas, but she couldn't make anything out, couldn't see the faces of the people battling all around her. Ducking and weaving, she made for the south side of the square, near the lake where Digsy had said he'd meet her.

A guard spotted her though, and moved towards her, so she picked a shard of broken glass from the ground, ignoring the pain as it sliced into her palm, and drove it into the guard's neck.

Staying low, and ducking from cover to cover, she passed by below the balconies, hugging the edge of the square, caked in mud, urine and blood, her pants clinging to her skin and her neck tender still from the rope that'd been wrapped around it.

Tearing off her sleeve, and wrapping it around her hand, she heard a scream from above, and looked up to see a guard above her falling from the balcony. He hit the ground with a sickening crunch as his neck snapped on impact, so she shuffled over to the dead guard, grabbed his rifle, and then scurried back to the cover of the buildings, ducking behind an upturned table.

Raul stepped towards Digsy, his sword out at arm's length, keeping the crowd at bay as they tried get around it. The crowd had thinned, but Raul was cut off from the other guards now. A circle had formed around he and Digsy, probing for a way to get past the blade that Raul strafed them with. A skinny fellow with a bald head made his move, pouncing at Raul whilst his back was turned, but he failed and was easily run through. A second tried much the same to much the same end, and the others quickly dispersed.

Digsy stepped back away from Raul, who stepped towards him, his bald head glimmering and an evil glint in his eye.

'Raul, mate, don't do this.'

Raul came closer still though, and somewhere deep inside, Digsy had known this day would come eventually. It had seemed almost inevitable of late. The last thing he wanted though, was to fight Raul. To fight his old friend, but Raul it seemed, wasn't so inclined. Stepping back from the stage, and with one eye on Raul, Digsy scoured the surroundings for a weapon, for anything he could use to defend himself, his hands up before him, begging Raul for clemency, appealing to the old Raul, who lunged forward without warning and thrust his blade at Digsy's head.

It was quick too, and it caught Digsy off guard, but he stepped to the side as the blade drove past him and threw a right hook, slamming his fist into Raul's jaw.

Bam!

Raul wasn't shaken though. His podge took the blow well, and he stepped back with a smile, adjusting his grip on the sword's hilt with a little shake of his head. Rounding the corner of the stage, with the willow behind him now, Digsy grasped a baseball bat from the mud beside him, stumbling to avoid the corpse it lay beside.

Again they faced each other down, the rain beating down around them, sporadic gunfire still sounding in the distance, a tattered sheet of plastic whipping by between them, lost on the strengthening breeze.

Raul stepped to the left and Digsy to the right, Raul to the right and Digsy the left. Digsy feigned a lunge with the baseball bat, hoping to wrong-foot his opponent, but his foot sank into the mud and his balance wavered, and Raul lunged in at him, slamming the hilt of his sword into Digsy's throat.

Crunch!

Down Digsy went, crumpling to the mud in choked daze. His breath was gone, and he clawed desperately at his collar, as if trying to make a hole for his breath to escape through. Thunder rolled, and Raul stepped exultantly over him, his sword at his side with a smile that negated any hope that Digsy had left for the future. He was beaming down at Digsy, like they were remembering the old times over a nice cold beer. The square seemed quieter suddenly. Digsy's world much smaller. Muted were the sounds of chaos now.

'No so clever now, ay bro!'

Digsy wanted to respond, but he couldn't. He could barely breathe. His windpipe was blocked it seemed, and his larynx crushed, his eyes bulging as he stared up at the mad man glaring down at him.

'All we wan was your mooshine, but you ha to rescue the woman, din you bro. You ha to be tha hero.'

A crazed look was about Raul. A hatred that Digsy couldn't fathom. He raised his sword high above him, his coat flapping wildly on the breeze, the rain belting down, the sleek blade glinting like a ray of light bursting through the clouds, when a pained hail from the left distracted him.

'Ahoy zer matey!'

The timing couldn't have been better. Tomas stepped around the stage and limped onto the scene with a garden fork held out before him.

'Vel Shiver mein timbers.'

His shirt was torn, his glasses gone, and blood dripped from his nose, the whites of his eyes swelling with fervour though, and shining almost, like a demon set free. He raised the fork he held up in mock salute, and then he charged, serving very well in postponing Digsy's imminent demise indeed.

With a disdainful huff, and stepping forwards from over Digsy, Raul raised his sword, sneering and shifting his feet as Tomas slopped through the mud towards him. Tom's arm was back, the fork held out like a javelin behind him, and he launched it forwards, but then a shot rang out and he faltered, his legs buckling as the fork dropped harmlessly before him, and he splashed face first into the mud with a tricky looking stain forming on his back.

Where the bullet had come from was unclear, but it had certainly served its purpose. Tom made no effort to move from there. He'd made the ultimate sacrifice, and Digsy knew what he had to do at that point. There was no room for sentiment, so he pulled the knife from his boot, thrusting it up, up through the skin and up between Raul's ribs, who screamed and dropped his sword, staggering back as Digsy drew the blade back out again with a trickle of warm blood flowing over his knuckles.

'Bro…'

Raul's eyes bulged as he gazed in surprise at the blood seeping down his jacket. He was ashen faced suddenly, an amazed air as if he'd thought himself obviously invincible, and he fell into the tree beside him, slopping to the mud with a pained gurgle.

A strange hush filled the square now. The aftermath of the chaos. Dropping exhausted to his knees, Digsy let the knife slip from his fingers, craning his head back to wash his face in the rain. It was exhilarating, but it didn't wash the guilt that was suddenly surging through him away. That would likely never leave him he knew.

A twinkling in the mud caught Digsy's eye. He could see his old 44 Magnum lying in the mud beside Raul, so he shuffled over and picked it up, wiping it down, and then took in the scene around him.

Most of the brawls seemed to have spilled out beyond the square now. Sporadic gunfire could still be heard, but only in the distance. He could see a solitary guard defending himself against three of the mob, battling well, but he was quickly forced back into one of the surrounding buildings, which collapsed in flames around him. People lay bloodied in the mud all across the square, moving and not, whimpering or silent.

Just the occasional scream cut the air now, the clash of steel, the crackle of the flames and the relentless beating of the torrent now coming down.

It was a scene of misery and mayhem, terror and slaughter that Digsy scanned, ignoring Raul as he sat bleeding against the willow, moaning midst spluttered profanities against Digsy and the world.

Indeed it was a terrible scene, but one that Digsy was sadly growing used to. Wiping the knife on a corpse beside him, he went to leave, but Raul grabbed his ankle, loosening his grip after a second though, as he didn't have the strength.

'Ere bro, have thees.'

Raul was smiling at Digsy, and then laughing, which made him cough, and then he gestured to his pocket, where Digsy found a roll of bullets which he took out and put in his own.

'You might nid 'em.'

Raul laughed again with a gurgle, blood seeping from his lips as he began to choke, and with an effort, pointed to Digsy's left.

'Break a leg bro.'

And it was an upsetting sight that Digsy saw when he turned to look. One that frightened the life out of him. Just when he thought it was all over too. Just when he'd thought he might actually survive the day. But to presume is to rue Digsy knew.

Not twenty meters away, Rodney was barely visible through the smog but for his sheer size. He was holding a man by the throat with his feet dangling two feet from the ground.

The man was grasping at Rodney's fingers, struggling to loosen them as his feet whipped around frantically below him. Rodney squeezed then, and the man went limp, dangling from his grip like a puppet.

Dropping the man to the mud, and like a terminator honing in on its target, Rodney turned to face Digsy.

Chapter 52

That was a brown trouser moment for Digsy. Absolutely terrifying, and he wasn't ashamed to admit that he'd leaked a touch at that point too.

The sword Raul had dropped lay in the mud at his feet, the blade submerged but for its hilt, so Digsy backed up and grabbed it, and then strafed the side of the stage, watching Rodney carefully as he approached.

He came on slowly to begin with, his movements measured and concise, and worryingly manicured. He was wearing body armour which hung limp from one strap, and was drenched in gore. Three of his dreadlocks were cut to stumps and a big gash traversed his cheek. Drawing a blade the side of Digsy's leg from behind him, wisps of smoke formed a charcoal wake as he slashed it through the haze.

A cough from his right distracted Rodney, and his eyes found Raul, slumped against the willow's trunk.

'Why did you kill the boss bro?'

A touch of sadness marked Rodney's voice. Raul was jabbering incoherently to himself now, and gazing off into the distance.

'You shouldn't have done that.'

He rolled the sword in his hand and pointed it at Digsy, clearly upset at seeing Raul bleeding in the mud and a tear glinting in his eye now. Digsy was running on fumes. The tank was empty. Rodney smiled at him, like a cat, if it were able to, would smile at a mouse, and then he charged, baring down on Digsy with the rage of a thousand ginger Nazis.

Crunch!

Their swords crashed together and Digsy staggered back. Somehow he kept his own blade from driving back into him, and he thrust himself back as the blade came at him again, falling back and under the stage and rolled to a halt beneath it.

The space beneath the stage was cramped and dark, and intertwined with makeshift supports with only room to crouch.

Pushing further back, a shudder went through him as he brushed past the corpses that were hanging from above. The space was small, and Rodney not so, but Rodney followed him under anyway, splinters flying as he battered through the timbers like they were matchsticks. Somehow Rodney had closed the gap between them, and he reached out for Digsy, clawing at him, and pulling him back. His grip was like steel, the power pulling at Digsy immense, until he slammed his other boot into Rodney's face, who let go, roaring in pain as Digsy scampered backwards and emerged from under the stage again.

The air was thick again suddenly, and stinking, and stinging Digsy's eyes. He could barely see through the smog now. Barely see the fights still going on and the aftermath of those just gone.

Something moved to his left, so he thrust his blade into the guard that came at him, and then crept up onto the stage, his footsteps muted by the pounding rain, and ducked out of sight behind Nursey's corpse.

Her blood had mostly been washed from the stage now. Nursey was just a piece of meat, but her laughing face danced into Digsy's mind as he strained to ignore the heat still radiating from her. Her bulk hid him well though, so he cowered behind her for a moment, catching his breath, and then placed the sword beside him, pulling back the pistol's hammer. The click as it obliged was almost too much for him to bear, and then tentatively he rose, the 44 held out before him, his elbows resting on Nursey's corpse as he strained to spot Rodney through the haze.

'Where you gone, bro?'

Emerging from under the stage, Rodney stepped away from it.

'Come and play, mate.'

His back was to Digsy. He was near the steps to the stage now, and only a few meters from it. This was it. This was the best chance Digsy would get. Rodney was a big target, and the gun's sight was centred between his shoulders, hovering there as Digsy's finger did likewise on the trigger. But yay, it wasn't to be, and yes dear reader, perhaps painfully predictably, the pistol was empty, a hollow click as the barrel spat out nothing but air.

Rodney turned.

'Peekaboo bro.'

And then he advanced, stepping towards the stage slowly to begin with. Tired now it appeared, but still one of the scariest things Digsy had ever seen.

Vengeance and passion oozed from Rodney. His chest heaved and his muscles rippled. The time was now, but Digsy was out of strength, out of time and out of ideas. It was now or never though. He was all shook up. Rodney broke into a run, charging up the steps to the stage, so Digsy dropped the gun, grabbing the sword and launched himself forward, vaulting over Nursey's corpse and into the air, and then brought the blade down with all he had left.

What happened from that point wasn't clear. It had all happened so fast. Digsy felt the blade cut into something, just for a split second, but then Rodney slammed into him, taking his breath and hurling him backwards over the stage as a horrific scream filled the air.

The next thing Digsy knew, he was on the ground, on his back in the mud beside the stage, winded and shaken, and all he remembered from then, was the vision of Rodney's face as it crashed down on him an instant later.

Chapter 53

The world was warped when Digsy re-joined it, somewhat dazed and slightly confused, not for the first time in his life, choking suddenly, and spitting the filth he'd inhaled back out. He found himself lying flat on his back, in some pain and half-submerged in the mud, but not in any immediate danger it seemed.

He thought he heard a gunshot as he sat up, but couldn't be entirely sure as to what the sound was. Again a gunshot though, so he pushed himself up, dizzy and wavering, and still not entirely comps-mentis.

He could hear screaming too – a man's scream, pained and hopeless, and he wondered what'd happened. His mind flicked from one fuzzy memory to the next, one nightmare to the next—the raid that began it all, his meeting Sinead and then Her Ladyship. The cliff top. Oh that terrible night. He remembered seeing Mary again, how Mary had shot him and he'd fallen from the cliff, and then nothing more until his brief stay at the camp.

Quickly his memories skipped to the present, and he remembered the executions and the riot moments before.

Barely anyone was left in the square now. The floor around him was awash with mud, filth and blood, most of the buildings surrounding blackened and roofless with flames blazing up through them. Rain was coming down at an angle now, and coming down hard, but not worrying the flames. A strong breeze whipped up the smoke, and through it Digsy could see corpses littered all around, bodies everywhere, guards and townsfolk alike.

Had The Order won?

Had Sinead survived?

What happened?

As he stepped around the stage, Digsy could see Raul, still hunched against the willow, and alive still, but only just. Rodney too. It was him that had been screaming. He was slumped in a recess by the stage, quiet now though. He was trying to push himself up, but was struggling, whimpering and groaning, and he slumped back down as the one arm he had quickly lost its strength, blood gushing from the stump where his other had been.

The gruesome sight elated Digsy though, the glimmer of hope he'd almost abandoned suddenly exploding in triumphant joy. He'd beaten Rodney! He'd beaten The Order's most formidable pawn. Rodney would be dead in minutes.

Mud caked Digsy and was ankle deep. He slipped and then leant against the stage to steady himself. He was okay. He wasn't leaking or damaged, and as far as he could tell, he was still in one piece.

There were many that weren't. He could see Her Ladyship slumped on the stage, lying face down a few feet from the corpse of Nursey, but it looked like she was stirring.

And Mo too. Digsy could see him lying at the opposite end of the stage, flat on his back with his hands to his stomach. He was still breathing, and he opened his eyes when he heard Digsy approaching, smiled, and then coughed a fountain of blood up which spilled down his cheeks.

'Hey bro…' he gurgled after a moment, his voice faint but calm, the pain clearly awful yet the smile resolute. A tear fell from Digsy's cheek. He grasped Mo's hand and clasped it in his. Mo smiled, and then he coughed again, another trickle of blood following the last.

'The little g… girl, bro…' he spluttered, choking on the blood that was trying to stop him as he breathed his dying breath.

'Th… the boat bro…e… engine r… room…Chur bro…'

Mo's grip went limp, and Digsy squeezed his hand one last time, choked up for a second, and then he steeled himself to get the job done. He had to find Sinead, and The Order still had Tom's daughter.

Only a couple of brawls were still going on around the square now. The guards had been driven away, but now it sounded like they were fighting back suddenly. The sounds of violence were louder and closer again now, coming from beyond the buildings surrounding, sporadic gunfire and shouting, but from too far away to concern Digsy.

He'd told Sinead to meet him at the south side of the square, by the lake, so he crossed the square, stumbling through the grime, and almost blind, his eyes watering and stinging viciously. He could see more people suddenly, the remnants of the mob, backing away from the buildings or running. They were on the retreat it seemed. He had to find Sinead and get out of there. He couldn't see her though. Where was she?

Digsy was starting to hurt now, the adrenaline wearing off, and injuries he hadn't been aware of were suddenly making themselves known. Stopping for a moment, the pistol in his hand felt heavy suddenly, and empty too he remembered as his mind flicked back to his encounter with Rodney, so he slid the bullets he'd taken from Raul into it, and flicked the barrel back into place.

That was when he saw her.

On the west side of the square. The building behind Sinead was ablaze, and Mary had a rifle trained on her, with her back to Digsy.

An unnerving urge was coursing through Mary, over which she had no control. It was like she was a different person. Like someone else was in charge of her, controlling her every move and thirsting for the blood she was so easily letting. Thriving off it even. She'd never wanted to be this evil, and yet here she was.

She had fifteen kills by her count already that day, and she was very proud of herself. A man lying bloodied in the mud beside her moaned, so she drove her blade into his mouth, twisted it, and then turned her attention back to the woman she'd been stalking – the Irish one that they'd tried to execute earlier. The one Mary had already tried to execute at the cliff that night. *Fair play to her* thought she. How the hell was she still alive?

Mary could see her now, cowering behind an upturned table at the square's periphery. She'd had a rifle moments before, and had tried to shoot Mary with it, but it was empty and now she was unarmed. The building behind her was in flames which danced dangerously close to her. She was a sitting duck.

Gunshots could still be heard in the distance, and screaming from much closer.

Such relaxing sounds.

Somehow Mary felt at peace amidst the chaos, and she cherished it dearly. Thunder again rolled, and lightning glowed through the haze an instant later, but Mary didn't flinch. She had her this time, pinned and disarmed.

She couldn't miss the butter-wouldn't-melt bitch.

The heavens roared as Digsy watched on.

He knew Sinead had nowhere to run, and he knew she'd surely die at Mary's hands unless he acted, so with a splendiferous effort, our man of the hour raised the 44 up to Mary, and yelled…

'Mary…stop!'

and he was pleasantly surprised when Mary obliged, looking back and frowning at the somewhat inevitable interruption.

Glistening in the heavenly deluge, like an angel sent from the deepest recesses of hell, she stood there with her gun aloft, soaked to the core as her ample chest heaved at the day's exertions. She looked amazing, and the heavens again roared in delight.

Spotting Digsy, Mary frowned, safe in the knowledge that Digsy was but a wilting rose, and would never harm his beloved. Never harm her,

'Don't do it Mary,' sobbed he, shaking the rain from his brow as his finger trembling precariously on the trigger.

'Don't make me do this.'

His arms were shaking furiously now, the barrel of the gun wobbling around like a conductor's stick before him. What the hell was he supposed to do? Such a cruel choice.

Mary, Sinead, Sinead, Mary...

How could this be happening? His dream was turning into a nightmare. He'd found the wife he'd thought long since dead, but now he was pointing a gun at her!

Closing his eyes for a second, a flash of lightning shone pink through Digsy's eyelids. He gripped the gun harder, praying for guidance, begging for strength and pleading for fortitude, every wrong deed and every hurtful remark he'd ever made to her crashing back into his mind in a torrent of torment.

Mary didn't turn as he called out to her this time.

'I'm not Mary,' was all she uttered.

The words cut Digsy like a knife. He was bewildered, shell shocked and heartbroken, and unsure as to what was real and what not now. His insides churned, his heart objected and his head gave up trying. The trigger felt cold and slippery, the pistol felt heavy and his arms felt weak.

What Digsy had to do didn't bear thinking about, but somehow, his path became clear to him suddenly, and a worrying calm became him at that point. The past was the past, and Mary wasn't Mary. Not his Mary anyway. This Mary wasn't a very nice person at all. So Digsy said his goodbyes then, and he made his apologies, and then, as he started to squeeze, his very soul, and his very essence, abandoned him.

Chapter 54

A strange feeling came over Mary. She didn't feel at all well suddenly. Her ears were ringing and she was confused, and dizzy all of a sudden too now. Two shots had been fired. She remembered that much, and for a moment she'd thought she was okay. The Irish woman had been in her sights moments before. Mary couldn't recall taking the shot, but it felt now like Digsy had.

She was cold and weak suddenly. Her grip failed her and the rifle fell from her hands, slopping to the mud as her knees buckled and she did likewise.

The cold that engulfed Mary then was a terrifying sensation, and she panicked, spluttering and struggling to keep her mouth from the puddle it'd found itself in.

She felt the pain in her chest, but numb everywhere else suddenly, and afraid too. If she was to meet this God she'd heard Raul harp on about she suddenly thought, she was in serious trouble. She could only remember a few years of her life, and they were spent mostly mischievously, mostly.

But what did Raul know anyway? If God is there, then why would he let us live like this?

She'd asked him that once, when they'd been on guard duty together.

'He med us, but we are responsible for owself,' Raul had replied, as if that was all that needed to be said.

Much as in humanity Mary had mused as she'd mulled it over later that day. The child always blames the parent for their own mistakes.

If only she hadn't been such a bitch though. That would be her downfall she knew. That's what would condemn her to hell if anything. The killing was one thing, and she knew deep down that it was wrong, but she'd only been following orders.

Mary didn't much like the sound of hell. Or purgatory for that matter, and if the Buddhists were right, then karma would most likely shit all over her in the next life she supposed. Worse of all though, was the thought of nothing. Absolutely nothing. Of course, she knew she wouldn't know about it should that be the case, but that scenario just hadn't seemed plausible to Mary. All those memories. All those experiences, pleasures and pains, loves and lives. All that energy, for nothing? Indeed, she'd pondered it a lot, what with her intimate relationship with death and excessive guard duty. Maybe there is a heaven she'd muse, maybe we turn into a tree or an ant or a groak on the planet Dave, or maybe we transcend to a higher plane, or regress to a lower one. But not nothing.

Maybe the Jedi order she'd heard tale of were right. Maybe the whole planet is connected, some kind of all-powerful force linking it all. Not a god, but a consciousness one can interact with, and manipulate even. Mary quite liked the sound of that.

She'd heard that the Jedi transcend into higher beings when they die, a bit like what Raul had told her happens to the good Buddhists. She liked the sound of that too, but then couldn't there then be something higher still?

It was all so confusing.

Either way though, the concept of God still seemed more realistic than the science books she'd read. We're all made out of minute particles that were formed in an exploding star hundreds of billions of light years away in a galaxy far, far away?! Really? She failed to see how that was easier to believe in than the existence of God, and more plausible somehow, and how it was for some reason seen as a more rational and enlightened belief.

*Uppity know it all wankers. I mean, come on people. Where's **your** proof?*

The words she'd read were all part of some wonderful universal theory she knew, but it was mostly still only a theory, and a theory developed by flawed human minds at that, and to Mary, it sounded by far the more farfetched.

Consciousness can't simply be electrical, or mathematical. It just didn't compute.

Either way, Mary might be finding out soon enough she knew.

She could see Raul, perched against the tree by the stage, his hat caked in mud beside him, clutching his ribs and muttering to himself as he tried to get up, screamed, and then flopped back down again.

Not far from him, lay Rodney, the blood pooled around him eclipsing the recess he'd fallen into. He wasn't moving, and it looked like he was floating in a pool of his own blood. Indeed, it reminded Mary of an antique toy she suddenly remembered playing with as a child—a plastic model of a spaceman, cryogenically frozen in molten something or other, the specifics she couldn't quite remember, what with her current distracted state.

The clap of the rifle had shocked Digsy, even though he'd pulled the trigger, and he grasped the rifle harder, keeping it levelled, and terrified of opening his eyes, and of what he'd maybe done.

How could he ever forgive himself?

He'd hoped for a retaliatory shot to put him out of his misery, but none came.

Screaming could be heard again, but from closer now. More gunfire too, the hush that had for a while taken the scene interrupted as a chill suddenly took Digsy. His arms started to quiver, the gun in his hands heavier still, so he lowered it, opening his eyes, and then there was Mary, lying crumpled and bloodied in the mud before him—His doing.

He ran to her and placed a hand on her shoulder, startling her as she looked up to him, frightened and confused, bleeding badly at her side and turning a ghostly white. She tried to speak, but she couldn't. The pain of opening her eyes was too much, so she closed them again. It felt better. Then she felt the hand on her cheek and opened them again, straining to see through the blur before her.

Gazing back at her, was a familiar face, gaunt yet broad, and drenched to the bone she noticed as it crouched down beside her. It was a man. He looked upset, and Mary recognised him a second later, but not just from recently she suddenly realised as a barrage of memories suddenly slammed into her mind. But from the old world too, and her heart melted as she pictured Digsy as she'd once known him, clean cut and shaven, always smiling at life's tribulations, and the first to crack a joke, albeit a bad one that silenced whatever room he was in.

She recognised Digsy, and remembered him now as the world started to fade around her, his face blurred further and a brilliant white light attacked her eyes.

Digsy.

Chapter 55

Gazing down at Mary, tears streamed down Digsy's face, trails of skin in the mud like war paint streaking down his cheeks. He hadn't wanted to shoot her of course. He'd aimed for her arm, but there she was anyway, quite possibly dying.

He cupped her face in his hand, keeping her mouth from the puddle it lay in.

He'd had to do it though, hadn't he?

He'd had to shoot Mary. Had to shoot his wife. She would have shot Sinead otherwise. And it wasn't his Mary anyway. Not really. Not the Mary he remembered worshipping in the old world—the caring, kind Mary that he'd spent half of his life with. This Mary had tried to kill him, and then tried to kill him again.

He gazed into her eyes as all this ploughed through his mind, and she smiled a warm smile, trying to speak, but moaned instead.

Did she recognise him? The thought cut Digsy to the bone.
Crack!

The clap of a rifle, and the square suddenly started ringing with noise again. Chaos had resumed. The Order had regained control it seemed, shot after shot resounding now, scores of people scurrying back through the buildings, back into the square, some falling dead, others tripping over the corpses, diving into the lake or taking cover behind whatever they could.

The people's revolt had failed.

'We have to go, now!'

Sinead placed a hand on Digsy's shoulder.

'NOW!' she urged louder.

She tugged at Digsy's jacket when he didn't respond, so he kissed Mary on the forehead, and then stood, stepping quickly back as people began charging past him, slipping in the mud, ducking behind the stage, sprinting off down the beach or jumping into the lake.

The Order's guards were starting to fill the balconies again, taking aim and opening fire. The smog was clearing quickly, their cover dissipating, the breeze swirling it around in a chaotic tango that seemed to mimic the day's events. Her Ladyship was coming around on the stage. Red helping her up.

'Find'em ya fak'n halfwit!'

So Digsy grabbed the sword from the mud, slid the Magnum into his belt, barricading Mary's image at the back of his mind.

It was time to move.

Staying low, he scampered across to the lake's edge in Sinead wake, and crouched beside the wall beside her.

'Tom's daughter…' he stammered between breaths, pointing at the TSS Earnslaw moored only meters beside them, smog whipping around it like a ship from below.

'Mo told me, she's on there.'

They charged up the gangplank and onto her bow, a couple of shots following them, splintering the wooden frame of the door before them. Through the hatch and down the ladder they went. There were no guards anywhere to be seen now, the narrow corridor silent but for an unnerving creak that resounded the entire vessel. Down a second ladder, and there before them was the engine room, at the end of a long corridor. That was where Mo had said the girl would be.

The door was partially open, but no sounds came from within, so they crept down the corridor, careful to make no sound as they passed a series of small doors to their right. The engine room was meters before them now. There was still no sound. The door was ajar, so Digsy pushed it back, the hinges creaking as it swung slowly in, and he stopped in his tracks as he saw the gun beyond it pointing back at him.

'Not so fast, mate.'

There was Tom's daughter, stood before the furnace with a guard stood beside her. Tiny and terrified, with a mass of filthy blonde hair hanging down to her waist, she was the image of Tomas, and the one innocent in this whole mess, and yet here she was, held in place by the worst humanity had to offer.

Digsy didn't recognise the guard to begin with. His face was swollen and bruised, his nose crooked and his top lip scarred. Sun bleached hair drooped in a centre parting down to his cheeks, and as he shifted his aim from Digsy to the girl, Sinead's heart fluttered. **She** recognised him. The guard held the girl in place with a pistol to her head.

'G'day, mate…'

The skinny guard had a twinkle in his malignant eyes, shifting his weight back and forth between his feet, nervous and on edge, but smiling and focused too it seemed, and willing to do the unthinkable.

Indeed, evil emanated from this fellow. A worse being it would be hard to imagine, and as the skinny guard's brow furrowed, his trigger finger tensed and his smile morphed into a frown, Sinead grabbed the 44 from Digsy's belt and blew the skinny guard's brains out.

Needless to say, dear devoted reader, there was to be one final obstacle for our valiant heroes to negotiate, for one couldn't expect their escape to have been such an easy one. Indeed no, for the ever tenacious Red and two more guards had followed them aboard, and blocked the corridor behind them now.

In latter tellings of the tale, his grandchildren on his knee with the fire blazing away beside them, Digsy would oft embellish his own ingenuity at this point. For it had been a proud moment for him, and a moment that had changed the future of New Queenstown he'd normally add for effect. He'd often go on somewhat of a tangent, and tell of grenades being tossed his way, of his fending off twenty of The Order's most fearsome guards, each one of them like Rodney on steroids he'd laugh. He'd tell of the Earnslaw burning and sinking around them, and various other death-defying feats; but most of all, how it was destiny that'd seen them through, and it was destiny that would see them ever onwards.

Digsy didn't believe in destiny of course. At least he didn't think he did, but he'd never been one to let the truth get in the way of a good tale.

Indeed no! What Digsy believed in was always being prepared.

He kept a glass hip-flask full of moonshine in his jacket pocket you see, strictly in case of emergencies, and in a rare moment of clarity, he reached into his pocket, slipped it from its case and threw it as hard as he could against the wall in front of the guards.

The plan worked too. He couldn't believe it, as he hadn't been entirely confident in it to begin with. Shooting the guards had seemed the most sensible of the alternatives in the time he'd had to consider it, but the hip-flask shattered on impact nevertheless, spraying the walls in moonshine as Sinead raised the Magnum once again and pulled the trigger.

Boom!

The Earnslaw's walls rattled, eardrums cried out in agony, flames leapt up the walls and across the ceiling, the ancient timbers shrouded suddenly in a blanket of raging blue that blocked the corridor nicely.

'Yous god-damned-sunuva-biaaatch!' yelled Red as Digsy turned down the adjoining corridor, ushering Sinead and the girl down it whilst the fire still kept the guards at bay. **'I'll git you yous god-damned-sunuva-biaaatch!'**

The corridor our heroes found themselves in led up to the main deck, where they found nothing to hinder their escape. The rain made a din like hundreds of drummer boys tapping away at the ship's decking, almost applauding their efforts it seemed, but there was no time for indulgence.

They could hear heavy footsteps moving up the gangplank, and see more of The Order's guards ashore moving towards the boat, so Digsy grabbed Tom's daughter and threw her over the boat's railings, her scream dying quickly as she hit the water with a splash.

Sinead seemed to object to this, which Digsy thought understandable. The throwing of minors into lakes was generally frowned upon he'd found, much to the chagrin of numerous unadventurous parents who didn't subscribe to the literal translation of "In at the deep end"; but she was thankfully lost for words too it seemed, so they both quickly followed, splashing down into the dark waters below.

The sky was dark now, though it was only mid-afternoon. A cloud of filth sat above the town, growing thicker by the minute, but the air was cleaner at lake level. A corpse floated past them, the back of its head missing and a sheen atop the water around it. Sinead pushed it onwards and followed, using the corpse to hide her as she swam for the shore. The others followed, pushing as quietly as they could through the water.

The Order had regained control of the square now it seemed. Digsy could hear Her Ladyship barking orders as he swam away, shots still sounding as black smoke billowed up from the Earnslaw's portholes, and up through her roof. Yet another relic of yesteryear, lost to time, relegated to a thing of memory at Digsy's own hands. Now wasn't the time for regrets though.

The water was bitterly cold, but their senses were numb to it, and they emerged onto dry land at the far side of the wharf by the town's southern exit.

They were out.

The road to Glenorchy was all that stood before them now, its winding path hemmed in by the lake to one side, and the mountains the other. A couple of guards were scouring the area, but they didn't prove to be an issue.

The chaos of moments before was but a memory to the three of them after a short while, all of them too tired to think, let alone speak. Making their way along the lake's shore, Sinead led the girl by the hand, so much like her father, the rain driving down still, but refreshing them more than anything, and giving them strength to push on.

They were on their way to see a friend at a camp called Moke Digsy told them after a while. A friend he hadn't seen since the fences went up. He was a most obliging fellow he assured them, who'd doubtless delight in lending assistance. He'd tend to their every need he promised as New Queenstown receded into the gloom behind them, thick plumbs of black smoke billowing up like cigarette smoke into the night.

Ah cigarettes thought Digsy, dreaming of the days he'd cough and splutter till it felt like his lungs would explode, tragically resigned now to only fresh, clean alpine air with which to fill his lungs.

The End